Passionate Seduction
Sexy Stories Collection

VOLUME 7

10 EROTIC SHORT STORIES

FAE DEROSE

Passionate Seduction/ Fae DeRose. -- 1st ed.
Xplicit Press, an imprint of TLM Media LLC

ISBN-13: 978-1-62327-537-2
ISBN-10: 1-62327-537-7
eISBN: 978-1-62327-588-4

Printed in the United States of America

CONTENTS

1 THE BANG IN THE BAR

Danny finished wiping down the bar and started cleaning the tables. His waitress had called in sick so he'd been running the place by himself basically. His buddy Steve had jumped in as bartender for a little while, but other than that, it had all been on Danny. It was a good thing that the Dug Out wasn't a fancy place that served complicated drinks.

Gathering up baskets filled with peanuts, Danny ran them back to the kitchen. When he returned to the bar, he was surprised to find a woman standing by the bar.

"Hi. Can I help you?" he asked.

She smiled at him and Danny's heart did a little flip-flop. She was an extraordinarily attractive young black woman. Her beautiful dark eyes reflected the light and her mouth was so pretty. Danny couldn't help but ogle her curvy figure in her jeans shorts and pink tank top.

"I hope so," she said taking a step towards Danny. "Are you the owner of the bar?"

Danny nodded. "Yeah. Why?"

She held out a hand to Danny. "I'm Tasha Williams. I'm new to Marshfield."

"Nice to meet you," Danny answered as he took her hand. It was small, strong and very pretty, like the rest of her. Her nails weren't long like talons, but shorter and nicely shaped.

"You, too," Tasha said and released his hand.

"So what can I do for you?" Danny asked. He didn't mean to look at her breasts, but couldn't help it. He could only imagine how pretty they were underneath her top and bra. His eyes lowered to them whenever she wasn't looking directly at him.

She slanted a sly look at him. He was a very cute white boy, she thought. Sandy-blonde hair, blue eyes, and it looked like he worked out a lot. Of course, running a bar and lifting beer kegs and cases of beer would certainly keep a guy in shape.

"I think, maybe, we can do something for each other," she said and moved closer still.

Danny cocked his head and smiled a little. His male mind couldn't help but jump into the gutter at her statement. "Like what?"

"I'm a singer and you own a bar. Singing and bars go together. I want to sing here once a week. I'll sing for tips," she said. "It won't cost you anything. I have my own equipment, too."

Danny looked into her eager face with those

sexy lips and knew that he'd already lost the battle. But was it really a battle? She would sing, if she was good, and he'd make money from the customers she drew once the word was out. He could sure use more business. It wasn't going to cost him anything, so what the hell?

"How do I know you're any good?" he said and arched an eyebrow.

Her confident smile mesmerized him. She broke into a soulful rendition of the Star Spangled Banner and Danny felt a certain part of him begin to stand to attention. Damn, but the girl could sing. Her movements while she sang were sensual and emotional.

When she was done, Danny found himself clapping. "That was beautiful. You got one hell of a set of pipes," he commented.

"Thank you," Tasha said modestly even though she knew she had skills.

"Okay, you're hired," Danny said.

Tasha couldn't believe her luck. She'd figured that she was going to have to do a lot more persuading than that. She clapped her hands and jumped up and down slightly.

"Thank you! You won't regret it. It's going to be so fun," she told him.

Danny laughed as he watched her tits bob up and down. "Yeah, I think it is, too. Hey, you wanna have a drink to celebrate our partnership?" he asked.

"You bet," Tasha answered and hopped up onto a barstool.

Danny got a good eye of her toned chocolate legs and almost groaned. "Let me go lock the door. We're closed and I don't want other people wandering in."

"Ok. I'll be here," she said. While he was gone, Tasha thought about her good fortune. Not only would she be able to make money doing what she loved, but she also got to work for such a good-looking guy. He had a nice ass, she'd noticed.

Danny returned. "What's your pleasure?" he asked.

Tasha almost said, "You," but instead said, "White wine, please?"

"You got it," Danny answered and poured her a glass. "So where'd you move from?"

"Philly. I lost my job down there and my aunt lives in Marshfield, so I moved here when I lost my apartment and stuff," she answered honestly.

Danny frowned. "Sorry to hear about your job and all, but I'm glad you're here and that you have family."

Tasha shrugged, touched by his concern even though she was a stranger to him. "It's okay. It was time for a change anyway."

Danny was a bartender and an observer of people. "Guy trouble?"

Tasha smiled. "Yeah, that's right. He was a loser and wouldn't give up when I told him it was over."

"I can understand not wanting to give up on a beautiful woman like you, but he shoulda treated you better," Danny said.

Tasha smiled up at him. She could tell he was attracted to her. "Thank you. You're very sweet."

Danny shook his head. "Nah. Just telling the truth."

Tasha watched him as he took a swig of his beer and then set about organizing things behind the bar.

"I'm sorry. I'm keeping you from your work. I'll get going and leave you to it." A thought occurred to Tasha. "Or, I could help you clean up, if you like. I've done that sort of work before," she offered.

Danny considered it for a moment. He was short-handed and if she helped him, he would get done faster. Plus, he didn't mind spending some more time with her.

"Okay. Sounds good. I'll pay you twenty-five bucks to help me," he said.

Tasha shook her head. "You don't have to pay me."

"Yes, I do. I'd be paying my waitress, Cindy, anyway. So you might as well make some money, too." Danny smiled at her. "Your first duty is to fill the napkin holders and salt and pepper shakers."

She gave him a salute. "On it, boss," she said and laughed.

Danny showed her where the salt, pepper, and napkins were kept and left her to it. He started bringing up kegs from the basement to get ready for the next night since it was dollar draft night. As he went to enter the kitchen on his way back to the basement, Tasha was coming out the door and they collided. He grabbed her around the waist to steady her so she didn't fall. Somehow his left hand ended up on her right breast.

"Oh, God! Sorry!" he said and moved it away.

Tasha smiled and said, "You can leave it

there if you want." She smiled at him coyly. She wasn't above coming on strong when she wanted something and she wanted Danny.

"Really?" Danny asked. He wasn't sure he'd heard correctly. "You want me to touch you?"

Tasha took a hold of his hand and placed it back on her breast. "Yeah. Squeeze it. Go ahead."

His blue eyes widened and then he smiled. He liked aggressive women because it saved time trying to figure out if they wanted it or not. He closed his hand around her tit and squeezed slightly. It felt good. Firm and rounded. He could feel her nipple harden against his palm so he rubbed his thumb over the small peak.

"Mmmm." Tasha murmured and ran a hand up his other arm. "More."

Danny bent down and bit her nipple through her shirt and bra and Tasha gasped.

"Ooh! Are you a hungry boy?"

"Starving," Danny said and pulled her shirt from her jeans shorts.

He ran his hand up under her shirt, enjoying the feel of the warm skin of her stomach. He found her bra and edged his finger underneath it until he found her bare nipple. He rubbed back and forth over it. Tasha felt her pussy start to tingle at his touch. She'd been horny for days and could tell it wasn't going to take much for her to be ready.

She grabbed her shirt and pulled it over her head. She backed into the kitchen as she took off her bra and released her full breasts. Danny had never been with a black girl and thought her incredibly beautiful. The rich brown of her skin was exciting to him. Her dark nipples reminded him of chocolate kisses in color and the way they stood up. Danny's mouth began to water and he wanted to taste them.

Tasha played with them, enticing him further. Danny closed in on her and captured her lush mouth with his. He asked for entry into the sweet recess beyond her lips and groaned when she opened to him and they touched tongues. She tasted so good and her little tongue met his eagerly. The kiss grew wet and hot and Danny grabbed her ass and brought her fully against his rapidly growing erection.

Moaning her approval, Tasha moved her hips over it and ran her hands up his strong back before grabbing his T-shirt and yanking it upwards. Danny threw the shirt on the floor and then caressed her breasts and toyed with her dark nipples. Tasha pressed into his hands harder, loving the sensations he was creating between her legs.

Danny dipped his head, took a nipple into his mouth and sucked hard.

"Oh, shit!" Tasha cried and let her head fall back.

Danny's tongue circled the turgid peak as he kept playing with her other nipple with his fingers. He let her go when her hips started moving again and unbuttoned her shorts.

Danny helped her out of them, sliding them down her silky smooth legs. He felt himself growing incredibly hard as he looked at the triangle of pink material that covered her pussy. Danny was intensely curious to see what a black pussy looked like in real life. He'd seen naked black women in videos, but that was it.

Tasha gyrated her hips for him, enjoying the lust in his eyes as he watched her. She reached a hand down under the flimsy fabric of her panties and started rubbing her cunt in circular motions while her other hand played with her tits.

"Shit, that's hot," Danny said in a husky voice.

"Like what you see?" Tasha said playfully.

Danny laughed. "You know I do, you bad girl. What's not to like?"

Tasha kept playing with her clit and felt herself getting wet. "Mmmm. I'm so horny."

"You're not the only one. Would you like me to do something about that?" Danny said as he stood up and began running his hands over her shoulders and down her back. He loved the contours of her shoulder blades and the sweet curve of her ass. He grabbed it and squeezed it. Then he smacked it a couple of times making Tasha squeal and laugh.

His hand joined hers on her crotch and they stroked together, which Danny found highly erotic. Suddenly he couldn't stand keeping his pants on with his huge erection. His dick needed to be free. Danny shed his jeans quickly while Tasha giggled as he hurried to complete the job.

"Oooh! Look at you, baby!" she said when she saw his big, hard cock. "No wonder you wanted to get those pants off." She got rid of her panties wanting to be naked, too.

Danny began working his cock while she watched. He could see that she wanted to touch him as much as he wanted to touch her. She backed up to a counter and hoisted herself up on it. She spread her legs open and Danny thought he'd never seen anything so pretty as her pussy. It was all chocolate on the outside but soft pink on the inside and he wanted nothing more than to lick it.

Tasha was getting wetter by the second and she parted her pussy lips while watching Danny stroke his dick. She toyed with her clit and moaned in excitement. Danny couldn't take any more and came over to the counter. He moved between her legs and ran his cock up and down the length of her slit letting the head of it rub her clit. It felt fantastic to feel the slick skin of her pretty cunt against his dick.

"Don't stop, baby. Faster. If you do it faster, I'm gonna cum," Tasha informed him as she watched what he was doing to her.

Danny complied with her wish. He moved his hips faster and pressed his cock down onto her clit harder. Tasha leaned back, letting her legs fall completely open to get the full effect of what he was doing. The sweet heat built inside her and she felt the first pulses of an orgasm.

"Yeah, that's it. That's it." Soon her moans became louder and her hips began vibrating as she neared the brink. "Danny, I'm gonna cum, baby. Oh shit. I'm almost there. It's so good."

"Good, baby. I wanna fuck your sweet cunt so good. I'm gonna fuck it all kinds of ways," Danny promised as he moved even faster.

"Oh, fuck!" Tasha screamed. "Mmmm! I'm cumming, I'm cumming." High-pitched whimpers came from her and Danny could have cum right then. Her ecstasy made him so excited, but he held back because he wasn't done with her yet.

"Oh, Danny," Tasha said as the orgasm began to subside. "That was amazing."

"That's what I was aiming for," he teased her with a grin. "Keep those sexy legs of yours spread. I'm hungry for dessert and chocolate pussy is what I want."

Tasha's eyes widened in amusement. "You say the nicest things, baby." She scooted her ass forward a little and repositioned her legs so that her pussy was completely open to him. "It's all yours, white boy."

"Mmmm mmmm." Danny knelt and rubbed his fingers over her cunt. She was silky smooth and wet with cum. He gently spread her lips apart and ran his tongue up her pink slit.

Tasha sighed and let her head fall back. "That feels so good. Your tongue is warm and wet."

Danny made his tongue hard and dipped it inside the entrance of her pussy. Her cum was sweet and salty and he loved her taste. He kept his tongue stiff and thrust it as deep as he could and then pulled out again, mimicking the movements his cock was going to make in a little while.

"Oh, you kinky boy." Tasha's eyes widened as his tongue continued diving in and out of her. She had never had that done to her and liked it a lot.

Then Danny began lapping at her pussy, licking up from her pussy hole and hitting her clit. It was very sensitive and every time Danny's tongue touched it, Tasha gave a little jerk forward. He was teasing her and she knew it. It drove her wild.

Danny flicked his tongue over her female erection and was rewarded by little moans and hip thrusts.

"Oh, Danny. You have a wicked tongue. You know just how to lick me," she said and meant it. He was barely touching her and yet she felt another orgasm looming.

Danny wanted to draw it out for her. He was in no hurry and it seemed like she wasn't either. It was his intent to pleasure the hell out of her and make her exhausted. Her movements grew more urgent and she became even wetter.

"Baby, it's so good. Oh, God, I need it. I need to come, please," Tasha urged as she watched his tongue roam over her clit. She loved watching and was fascinated with how fast he could make his tongue go.

"I'll give it to you. Don't worry," he said stopping long enough to respond to her.

Tasha thought she would scream with need and was relieved when he started up again. "Yeah, yeah."

"Mmmm," Danny said against her cunt and licked her a little harder.

"Baby? Baby?"

"Hmm?"

"Oh, oh! Yeah! I'm cumming, I'm cumming! Oh, Danny, it's so intense! Don't stop yet. Don't stop." Her words dissolved into cries of pleasure.

Danny held her thighs still as he licked and sucked her clit while she came, each noise from her music to his ears. He drew it out as long as he could for her.

Tasha started coming down from her blissful high. She laughed and said, "You are fantastic."

Danny wiped his mouth and said, "Thanks. Your pussy tastes so good. We ain't done yet, though."

Tasha looked hungrily at his erect penis. "I hope not. I want that cock inside me."

Danny snagged a condom from his jeans and ripped it open. Tasha giggled and snatched it out of his hand. "Allow me," she teased.

Danny watched her dexterous fingers unroll the condom down over his pulsing dick. Her hands felt so good as they smoothed it and then worked up and down in long, lazy strokes. The sight of her dark hands against his white cock was very exotic and increased his excitement.

Tasha leaned back and spread her legs for him again. She parted her pussy lips so Danny could see her hole. "There, Danny.

Please get that hot rod in there," she coaxed.

Gently at first, Danny eased his cock inside her giving her time to adjust. The last thing he wanted to do was hurt her.

"Deeper," Tasha said. Danny was nice and thick and long and she wanted to feel him all the way inside.

Danny encircled her waist and pressed harder. Her cunt was so hot and tight.

Tasha wrapped her legs around him and squeezed. "All the way, Danny. All the way."

Sensing that he didn't have to be as careful with Tasha as he had other girls, Danny gave her what she wanted. He grabbed her hips and quickly pushed all the way inside her tight pussy.

"Yeah, baby. That feels so good," Tasha said kissing his neck.

Danny began moving his hips and kissing her. She tasted so good everywhere, he noted. Tasha moaned into his mouth and then bit his tongue.

Danny said, "Ow!" and then laughed at her playfulness. "You're such a bad girl," he told her and slapped her ass.

"That's right, I am. You're gonna have to teach me a lesson," Tasha answered.

Danny's response was to start pounding at her, ramming his dick deep inside. She ignited such passion in him and he captured her mouth again even as she moaned and whimpered her approval. He trailed kisses down her neck and then slowed his rhythm. Tasha protested but Danny kept the pace the same for a minute then suddenly sped up again.

"You're such a tease," Tasha said with a big smile.

Danny just laughed and moved faster.

"Oh, shit! Yeah, like that. Fuck my pussy! I love it hard like that," Tasha said in between moans.

Her orgasm started and Danny felt her clench around his dick and she became even wetter. "Yeah, come on my cock, baby. That's it." Danny didn't slow down and he felt the tension start again in Tasha. "Was that good, Tasha?"

Tasha nodded her head up and down vigorously. "Uh huh. So good. Don't stop, oh, please, don't stop!"

Danny gripped her hips even tighter and pulled her towards him while he thrust forward. She shouted her pleasure as an even more powerful orgasm racked her body. Tasha thought she was going to die and she'd have died happily if she did. It was so intense that she didn't know anything but what was happening in her most intimate place. Waves crashed over her as she came and she felt herself spurt a little. It was so amazing.

Her cum covered them and dripped to the floor. Danny had never experienced anything like that before and found it unbelievably erotic. He felt his own release nearing and needed it badly. Tasha was so exciting and hot. He growled and moaned as he neared the brink.

Tasha could see it in Danny's eyes and hear it in the noises he was making that he was going to cum.

"You gonna cum for me, Danny? You gonna

shoot that load of yours?" she coaxed.

"Oh, yeah. Oh, God, you feel so good. Your pussy is so tight and wet and hot. Oh, fuck!" He grabbed Tasha tight and humped for all he was worth as his hot sperm spurted from him. He pumped in and out and he felt Tasha have another smaller orgasm. Her nails dug deep into his back and he relished the feeling as he began drifting down from his high.

"Oh, shit, Tasha," he said pulling back so he could look into her beautiful eyes. "You are unbelievable, baby. Do you know that?" he asked and kissed her.

Tasha kissed him back. Danny was a great kisser and it felt good kissing him with his softening cock inside her. It felt sexy. "I'm not the only one," she said when the kiss ended. "I think I'm really going to like working here. Especially if one of the fringe benefits is getting to fuck you," she said.

Danny laughed and said, "Baby, you can have me anytime you want. I'm all yours," he said honestly. He withdrew slowly from her and looked down at the wet floor. "I guess I'm gonna need a mop," he said with a grin.

Tasha smiled shyly and giggled. "Sorry about that. I can't help it. That happens sometimes."

"Don't apologize. I loved it." He gave each of her nipples a last kiss and stepped back.

Together they cleaned up the kitchen and each other, laughing and teasing the whole time. Once they were done, Danny walked Tasha to her car since it was so late. Marshfield was a small town, but he didn't want to take any chances that someone would mess with Tasha.

He put his arms around her waist and pulled her close for a goodnight kiss. Tasha was amazed by how tender he was with her. When it ended, she smiled up at him and said, "See you tomorrow night?"

Danny nodded. "Definitely. I'm really looking forward to hearing you sing more. You have an amazing voice."

"Thanks. Bye," she said as she got in her car. She turned the ignition switch, gave him a little wave and drove away.

Danny stood there looking after her. He couldn't help feeling that his life had changed and definitely for the better. He set off for home with a smile on his face and a song in his   heart.

2 CRIME AND PASSION

"Damn it! How did she get here so soon?" Lt. Darryl Rodgers griped as he saw Rikki Showers, a local reporter, on the fringe of the crime scene.

She was snapping pictures and talking to a couple of the uniforms who were guarding the perimeter. Her platinum blonde hair was pulled back into a ponytail that whipped around her neck when the wind blew. She wore a bulky winter coat, but Darryl knew that the coat hid a sinfully beautiful body that he had a hard time not looking at when she didn't know it.

"Showers!" he angrily called out.

Rikki jerked and turned her head towards the voice that she knew so well. As always, she experienced a flutter in her stomach when she met Rodgers' smoldering dark eyes. His broad shoulders and wide chest were encased in a black leather coat and form-fitting jeans showed off his long legs. His short-cropped dark hair only emphasized his strong jaw line. The man was a god, and he didn't even know it.

She stopped taking pictures as he stomped up to her and glared down into her eyes. "What's up, Rodgers?" she flippantly asked.

His scowl became even darker. Rodgers suspected that she often made him mad on purpose, but he didn't know how much his anger turned her on. There was nothing she loved more than watching him yell at people in the interrogation room or taking down a criminal out in the field. In her eyes, he was poetry in motion when he was riled up.

"What's up is that I don't need you nosing around another crime scene. Get gone, will ya?" Rodgers commanded. He didn't hold out much hope that Rikki would leave. The woman was as stubborn as she was beautiful.

"C'mon, Rodgers. This is going to be a big story, and you know it. You also know that I'll give the cops good press, and I promise I won't publish anything that you don't personally approve. You can't say no to that," she coaxed.

Rodgers' expression softened a little. Damn her, he thought. She always knows what to say to get her own way, and I'm an idiot to let her manipulate me. But the fact is that we do need some good press right now.

"All right. But just like you said, you print nothing without my express approval," he relented.

Rikki was thrilled that he was giving in and vowed that he wouldn't regret it. "Great! I could kiss you! So what do you know so far?"

Rodgers laughed at her enthusiasm. "All I know is that we got a dead guy in this park, and it looks like he was stabbed repeatedly. Now get back. I'll talk to you after all the preliminary stuff is done."

Rikki gave him a mock salute, her dark eyes laughing the whole time. "Yes sir! Off I go, sir!" She turned and made her way through the crowd.

Darryl watched her go, wishing that her coat didn't cover her fine ass. It might be the best thing he saw all day.

"So you don't know anything about what your buddy might have gotten into?" Darryl said with a glower. He sat across the interrogation table from a grad student who was a friend of the deceased, one Mr. Robert Chambers.

The student, Chris Tompkins, shook his head, his blue eyes darting around the room. Sweat trickled down his forehead from his scalp, and he kept wiping it with a tissue. "No. I swear. Bobby was kinda secretive sometimes."

Darryl's square jaw tightened and Rikki, who was watching in the observation room, knew what was coming. She'd seen it a hundred times and never tired of it. Her heartbeat ramped up in anticipation.

"I'm gonna do some swearing of my own, Chris. Bullshit! You know damn well what was going on with Bobby!"

Chris flinched as Darryl brought a big fist down on the table creating thunder in the small room.

"You know how I know?" Darryl continued. "Because you're sweating bullets, and you can't even look me in the eye when you say you don't know. I'm not some dumb, green cop, buddy. I've broke guys who would eat you for breakfast just because they could, guys who would slit your neck if you gave them the slightest chance."

"I don't know!" Chris insisted, which only earned him more of Darryl's wrath.

Darryl rose from the table and strode over to the mirror set into the wall in front of Chris. Rikki was close enough that she could have touched Darryl if the barrier hadn't been there, and she wanted to touch him. Badly. She dreamt of it all the time.

Darryl looked through the window, knowing that Rikki was there. He looked at the spot where he imagined her eyes would be and gave her a huge grin and mouthed, watch this. He knew how much she liked watching him work over a suspect, and damn it, he couldn't help but want to please the woman even though she often infuriated him.

He whirled around from the window and stomped around the table, coming at Chris like a freight train. He whipped Chris' chair around like it weighed five pounds and put his face three inches from Chris'. The younger man's eyes bugged out of his face in abject terror.

"Fucking listen to me, Chris! You know

more than you're telling me. I can hold you for twenty-four hours. I'll put you in lock-up with God knows what kind of creeps, and I'll make your life a living hell. At the end of it all, you will tell me what I want to know. Or, we can do it the easy way. You just tell me what you know now, and then you can go home. What'll it be?"

Darryl kept the pressure on, now moving an inch away from Chris. To the kid's credit, he didn't say a word. Darryl reached across the table and grabbed the case file. He opened it to Bobby's crime scene photo and shoved it in Chris' face. "You see this? This is what happened to your friend."

Chris tried to look away from the sight of Bobby's bloody, mutilated body, but Darryl wouldn't let him. "If you're involved in this thing, if you know why he was killed and by whom, they may be after you next. Is that what you want?"

Chris broke down then and Darryl shifted into the role of comforter. He knelt on the floor next to Chris. "Hey, buddy. I know this is scary, but that's what we're here for. I'm sorry I was so hard on you, but this is really important."

Chris nodded and opened his mouth to speak, but vomited all over Darryl's shirt front instead.

Darryl froze in disbelief for a moment then shot to his feet. "Fuck! Couldn't you have warned me? Holy shit," Darryl said and took off his shirt quickly. He still ended up with puke on his chest. "Son of a bitch! This was a brand new shirt," he said as he wiped off his chest with an unsoiled part of it. He heaved it into the trash can and then exited the room.

When he entered the bullpen shirtless, whistles came from all directions. Despite his earlier disgust, he grinned. He stopped and did a complete turn, showing off his excellent physique. "Glad you like what you see, but how about you put your money with your mouths are? Singles are accepted, but I prefer tens and twenties," he joked.

Rikki jogged after him, admiring the way his muscles rolled under the skin of his back as she followed.

Captain Dennison came out of his office, his craggy face drawn in lines of disapproval. "Rodgers, go get some clothes on, will ya?"

"On my way, sir," Darryl called out over his shoulder.

Rikki caught up with him. "Oh my God! That was fantastic!" she said.

"What? Getting puked on? Yeah, that was awesome."

"No, you jerk. The way you went after that kid," Rikki responded as Darryl went through the door to the shower room. She followed him right in.

"Hey!" he said and turned on her. "You can't be in here. Get out!"

"What's the big deal?" she teased.

His face settled into a frown. "You know what. Guys only. Out."

Rikki crossed her arms over her chest and said, "No."

"Fine," Darryl said and stepped in front of one of the showers. "Last chance to leave," he told her.

"I'm fine right where I am," she returned.

He arched an eyebrow and shrugged. Darryl undid the button of his stonewashed jeans and drew the zipper down revealing black boxer briefs. He pulled the jeans down over his hips then looked up at Rikki again. The woman was rummaging in her purse for something, not even watching him. He stepped out of his jeans and folded them, setting them on a bench.

"What the hell are you doing?" he asked.

Rikki gave him a triumphant grin and pulled out a wad of money. "Singles!" she announced.

Darryl laughed so hard he had to sit down on the bench. Rikki laughed with him and then said, "C'mon. I got the money, I want my show."

Darryl stood up and said, "You do know that you're propositioning an officer of the law, right?"

"So arrest me."

Shaking his head, Darryl approached her. "Turn around. I'll get ready and then you can have your show."

"Yeah, right. I don't think so," Rikki said distrustfully.

Darryl's lopsided grin did things to her body that Rikki couldn't really define. "C'mon, Rikki."

Reluctantly, Rikki turned around. The next thing she knew, Darryl yanked the money out of her hand and danced away from her. Rikki whirled around and made a grab for it. Darryl laughed and held it way above her head. Her five-feet, four inches were no match for his six-foot, three-inch height.

Rikki didn't waste anymore time jumping for it, she aimed a hard blow to his solar plexus.

"Ooof!" Darryl said and brought his arm down low enough for Rikki to retrieve her funds.

"Ha!" she said and scooted out of his reach.

"Who taught you to hit like that?" Darryl asked rubbing his chest and looking at her with new respect.

"My uncle. He was a Navy seal and has a black and red belt in jujitsu," she informed Darryl.

"Really? That's cool. I didn't know that," he said.

"There's a lot you don't know about me. So see? I can handle myself in tough situations," Rikki said. "I have a brown belt myself. So don't think I can't take you down."

"Ha! I'd like to see that."

Rikki grinned. "We'll have to get on the mats sometime."

"You're on," Darryl said. "Now, seriously, Showers. Get out before the captain comes in here, ok?"

"All right. See you later," Rikki said with a little wave and was gone.

Darryl blew out a breath. What he really wanted was to strip her down and get her in the shower with him. Pushing that thought aside, he showered quickly and dressed, heading back out to work.

Darryl stretched out on his couch, put the Steelers game on, and popped open a beer. He guzzled some and proceeded to stuff a hoagie in his mouth. Ripping off a bite, he chewed as he watched the pregame show and thought about his current case. He found that football helped him think.

Chris had told him that Bobby had gotten involved with a guy who sold drugs, but that he didn't know the guy's name. He'd only seen this man twice. Darryl and his partner, Brian Sellers, had been trying to track the guy down based on a composite sketch made from Chris' description.

Darryl wasn't completely sure that Chris wasn't snowing them, but he couldn't prove it. At least not yet. They would get to the bottom of it, though. He wasn't cocky, but he had confidence in his and Brian's abilities to solve cases. Their track record spoke for itself. Brian's out-of-the-box thinking, and Darryl's analytical skills were a great combination.

The game just started when his doorbell rang.

"Shit," he said and pushed off the couch.

Always the cop, Darryl looked through the peephole to see Rikki standing outside the door. He certainly hadn't expected to see her.

Opening the door he said, "Hey, what are you doing here?"

Rikki rushed past him, drawn to the TV. "Did it start? Did I miss anything important?"

" 'Come on in, Showers. Why, thank you, Rodgers,' " Darryl said sarcastically as he closed the door.

"Shhh! Ben has the ball! Shit! He has to

scramble. Where are the fucking blockers? Damn it, he's down," Rikki lamented.

Darryl's eyebrows rose in surprise over her correct play-by-play calls. "You watch football and you're a Steelers fan?"

"Hell, yeah! I live and grew up in Pittsburgh, didn't I?" she said cutting him a scathing glance.

"Yeah, I know. Just didn't figure you were a football fanatic," Darryl said. "You want a beer?"

"Yeah, sure."

Darryl retrieved one for her. When he came back into the living room, she had taken off her coat and was sitting on the couch Indian style. Darryl scowled at the fact that she'd taken his seat, but gave Rikki her beer without comment.

"What do you mean that was out of bounds!" she hollered at the TV. "Goddam ref is blind!"

Darryl couldn't help but laugh at her. She was as vocal over football as any guy he knew. It was pretty cool, and sexy somehow.

Rikki looked at him and grinned. She liked hearing him laugh. She liked making him laugh. "Stop laughing at me."

"I just think it's cute that you like football so much. I didn't expect it," he said with a shrug as he sat down in a recliner. "So did you come over here just to watch football or was there something else you wanted?"

Rikki almost said "you" but didn't. She wanted Darryl in the worst way, but wasn't going to just blurt it out.

"I have some information for you on the

Chambers case," she said.

That got Darryl's attention. "Really?" He didn't discount what Showers said. She'd come up with reliable information in the past, so he took her seriously.

"Yeah. You know that unknown guy you're looking for? Here's some information about him," she said pulling a folded piece of paper from her hip pocket.

Darryl took it from her and scanned it. In the morning, he would get right on plugging the information into the database and seeing what came up. For right now, though, he was going to enjoy watching football with Rikki and seeing what other things he found out about her.

"Damn, she's good," Brian said to Darryl the next morning. The information that Rikki had given them had panned out.

The two cops had gone looking for the goon that Chris had described and that Rikki had collected info on. The creep had holed up in a rotten part of Pittsburgh called Homewood. He'd tried to run when they caught up with him at one of his girlfriends' apartments.

Now, they had him in custody and were on the way back to the precinct. Darryl decided to call Rikki and tell her the good news. He hit the speed dial button for her and waited until she picked up.

"Hey, big guy. What's up?" she said.

Darryl smiled upon hearing her voice. He

liked hearing it way too much, he decided, but carried on. "I just thought you'd like to know that we found Waters. He was shacked up with a girlfriend in Homewood, just like your source said. So you can tell your source that they did a good job."

"Glad to hear it. You bringing him in, I take it?" Rikki said eagerly. She relished the chance to watch Darryl and him work on the guy.

Darryl knew what she was after and was only too happy to comply. "Yes. Would you like a ringside seat?"

"You know I would," she said with a soft laugh.

"Ok. We'll be there in twenty," Darryl told her and hung up.

In the passenger seat, Brian laughed. His white teeth created a stark contrast to his caramel skin.

Darryl frowned and looked at him. "What?"

"For a guy who keeps saying what a pain in the ass Rikki is, you seem to like her an awful lot," Brian commented.

"She's useful, that's all. So I pay her back by letting her see some police work. What's wrong with that?" Darryl said.

Brian grinned. "How useful was she last night watching football?"

"That was a one-time thing. She came with the info and didn't want to miss any of the game. Who am I to deny her that?" Darryl said with a shrug.

"Whatever you say," Brian said and dropped the subject.

Darryl scowled and thought about what

Brian said. Did he have feelings for Rikki that went beyond a working relationship? He had to admit the woman got his juices flowing, both because she was annoying as hell and because she was hotter than hell to look at.

Plus, he liked her pluck and the fact that she wasn't afraid of his temper. It actually seemed like she enjoyed it. He'd picked up on that since she liked watching him in interrogation so much. Maybe he should explore this a little more, he thought.

Darryl swept Jamal Waters' feet off the interrogation table when he entered the room. Brian followed him in and sat in one of the chairs. He flipped open the case file and thrust the autopsy and crime scene photos at Waters.

"You recognize this guy, Jamal?" Brian asked in a no-nonsense voice.

Waters didn't even look at the pictures. "Nope."

Darryl leaned against the one wall, arms crossed over his impressive chest. He didn't say anything, just fixed Waters with a steely glare.

He was making Waters a little nervous, but Jamal wasn't going to let it show.

Brian sat forward. "You didn't even look at it," he said shoving the picture in his face.

Jamal looked at it briefly and blanched under his black skin. "Man, get that thing away from me," he said.

The next thing he knew, a hand clamped down on his neck with an iron grip and forced him to look at the pictures. "Take a good long look, dirt bag." Darryl growled into Waters' ear. "Your future depends on it."

Waters didn't cry out even though the grip on his neck was excruciating. He let his gaze linger on the picture a few moments. "I still don't know the guy," he said.

The grip on his neck tightened further. "And I still don't believe you."

Waters tried to shrug Darryl off, but the cop was too strong. "Fuck you!" he responded.

Darryl slammed Waters' face down onto the table. "I think you'd better start showing some respect."

"I swear that I don't know him! I swear!" Waters' voice was somewhat muffled by the table.

Rikki watched Darryl do his thing. The man was in his element that was for sure. The action in the interrogation room died down, which meant that both cops knew they'd gotten all they were getting out of Waters. Damn.

Rikki joined Brian and Darryl in the corridor. "So now what?" Rikki asked as they entered the bullpen.

"Now we go back to security cameras and to Chris Tompkins. He lied to us," Darryl said.

Rikki felt the anger thrumming around Darryl and knew that she'd hate to be on the receiving end of it. "So where are we going?" she asked.

Darryl rounded on her. "You're not going anywhere except back to the paper. Don't you have a story to write or something?" he said with a stony look and a nasty tone.

Stung, Rikki stopped in her tracks. "Yeah, that's right. I've got a lot more important things to do than hang around with your ass," she snapped back.

Brian gave her an apologetic look before following Rodgers from the precinct.

Snow swirled outside her living room window and Rikki sipped her coffee. She was working on her nonfiction book about Pittsburgh crime. Working with Rodgers and Sellers was giving her a wealth of material to draw from and this case would be no exception.

Deciding that a break was in order after two straight hours of writing, Rikki got up and stretched. Someone knocked on her door and Rikki looked down at her shorts and T-shirt. She wasn't exactly dressed for company.

"Oh well," she said. "Their problem, not mine." She looked through her peephole. Darryl stood well back from the door so she could see that it was him.

She pulled open the door and said, "To what do I owe this pleasure?"

"Thought you'd like an update on the case," he said and stepped inside. Her small apartment was a disaster. She was no housekeeper. It was hotter than hell in there, too. He took off his coat immediately before he started to sweat. "Shit, Showers. What's with the sauna?"

"I like to wear shorts and I hate the cold," she said.

He gave her the lopsided grin she loved.

"Your heating bill must be high as hell."

Rikki shrugged. "I can afford it. So what is it you wanted to tell me now that you've decided I'm good enough to be around you?"

"C'mon, Rikki, you know you can't go everywhere with us. There are just some things that Bry and I have to do on our own."

Rikki padded into her kitchenette and returned with a beer, which she thrust at Darryl. "Whatever. Here. Figured I owed you one."

Darryl rolled his eyes at her attitude and said, "Thanks." He sat on one of the stools at the breakfast bar that separated the kitchenette from the living room area. "Turns out that Chris was the one involved with Waters. When we showed Waters a picture of Chris, he ID'd him right away. Problem is, it looks like Chris split town. We've got an APB out on him. We'll get him."

"I'm sure you will."

"You're partly responsible, you know. You got the info on Waters," Darryl said.

"Wow. What's wrong with you? Are you sick? You're being so generous," Rikki's dark eyes eyed him suspiciously.

Darryl took a swig of his beer as he thought about his next words. "Maybe I'm just coming to realize that you're helpful sometimes, that's all."

Rikki blinked. She wasn't sure she'd heard right. "You just gave me a compliment."

"It happens," Darryl said with a scowl. "Don't be so shocked."

"It doesn't happen to me," she stated. "That's the first time I think you said anything actually nice to me regarding my professional abilities."

Darryl's deep brown eyes speared her. "If I didn't respect your professional abilities, I would let you hang around so much."

Rikki's ire rose. "Let me hang around? What, like I'm some puppy? Is that what you mean?"

Uh oh, Darryl thought. Now you stepped in it.

"No. That's not what I meant and you know it. I'm saying that no other reporter is privy to the information I give you and that's a fact. I let you ride along with us sometimes and watch interrogations. I don't do that for anyone else, Rikki," he explained.

Rikki's expression changed to a smile. "So does that mean that you like me?"

Darryl nodded. "Yeah, I like you."

Closing the distance between them, Rikki said, "No, Rodgers, I mean do you like me... the way a man likes a woman?"

With her beautiful face only inches away from his, what red-blooded man could say anything but yes? Darryl looked at her pretty mouth, her slightly pert nose, and her big brown eyes, and knew he'd lost the battle with himself.

Rikki saw it coming in his eyes, knew he was going to kiss her, and she was ready for it. It was a rough, searing kiss, and she loved the harshness of it. Darryl's lips were surprisingly sensual and soft even though the kiss was hard. One of his powerful arms slipped around her waist and pulled her closer.

Darryl felt Rikki's arms go around his neck, pressing her breasts against his chest. He could tell that she wasn't wearing a bra, and it set him on fire. He yanked her T-shirt up and ran his hands up her back. Rikki gasped as she opened her mouth, inviting Darryl in. Darryl's deft fingers massaged her back as he kissed her, touching her tongue with his and running it across her bottom lip.

He sucked her lips in turn, and Rikki shivered deliciously, her nipples tightening in response. Darryl felt the change against his chest and needed to touch her breasts before he went crazy. He drew her T-shirt up and Rikki gladly raised her arms so that Darryl could take it off her.

Rikki's breasts weren't huge, about a 36B, Darryl judged, but they were beautifully formed, and the pale pink nipples stood out against her creamy skin in a pretty contrast. Darryl palmed them, rubbing his roughened hands over them, making Rikki's nipples tighten even more. Rikki sighed and placed her hands on top of his as she closed her eyes.

Darryl smiled at her obvious pleasure. He flicked his thumb over a nipple, and Rikki gave a sharp gasp and a small moan. He was surprised when she grabbed his other hand and drew it down to her shorts to cover her crotch. She opened her eyes, which had darkened with desire and smiled at Darryl's shocked expression.

"Go on, big guy. Have at it. God knows I've wanted this for a long time," she said.

Her honesty was a little humbling. "You have?" he asked. He'd had a hunch that she liked him, but the confirmation was welcomed.

"Yeah. Oh, that feels good," she said as Darryl's hand moved over her sex in a circular motion and then delved between her legs.

He squeezed her nipple and said, "The feeling has been mutual."

She smiled. "I know. You just weren't going to admit it to yourself much less to me."

"I guess I'm easier to read than I thought," Darryl said with a short laugh.

"Maybe just to me," Rikki replied as small shock waves danced through her as Darryl's fingers kept hitting her clit.

Darryl's hands withdrew from her crotch and breast, and Rikki opened her eyes again to see why he'd stopped. He pushed her away a little so he could take his shirt off, then snaked his arms around her waist to pull her closer again. He ducked his head and took a nipple in his mouth but didn't suck. He ran his tongue around her areola, leaving a hot, wet trail around the sensitive area.

Rikki's fingers glided through his short-cropped hair, the short strands tickling her palm. Suddenly, Darryl's mouth closed around the tight bud and sucked hard and Rikki thought she was going to come right there.

"Oh yeah!" she said.

His other hand toyed with her other nipple and ripples of pleasure spread through Rikki's lower body.

"Darryl, oh God."

Then his mouth left her breast to fuse with hers again. Her breasts came into contact with his hard chest, and Rikki felt like she was going to melt. Her hands found the snap of his jeans and undid it. She slipped a hand inside them and felt along the hardening length of his cock. Judging by the feel of it, it was as big as the rest of him and suddenly she was wild to have him.

She broke the kiss and backed away from Darryl. He was confused for a moment. He thought she'd changed her mind until she tugged her shorts off and ran naked from the kitchen. He grinned and shed his jeans and underwear and followed at a slightly more sedate rate.

He didn't know which room was her bedroom at first, but then he found it. She was standing in the middle of the bed bouncing up and down. He watched her tits jiggle up and down and laughed. Rikki giggled and crooked a finger at him. He walked to the edge of the bed and Rikki bounced over to him and put her arms around his neck. She leaned forward and whispered, "Fuck me, now," into his ear.

Darryl didn't wait for another invitation. He hooked an arm around the back of her knees, took her down and fell on her, his mouth and hands everywhere. His five o'clock shadow scraped pleasurably against Rikki's sensitive skin as he dragged his face from her breasts to her pussy.

He spread her legs apart roughly and then gently opened her pussy lips. He raised his eyes to hers and watched her reaction as he started licking her clit in earnest. Rikki propped herself up on her elbows so that she could watch him tongue fuck her.

"Yeah, lick my pussy, big guy," she said.

Darryl licked faster and harder, merciless in his motions. He wasn't going to take it easy on her, sensing that she didn't want him to. Rikki's eyes widened and her hands fisted at her sides. He growled as she quivered against his mouth and then burst into a swift orgasm. She let her head fall back and she let out a high-pitched yell.

He'd wondered if she was a screamer and figured he'd just found out the answer. Her slightly husky voice echoing off the bedroom walls was music to his ears, and his cock was rock-hard in response. Her hips moved in little thrusts as she came, and he tasted her pussy juice as he continued licking.

Rikki barely waited until the orgasm passed before she sat up and showed him the condom she'd been holding in her hand. Darryl arched an eyebrow at her and then smiled. He snatched it from her hand and ripped it open with his teeth.

Rikki grasped his cock and worked it up and down, loving the feel of it in her hand. He was big and hard and hot, and she wanted that dick inside her cunt.

"Hurry!" she demanded.

Quickly, Darryl rolled the condom down over his cock and spread her legs apart again. As he buried himself in her slick flesh, Rikki wrapped her legs around his waist, drawing Darryl deep inside her.

"God, your cunt is so tight, Rikki," he groaned.

"Good," she panted as he drove into her

over and over. "Fuck it, baby. Yes! I've wanted you to fuck me like this for so long. Dreamt of it, got off thinking about it," she confessed.

That excited him even more and his pace increased until he felt like a jackhammer hitting her. Rikki screamed as he made her cum again. It was so much more intense than the last time, and there was no way she was able to keep quiet.

"Yeah, cum, Rikki! That's it. And I'm not done with you yet, either," he warned her.

Rikki whimpered in his arms. "More, more!" she pleaded.

"More, what?" he asked with a snarl. She seemed to like it when he was mean to suspects and wondered if she'd like it in the bedroom.

"More, please, Lt. R-Rodgers," she panted. "Please, Darryl!"

Darryl rolled over, taking her with him, barely stopping his hip action, driving into her from a different direction. He grabbed her hair, pulled on it playfully and bit her neck while filling her repeatedly with his hard dick.

Rikki felt like she was being pleasantly split in half as Darryl pounded in her. She couldn't even articulate words as her next orgasm overtook her. Another scream announced her climax, and she took Darryl with her. He buried his face in her neck and his harsh shout joined her moans as his hot cum filled the condom.

Darryl fell back on the bed, Rikki falling on top of him.

They lay panting, letting their breathing return to normal. Rikki started to giggle then laugh, shaking against Darryl's chest.

"What's so funny?" he wanted to know as he smiled against her hair.

She raised her head to look at him and then gave him a light punch on the arm.

"Hey!" Darryl protested. "What was that for?"

"Waiting so long for you to make a move," she said.

Darryl chuckled. "I didn't see you making any moves," he said.

"Yeah, I know. That's why I didn't hit you harder," Rikki said. "Oh my God, Darryl. We shouldn't have wasted so much time. We coulda been fucking like bunnies long before now."

Darryl's laugh rang out. "You are so funny. 'Fucking like bunnies.' I love it."

Rikki slid off him and sat up on her knees. "Are you hungry?" she asked. "Screwing makes me hungry."

"You have a potty mouth," Darryl said.

"Is that a complaint?" she challenged him.

"Nope. Just an observation," Darryl answered. "You're hungry? Me, too. What are you going to feed me?"

"Take out," she announced and hopped off the bed and left the room. Then Darryl heard the shower and Rikki call out, "Lt. Rodgers, I have an emergency in here. Can I count on your assistance?"

Darryl moved off the bed and made his way to the bathroom. He followed Rikki into the shower. "Is this where the emergency is?"

"Yes. There's a fire in here and I need your hose to put it out," she told him with a laugh.

"I'm not a fireman, but I do have a nice hose," Darryl told her as he picked up a tube of shower gel and squirted some on his hands. He lathered up and set to work on her body.

They had a very satisfying shower romp and then ordered Italian from a place not far from her apartment. They spent the next hour eating and getting to know each other. Then Darryl said goodnight after giving her a lingering kiss that almost made them go back to the bedroom.

Rikki sat down at her computer again with a sigh, reliving her evening with Darryl. She grinned as images of their naked bodies together came back to her. She was still lost in her daydream when a knock on her door interrupted it. Smiling, she opened the door thinking it was Darryl since he'd only left a few minutes before. It wasn't. The guy standing there didn't even announce who he was; he just pushed Rikki inside and slammed the door shut.

Rikki backed up quickly. "Who are you?" she asked while assuming a fighting stance.

"You're the fucking nosey reporter," the guy said. His cruel blue eyes bore into Rikki. "I'm going to teach you to mind your own business," he said and struck out at her.

Rikki parried and lashed out with her foot, catching the guy's side. He was quick and got a hold of her foot and swung her around. Rikki used the momentum and pirouetted into a roundhouse kick that whacked him across his face.

Rikki was an excellent fighter, and she fought valiantly, but it quickly became apparent that this guy was better. Plus, he had about forty pounds of muscle on her. Rikki knew she'd have to get creative. Her windows were wired with an alarm. She picked up a paperweight from her desk and hurled it at her living room window, which looked down on the front street.

The glass smashed and the paperweight hurtled through the night air. Darryl stood down on the sidewalk, smoking a cigarette, something he rarely did, when he heard glass break above him and something hit his car roof with a deafening bang a moment later. He crouched low as an alarm sounded a moment later.

"What the fuck?" he said and looked upward.

He heard a woman's scream and recognized Rikki's voice. He threw the cigarette in the street and darted back inside the building. He took the stairs three at a time until he reached the second floor and barreled down the hallway to Rikki's door.

When Rikki saw Darryl bulldoze through her door, there was no describing the depth of her gratitude. She was still fighting but knew it was a losing battle. At least, she'd been able to hold the guy off long enough for help to arrive.

Darryl took a split second to appraise what was happening and then jumped the guy in the blue coat. It was then that Rikki learned just how lethal Darryl could be. What she'd seen of his temper until that moment was a pale representation of his fighting prowess and viciousness.

The kicks and blows that Darryl rained down on the creep drove him against the wall. Blood spurted from the guy's mouth and nose, and he seemed like he was almost passing out. Darryl didn't stop. He was seeing red because the guy had dared to attack Rikki, and he wasn't finished meting out justice.

Rikki watched as Darryl's fists kept pummeling the guy in his midsection. When the intruder doubled over, Darryl kneed him in the face and the guy did pass out. He slumped to the floor and Darryl stood over him, chest heaving and sweat pouring down his face. Rikki stood where she was, mesmerized and a little afraid of Darryl at that moment. Underneath that, she was incredibly turned on, however, and wondered what was wrong with her.

Darryl seemed to remember her then and looked at her, his dark eyes shining with a wild light. "You ok?" he asked in a rough voice.

Rikki simply nodded.

Darryl nodded back and then flipped the guy over and cuffed him. Next, he pulled out the guy's ID.

"Jack Parker," he said. "Well, Jack Parker, let's find out just who you are." Darryl kept looking at Rikki as he called dispatch and relayed the information and requested a squad car come pick up Parker.

Once that was done, he came to stand in front of Rikki. He noticed that she had a few cuts and bruises in various places. "Are you sure you're ok?"

Rikki cleared her throat. "Yeah. I'm ok."

"Do you want to go to the hospital?" he asked. This earned him a scathing look. "All right. No hospital."

"I'll live, I promise. I've gotten worse than this during practice. Believe me," she said.

"Ok. After backup gets here, we'll get you cleaned up," Darryl promised her. "Then I'm going to stay the night."

Rikki laid a hand on Darryl's cheek. "You're sweet, but it's not necessary. I don't think anyone else will be coming after me tonight."

Darryl took her hand and kissed the palm. "I'm not taking any chances."

The sound of feet on the stairs stopped him from kissing more than her hand. The uniformed cops helped the paramedics get Parker down the stairs since he was still unconscious. Once Darryl and Rikki had answered some questions, everyone else left. Darryl took his coat off and set to work to temporarily fix the window for the night. They used some cardboard and duct tape to do the job. Then he saw to Rikki's cuts and bruises. Rikki was touched by his tenderness as he administered antibiotic ointment and a couple of Band-Aids.

When he finished, Darryl smiled at her and said, "You got any whiskey?"

Rikki shook her head, "No, but I have some vodka."

"That'll do. Where?"

"In the cupboard above the fridge," she told him.

At his height, Darryl had no trouble reaching it, and he retrieved two glasses and brought them to the living room where they'd been sitting. He poured each of them a small amount and handed a glass to her.

Despite her protests that she was fine, Rikki's hand shook a little as she drank it. The fiery liquid did the trick and relaxed her a little. Darryl tossed his back and then poured a little more, which they both drank slower.

"There, that's better," Darryl said. "You're a hell of a fighter. You were holding your own there, from what I could see."

Rikki smiled. "Thanks, but he was wearing me down. In fact, I'm not sure how much longer I could have gone on. That's why I threw a paperweight through the window. They're alarmed and I thought that it might scare him off and knew it would signal the police."

Darryl nodded. "Good thinking. I heard glass break, something hit my car roof and then an alarm went off. I heard you scream and came on the run. I hadn't left yet. I was having a smoke."

Rikki cocked her head. "You smoke?" she asked disapprovingly.

"Yeah. Well, only every so often when the urge strikes me," Darryl told her with a smile.

"Oh. Ok. Is your car ok?" Rikki asked as she finished her drink and set her glass on the coffee table.

"Yeah, it's fine," Darryl answered even though he had no idea what damage the paperweight might have caused.

"Good. I'm exhausted."

"Let's go to bed, then," Darryl said.

Rikki gave him an annoyed look. "I don't need a babysitter."

"Maybe not, but I'm not gonna sleep unless I know you're ok," he said with a serious expression. "Have pity on me."

Rikki regarded him for a moment and saw that he was telling her the truth.

"Ok. Come on," she said and took his hand.

Rikki changed into her jammies and Darryl stripped down to his underwear. They crawled into Rikki's bed and covered up. It felt as natural to them both as breathing. Soon Rikki was asleep, tired out by the events of that evening. Darryl didn't go to sleep right away, still bothered by what had happened.

The fact that Rikki had been attacked meant that the investigation was making someone nervous. It also meant that it was someone who knew that Rikki was working on the case with them. That could be a lot of people, he realized. Rikki curled up with her back to him, her warm little body resting against him.

Darryl rolled over, spooning her. He put his arm around her and kissed her hair. Rikki smiled in her sleep and sighed. Darryl smiled as he remembered the way Rikki had fought Parker off. Her moves were quick, sure, and accurate. Her uncle had taught her well.

He frowned as he realized that if they sent one guy after Rikki, they might send someone else after her, too. His embrace tightened as anger slithered through him at the thought of anyone hurting her. Darryl vowed that he wouldn't let that happen at any cost.

Darryl smiled. He was having one hell of a good sex dream. He had a powerful hard on, and some chick was licking and sucking it. Shit, it felt incredible. He reached his hands down to touch her hair and was jolted awake by the realization that he was actually physically touching someone real.

He felt a hand run down his thigh while another one held the base of his penis. Recognizing that he was still in Rikki's bedroom, he grinned and laughed at himself.

Rikki stopped what she was doing and looked up at him.

"Why are you laughing at me?" she asked with a frown.

"I'm not laughing at you. I'm laughing at me. You scared the hell out of me for a second or two," he told her and stroked her cheek.

Rikki giggled and went back to the task at hand. Darryl watched her small pink tongue flick over the head of his cock, and he growled as frissons of heat seared his loins. His cock disappeared into her mouth, and his eyebrows rose as he watched her take him deep. Darryl could kick himself for not coming on to Rikki a long time ago. He'd had no idea she was so talented in the bedroom.

He felt Rikki's pussy rubbing on his other thigh and realized that she was straddling it. It was soft and hot and thinking about it made him even harder. Rikki pulled back, sucking hard on Darryl's dick. He tasted so good and felt amazing in her hand. She played with his balls, enjoying the softness of his skin and the coarseness of his pubic hair.

Darryl sucked in a breath as she moved

faster. Her suction was flawless, and the way she worked him with her hand at the same time was like watching a ballet he decided.

"Uh, Rikki?"

"Hmm?"

"You do realize what's going to happen if you keep doing that, right?" he asked. His teeth gritted as he held back.

"Mmm hmm," she answered in the affirmative never breaking her rhythm.

"No, I mean, uh, shit." He didn't know how to ask what he was getting at. Not all women liked to swallow, and he needed her to understand that he was on the verge of cumming.

He moved to sit up, cupping her head in his hand. She surprised him by knocking his hand away and pushing him back down. Darryl flopped back and said, "Ok. I guess you know what I'm saying."

"Mmm hmm," she said again.

Rikki appreciated Darryl's consideration, but she wanted to taste his cum, wanted to do that for him. Her hand gripped his cock a little harder, and she moved her head faster. She felt Darryl's large body tense and his ball sac tighten and knew that it would only be a matter seconds.

Darryl thought he was going to go crazy at the intensity of his orgasm when it happened. He came up off the bed and couldn't even shout for a few seconds. Rikki tasted the first of his cum and switched positions, taking him deeper and swallowing repeatedly as Darryl groaned louder and louder. The stream slowed and then stopped. Ever so gently, she licked

Darryl's cock a little and then released him.

Darryl sunk back on the bed, his heart pounding like a freight train in his chest. That was one of the most extraordinary things he'd ever felt, he thought. He lay completely still, contemplating that fact along with knowing that Rikki had done something few women actually enjoyed doing.

The next thing he knew, Rikki was swinging her leg over his chest, and he was facing her pretty pussy.

"Turnabout is fair play," she told him with a laugh.

"Ok," Darryl's voice gave out and Rikki laughed harder. He cleared his throat and laughed, too. "Damn, Rikki. That was... there are no words for what that was. I'll just show you what that was."

Rikki gasped when she felt Darryl slide two fingers inside her and begin sawing in and out. Then he added his nimble, hot tongue and licked and sucked her clit. Rikki grabbed the sheets in her hands and held on as Darryl took her on a sensual ride. He sped up and slowed down only to speed up again.

He was teasing her and obviously was in no hurry, and she loved it that he was playful and generous as a lover. She felt herself tighten around his fingers as her excitement grew to a fever pitch. Rikki needed to reach the summit, and she had every confidence in Darryl's ability to do it.

Darryl found the small patch of raised skin inside Rikki and started to move his fingers in trigger-squeezing motion and changed the rhythm of his tongue. Rikki shouted, "Fuck!"

and came in a blinding climax. She couldn't move, couldn't think. Darryl kept going until he heard her loud cries of delight trail off.

He placed a couple of kisses on her pussy as she collapsed on top of him. Rikki moved off of Darryl and flipped around the other way so she could see him. Darryl was still enjoying the taste of her on his lips.

"Damn, you taste good," he said as Rikki settled on top of him.

"So do you," Rikki said with a smile.

Darryl cleared his throat. "Thanks. It's unusual for women to want to or be willing to, well, you know..."

Rikki laughed softly, enjoying his discomfort. "You mean swallow?"

"Yeah, that." Darryl was relieved that she'd said it so he didn't have to.

"Men are so funny about that." She shrugged. "It's no big deal to me. I like doing it."

"That's amazing." Darryl rubbed her back. "You're amazing," he said.

Rikki snuggled closer to him. "You're not so bad yourself."

Darryl kissed her forehead and then asked, "What time is it?"

"Early. Don't worry. I have my alarm set for six. I think it's about four-thirty. I woke up and you were wrapped around me, and it made me hornier than hell. Hence, the wake-up call."

"And what a wake-up call it was," Darryl commented with a chuckle. "We have time for a nap."

Rikki was already drowsy. "Mmm hmm."

Darryl sensed her drifting and scooted her off of him long enough to grab the covers and pull them up over their cooling bodies. He gathered her to his side again and they sunk down into a deep sleep.

"That's the third time you've yawned in the past ten minutes," Brian said. "I'd say you had a busy night at Rikki's place." Brian gave Darryl a broad grin. He had come into the station after Darryl had called to inform him about what had happened at her place. He'd been working through the night on various leads, checking out Parker's priors and trying to find the connection to Tompkins.

Darryl gave him a dark look. "None of your business, Bry. I'm gonna call the hospital and see if Parker is up for a visit."

Brian let out a low whistle. "From what I hear, you really fucked him up good."

The smile that Darryl sent Brian was full of malice and made the hair on Brian's neck stand up. "He deserved it. He was going to kill Rikki. I'm just glad that she can fight the way she does. Did you know she has a brown belt in jujitsu?"

"No. I didn't know that. Cool. At least she can take care of herself," Brian remarked as Darryl picked up his desk phone.

"It was just luck that I was still outside her place when it went down. This guy is a pro and would have eventually overpowered her. I'm glad I was there," Darryl said.

Brian smiled. "And what were you doing there?"

"Updating her on the case," Darryl said.

"Is that what they're calling it these days?" Brian said with a short laugh.

Darryl grinned. "Ok," he said in a low voice. "It started out as just updating her, but it, uh, well it led to other things."

"I knew it!" Brian said.

"Shh! Not so loud, dumbass," Darryl reprimanded Brian. "I don't want a bunch of people knowing. We're just seeing where things go."

"I'm really happy for you, bro. It's about damn time you guys got it going," Brian said.

Darryl started dialing the hospital. "Thanks, man. That means a lot. Just keep it to yourself, ok?"

"You got it," Brian assured him.

The hospital operator picked up, and Darryl set about finding information on Parker's condition.

When Darryl and Brian arrived later at the hospital, Parker was uncooperative and lawyered up after seeing Darryl again. His fear of the lieutenant was palpable, and Darryl hadn't stuck around too long. He waited out in the hall for Brian who usually played good cop.

"Did you get anything out of him?" Darryl asked when Brian emerged from Parker's room.

Brian shook his head. "The only thing he would say is that Tompkins had all the answers and that he doubts that Tompkins will be talking to anyone."

"Shit. You know what that means," Darryl said.

"Yeah. He's dead. Unless Parker's lying to keep us away from Tompkins," Brian responded.

Darryl's cell rang. Rikki's face appeared on the caller ID. Darryl smiled then noticed Brian smiling at him. He punched Brian's shoulder playfully. "Shut up," he said to Brian then answered his phone.

"Hey. What's up?" Darryl asked.

Rikki's heart did a little skip upon hearing his slightly rough voice. "Hey. How are you?"

"I'm great. How are you?" Darryl asked as he took another swipe at Brian's teasing demeanor. He walked away from his partner, going down the hallway.

"I'm good and you're going to be even better."

Darryl's sensual mouth turned up in a grin. "Oh yeah? What'd you have in mind?"

Rikki laughed at the direction Darryl's mind had taken. It wasn't far from her mind either. "Well, there's always that, but not now."

"Oh." Darryl said. His voice registered his disappointment.

"Your boy Tompkins? I found him," Rikki said and doodled on the tablet in front of her.

"What? How? Where is he?" Darryl's raised voice carried to Brian who jogged down the hall to join him.

"What's going on?" Brian asked.

"Rikki found Tompkins," Darryl told him.

"Seriously? Where?"

"That's what I'm trying to find out," Darryl said sarcastically.

Rikki's laugh came through his phone, and Darryl saw her naked in her bed in his mind. "I'll meet you at the station and fill you in on everything. Oh, and by the way, he'll be arriving at the precinct soon."

A thrill of victory ran through Darryl, and he wished he could kiss Rikki through the phone. "Ok. We'll see you there."

Rikki ended the call and sat back in her desk chair. She craved seeing Darryl again and also watching him do what he did best. Well, what he did second best, she amended her thought with a smile. Then she gathered up her coat and purse and headed for Darryl's precinct.

Darryl looked up from his typing to see Rikki coming down the hall towards the bullpen, and he felt like someone slammed him in the chest with a sledgehammer. She looked so damn pretty in her mid-length ruffled skirt, matching blouse and heels. Enough of her well-toned calves showed to be tantalizing, and Darryl remembered how they'd felt locked around his hips. He shifted slightly in his chair at the memory.

Several male heads turned as she walked by them and Darryl scowled in jealously.

"Hey, big guy," Rikki said softly in greeting, her dark eyes shining as she looked at him.

Darryl wanted to grab her and kiss her. He wanted to take her hair out of the chignon she wore and spread it over her shoulders. Darryl forced the images out of his mind and smiled back at her.

"Hey yourself. You look pretty," he greeted her.

Rikki blushed a little. "Thank you. So do you," she teased.

Darryl laughed. "Thanks. Brian will be back in a minute, and you can tell us how this miracle happened."

"Sounds good."

Brian returned just then with two cups of coffee. "Oh, hey, Rikki. I'm sorry," he said indicating the coffee. "I didn't know you were here or I'd have brought some for you."

Rikki held up a hand. "No sweat. I've had enough coffee for one day."

Darryl said, "So tell us what happened."

"I have a friend in the FBI," Rikki said as she propped a hip on Darryl's desk. "He's a tech whiz. Not that I'm knocking your department's tech staff," she clarified. "He's one of the best in the country. He's able to pull footage from all traffic lights and run facial recognition and license plates. Not just in the city, but throughout the state and a couple of the surrounding states."

"Wow," Brian said. "That's really cool."

"So that's how they got him, huh?" Darryl asked. He was envious that this fed had this capability.

"Yeah, they found him just crossing the border into Ohio. Addison had the staties retrieve him," Rikki said.

"We need to send the man a gift," Brian said.

"Yeah," Darryl agreed. "You do good work, Rikki."

"Thanks, but Addison did all the work," she replied.

Brian stood up. "Well, shall we talk to the

punk?" he said to Darryl.

"Oh yeah," Darryl said. The angry look on his face gave Rikki a chill of anticipation.

After a half hour of abuse from Darryl and calm caring from Brian, Tompkins didn't know which way to turn. Darryl had scared the crap out of him again. He hadn't disappointed Rikki and in fact had seemed to turn up the heat just for her benefit.

By the time Brian and Darryl were done with Tompkins, they'd gotten a name from him and he'd confessed to several crimes. None of them were killing Robert Chambers, however.

Darryl and Brian were pleased with the information they had, though. It was a huge help, and now, they had a lot more to go on. Rikki came out the interrogation room and joined the two men. Darryl placed a hand on the small of Rikki's back, something he'd never done before. Rikki liked it.

"Thanks for your help," Darryl said to her as they reached their desks. "Now we get to go run down leads."

"Well, I'd love to go with you, but I have to get back and get my story done before John, my editor, has a conniption," Rikki told the partners. "Let me know how things are going."

"I'll do you one better than that," Darryl said. He was going to make a huge leap. "I'll pick you up at seven for dinner."

Rikki stopped in her tracks and blinked at Darryl. "Really?"

Darryl smiled at her surprise. "Yeah, really."

"I'll be ready," she said. There was no way

she was going to turn down a real date with Darryl.

"Good." Then he surprised her even further by leaning down and giving her a light kiss on her mouth. "See you then."

"S-see you then," she said and walked off in a daze. He'd kissed her in public at his place of work. She couldn't believe it. What had gotten into him? Not that she wasn't ecstatic about it, but it was so out of character for Darryl. Maybe that tough exterior was starting to soften a little, she mused, and continued on her way.

Two hours later found Darryl and Brian in a shoot-out after approaching Raymond DuPont. His name was the one that Tompkins had given them that morning. DuPont had ordered his goons to take Brian and Darryl out when they'd visited him at one of his warehouses.

The two cops had taken cover immediately and were now pinned down behind a pile of scrap metal. Brian had called for backup, but it would be at least five or ten minutes before someone showed up.

Darryl checked his ammo. He had three more clips, so he was confident that he and Brian could hold off the assholes shooting at them. The gunfire stopped for a moment, and Darryl took the opportunity to rise up carefully and aim at one of the guys who was trying to sneak up on them.

His bullet hit the guy in the shoulder, and he spun around and fell. Gunfire opened up again and Darryl ducked down. Brian smiled at him. "Nice shot."

"Thanks. Where the hell is backup?" he growled. "Taking their good old time," he said.

"Yeah, we need them, that's for sure," agreed Brian.

The rain of bullets stopped again and the cops assumed they were trying to reload.

"Time to go on the offensive," Darryl said.

"I'll go this way and you go that way. We'll keep each other covered," Brian said.

Darryl nodded and took off. He kept crouched down to make himself as small a target as possible. He wanted to get into that warehouse before DuPont took off. He rounded a corner of another pile of scrap metal to find one of DuPont's men pointing a gun at him.

Darryl dove for cover, throwing himself behind a few metal barrels to his right. Several shots rang out and Darryl felt something slam into his left ankle. Intensely hot pain hit him, and he gasped and gritted his teeth against the pain as he smashed to the ground.

The guy came around the barrel. Darryl twisted around and shot the guy in the head. He wasn't fooling around. A siren sounded close by and Darryl knew that backup had finally arrived. Darryl used one of the barrels to haul himself up on his feet. The leg that had been shot gave out and he fell back down again.

Rising once more, Darryl hopped around the barrels, keeping behind the metal piles as much as possible. He almost tripped over Brian who lay on his face in the dirt. Darryl dropped to the ground and flipped Brian over. His partner was unconscious but had a pulse.

When Darryl spotted a cruiser, he waved to the cop inside. Officer Mike Harris ran over to Darryl.

"Got one down. He's my partner. I'm hit. We need a bus," Darryl said.

Harris called for a bus and then left them to go help apprehend what men hadn't run when they'd showed up. The ambulance came and took both men away.

It was funny, Darryl thought. The first person he'd wanted to call was Rikki, not only because dinner wasn't going to happen, but also because she was the one he wanted to come to the hospital.

He dialed her number and smiled through the pain in his leg when she answered.

"Hey, big guy," she said. "Couldn't wait until dinner, huh?"

"Uh, no, but not for the reason you think," he told her. Then he filled her in on what had taken place.

Tears spilled from her eyes onto her desk as she listened to Darryl's story. She wiped them away and said, "I'll be right there." She hung up and practically flew out of the building.

Rikki arrived at the hospital and hurried to the ER waiting room and checked with the desk clerk. She was informed that the clerk would tell the doctor she was there and that she'd have to wait in the waiting room.

Rikki sat there for about five minutes and then decided to try to sneak back to the ER exam rooms. She made her way down a hall, turned right, and asked an orderly how to get back into the exam rooms. She lied and told him she'd gone to the bathroom and needed to get back to her fiancé.

He pointed the way and Rikki took off. She searched the rooms until she saw Darryl lying on a table in a small room. He wore a hospital gown and looked.

"Darryl!"

Darryl opened his eyes. He was a little groggy from the pain meds they'd forced on him. "Hi, honey," he said with a goofy smile.

Rikki sniggered a little at his condition. That he was hopped up on painkillers was very apparent. In his right mind, Darryl would have never said such a thing to her.

"Hi. How are you feeling?" she asked.

Darryl took her hand as she came to stand beside him and kissed it. Despite the fact that he was drugged up, his kiss still had an effect on Rikki.

"I'm glad you're here," he told her. "You were the only person I called."

Rikki was touched by his admission. "Really?"

Darryl nodded. "Yeah."

Rikki squeezed his hand. "Well, here I am. Have you heard anything about Brian?"

"Nope. Not since they took him to surgery. He took a shot to the stomach. They need to repair any internal damage." A dangerous light entered Darryl's eyes, and it seemed as if the haze of drugs lifted a little. "If he doesn't make it, I'm gonna kill every fucking one of them. I swear it," he said.

Rikki was surprised to see a tear leak from Darryl's right eye. She reached out and wiped it away. Her tenderness undid Darryl's control and he broke down. Rikki held him while he cried, knowing that this, too, would have never happened without the drugs in his system. She knew how close Brian and he were and was infuriated about Brian being shot, too.

His tears subsided, and he wiped them away just before the doctor entered the room. Darryl was going to have to have surgery on his ankle, and they were setting up the OR right then. Rikki stayed with him until they took him.

Four hours later, Rikki was notified that Darryl was out of surgery and doing well. She would be able to go see him in half an hour. When she entered Darryl's room, he was pressing the button that controlled his morphine drip. His face was tight with pain when he looked at Rikki.

"Looks like you're in some pain," she said kindly as she sat on the edge of the bed.

"Yeah, you could say that. Burns like a mother," he said.

"I'm sure the morphine will kick in soon," Rikki said soothingly.

Darryl nodded. "Brian's gonna be ok. One of the nurses told me," he said as he looked into her dark eyes.

Relief flowed through Rikki. "God, that's fantastic."

"I know," Darryl said sleepily as the morphine took hold of him. He fell asleep moments later and Rikki took the chair beside him.

Two days later, Rikki showed up at Darryl's apartment with a pizza and beer. She knocked and waited for him to answer the door. Thumping sounds came from inside, and she knew then that Darryl was on his way to the door.

He opened it and gave her a big smile. "Damn, talk about service," he said and moved back so she could enter.

She sat the pizza on the table and moved to one of his cupboards to get some paper plates and napkins. Darryl carefully sat down on a chair and propped his crutches against the wall next to him.

"How do you feel?" she asked as she placed slices of pizza on the plates.

"Better," Darryl said and took a huge slice of pizza. "Physically, anyway. I'm pissed that I can't follow this case to the end now."

Rikki bit into her own slice and said, "Yeah, but you guys did all of the legwork on it. You're practically handing them the case solved. You guys will still get the collar, so it's all good."

Darryl shrugged. "I guess. I just like to finish things that I start."

"Well, it's not like you can help it, you know," she said looking into his chocolate eyes. Her desire for him was never far away.

Darryl's gaze traveled over her lithe form. She was dressed in jeans and a deep purple sweater and looked good enough to eat. That analogy gave Darryl ideas, and he moved a little restlessly in his chair.

Rikki saw him move and asked, "Does your ankle hurt?"

Darryl nodded. "Some. Not too bad."

"Well, we're going to watch the game, and you can lay on the couch with your leg propped up, ok?" she said.

"Ok, Nurse Showers. Whatever you say. You gonna stay over?" he asked hopefully.

"Yeah, if you want me to," she said with a teasing smile.

"Of course I do, woman."

After the game, which the Steelers won, they headed off to bed. Darryl lay on his back with a pillow under his ankle. Rikki came into the room from down the hall. She wore a red bra and thong. Darryl swallowed at the desire that struck him.

She crawled onto the bed and lay down beside him. She put her hand on his hairless chest and began rubbing back and forth.

"How come you wax your chest?" she asked.

Darryl laughed at the question. It had come out of left field, which was typical for Rikki. "Because it doesn't grow in right, so it looks much better shaved."

"I like it very much," Rikki said making little circles on his smooth skin. She brushed her fingertips over one of Darryl's nipples and he sucked in a breath.

"If you're trying to torture me, you're doing a good job," he told her.

Rikki giggled. "But it's a nice kind of

torture, yes?" she said in a fake French accent.

"Yes, it is," Darryl admitted. "But where's it leading?"

"Right down here," Rikki said. Her fingers trailed down over his six-pack abs until they reached his underwear. "We're going to have to get rid of these." Rikki played with his package through the boxer-briefs and felt Darryl's cock start to come to life.

"You're gonna have to help me," Darryl said.

"No problem," Rikki replied.

Darryl raised his hips up with his good leg while keeping his bad leg still. Rikki pulled his underwear down over his ass and slid them down his legs. She took them off his good leg first and then gently took them off the injured leg. It only caused Darryl a short twinge of pain, a small price to pay for what he knew was in store.

Rikki carefully straddled his good leg and bent down to place a kiss on his penis, which was starting to throb slightly. She licked his ball sac and then took his cock in her hand and stroked him up and down. Rikki moaned at how good he felt to touch and ran her tongue around the head of his dick.

Darryl groaned and laid his head back. Then she was gone and he looked up to find her standing by the bed taking off her bra and thong. She placed one of her feet on the bed and spread her legs wide. She opened her pussy lips so that Darryl could see her center.

"Like what you see?" she asked in a saucy tone.

"Oh yeah. It's one of my favorite things to look at."

He watched transfixed as she put her hand over her pussy and slid a finger inside. Rikki stroked herself, going as deep as she could, then coming out and rubbing her clit.

"Now you," she said. "I want to see you stroke yourself."

Darryl did as she requested, grasping his hardening dick and working it while he watched her stroke her clit. Rikki stopped and went back to fingering herself then rubbing her clit. She kept going back and forth like that and Darryl kept stroking his cock.

Then Rikki stopped what she was doing and climbed back on the bed. She held out her fingers to Darryl and he grabbed her wrist and proceeded to suck her fingers, relishing the taste of her cunt. Both of them were so excited that Darryl didn't know how they'd kept from coming as they watched each other masturbate.

Darryl kissed Rikki long and deeply, cupping the back of her head with one hand and teasing a nipple with his other. Rikki moaned deep in her throat and her hips moved as little shock waves made their way to her pussy.

"I want you so much," Darryl said. He reached for his bedside table and opened the drawer where he kept condoms.

Rikki stopped him. "No need. I trust you and I'm on very reliable birth control. I want to feel you inside me with nothing between us," she said.

That sounded great to Darryl, and he

brought his hand back to run it down Rikki's arm. "If you're sure."

"I'm sure," she said and straddled his hips. "Don't worry, I'll do all the work. I don't want to hurt your ankle."

"Oh, don't worry about that. I'm feeling just fine," Darryl assured her.

She reached between them and eased his cock inside her pussy. She relaxed and took him all the way in. As her clit hit his lower abdomen, a fiery sensation flowed through her and Rikki could tell it wasn't going to take much for either of them to come. That had been the idea behind masturbating. It was the best way to satisfy their need for each other without causing Darryl pain.

Darryl growled as she rose up and came back down again. She was so tight and hot and wet, and he didn't know how long he'd be able to hold out.

"Oh, God, Rikki. You feel so good. It's not going to take long I'm afraid," he said honestly.

"For me, either, so don't feel bad. I'm so fucking horny right now, and I need to come so bad, baby," Rikki answered.

She lay down on top of him and moved back and forward, taking him in and withdrawing. Her clit kept hitting him and his cock kept filling her and stroking her G-spot. For Darryl, her cunt was so tight that it felt like it was milking him. He felt his orgasm building and knew it was imminent.

"Rikki. You feel so good. I'm gonna cum soon," he warned her.

"Good. I want you to come. Oh, your cock is

so hard and big and feels so good inside my pussy."

She slid down a little harder and moved back faster. Darryl bent his one good leg and pushed his hips up. His muscular thigh and hard ass muscles helped him and kept his other leg still. Rikki smiled down at him and rode the new rhythm he was creating. She saw the cords and muscles stand out in his neck and knew he was going to cum.

"Yeah, big guy, cum for me. Cum hard and fill my twat with that hot cum of yours," she coaxed and moaned as she felt a small spasm that announced her impending orgasm.

Darryl slid his arms around her waist and clasped her to him as he rose up hard, backed out and repeated the motion. As she came back down on him, Darryl soared into a mighty orgasm that made him feel like he was being turned inside out. Rikki reveled in the knowledge that she did that to him and the sensation of his hot seed spurting deep inside her.

As Darryl continued to thrust inside her, Rikki climaxed, her pussy clenching around his dick. Rikki shouted her pleasure, squeezing Darryl's big biceps and shuddering against him. They drifted down from their pleasure haze gradually, lingering in the ecstasy they created together.

Dimly, Darryl began to realize that his ankle was throbbing, but he didn't care because he felt so good. It was worth some pain, he decided. Rikki slid off him and lay down while she caught her breath.

"Jesus," Darryl said. "Where the hell did

you come from?"

Rikki laughed and propped herself up on an elbow so she could look at him. "What does that mean?"

"It means that I've never been with such an erotic woman before. You're not afraid to do anything," he replied with a huge smile.

"Why should I be? Sex is natural. It's a good thing. Too many people are too ashamed about sex," Rikki said seriously.

Darryl kissed her. "I like your attitude, Showers."

"I can tell," she said scooting off the bed. "I'm going to clean you up and then take a shower ok?"

"I can come in there and do it myself, you know," he informed her and made a move to get up. A hammering pain moved through his ankle and up his calf. Darryl hissed with the pain.

"Yeah, sure. You're doing great so far," she said sarcastically.

Darryl gritted his teeth and then shouted, "Fuck! I hate this."

"Shh," Rikki soothed and ran her hand over his forehead. "You'll be better before you know it."

She left him and then returned with a washcloth and towel. When she was done, Darryl decided it wasn't so bad having a personal nurse. She'd made it fun and not embarrassing at all. She kept teasing him about getting shot on purpose just so he could get sponge baths.

Then she gave him one of his painkillers and settled in beside him.

Six weeks later, Darryl was back to work at almost full capacity. He was temporarily partnered with a young detective named Tim Johnson. The kid was annoying as hell because he didn't know anything about real police work and thought he was Dirty Harry. Rikki kept reminding Darryl that he had been green at one time, too, and that he should be nice and teach Tim.

Some days Darryl could do it and some days not. He counted the minutes until Brian would be back. He was happy, however, that DuPont had been arrested for the murder of Robert Chambers and was being held over for trial. The man had been running drugs and weapons. It was a big operation, and there were a lot of crooks going to jail as a result.

Rikki had gotten her story and had painted Brian and Darryl as the heroes they were. Darryl wasn't happy that Rikki hadn't mentioned her own role in solving the case, but she'd insisted that she hadn't done much. He eventually let it go.

His and Tim's current case involved the homicide of a middle-aged housewife, and the husband was looking good for it. Rikki stood in the observation room while they grilled the guy. Tim was much more reserved and respectful, much like Brian, while Darryl prowled up and down the room and shot threatening looks at Mr. Hammond.

When Darryl had finally had enough of the

husband sidestepping questions, he came over to the mirror and looked at Rikki. He used his big body to hide the heart shape he made with his hands and winked at her. Then he spun around and whipped the case file that was tucked up under his arm across the room, papers flying everywhere.

Mr. Hammond was shocked and jumped out of his chair as Darryl approached him. Tim was scared shitless, and Rikki couldn't help but laugh as the poor kid scrambled to pick up the file and put it back together. Mr. Hammond backed against the wall, and Darryl put both hands on either side of his head and leaned in close. Five minutes later, Mr. Hammond was confessing and signing an affidavit.

Darryl clapped Tim on the back and left him to oversee the rest of it. Then he left the interrogation room and headed towards the observation room. Rikki was just coming out of it. He pushed her back in roughly and locked the door behind him. Rikki laughed at his treatment. It was just his way of playing, she knew.

Darryl undid his jeans and pushed them down, then he backed Rikki up against the wall, reached under her skirt, and ripped her panties right off her. Rikki objected until he promised to replace them and then stopped her protest altogether when he lifted her up and sat her down on his hard penis.

As he slid inside her, they were both lost, knowing only the bliss they created in each other. The crime around them faded away as their bodies gave into the passion they created together.

3 TOUCHDOWN

Hot sunlight glinted off Alex's next door neighbor's bare chest and back as he moved. She watched in fascination as sweat ran down his brown skin and dripped onto the grass. Alex got so caught up in watching Mike Sanchez saw off portions of two-by-fours that she didn't realize that she'd reached her kitchen door until she ran into it.

She swore under her breath when she heard the eggs break in one of the grocery bags she carried. They were for a cake she was baking for a client, and she didn't need the delay of going back to the store for more. She hoped there was enough left intact to do the job.

Mike had noticed Alex's preoccupation with him but had just continued his work. Now, as he watched her bump into her door and try to act nonchalant about it, Mike smiled to himself. It wasn't the first time he'd caught her looking at him. Mike wasn't overly vain, but he knew he was a great looking guy and that women liked him.

Trying to spare Alex some humiliation, he acted as if he hadn't seen her blunder. However, after watching her fail three times at unlocking her door, Mike took further pity on her.

"Hey there," he said, acting as if he'd just spotted her. "You need some help there?" he asked, trotting across the yard.

Alex couldn't believe that the object of her obsession was actually coming her way. "Oh, no. I'm fine, really. Just a little clumsy today, that's all."

Mike smiled at her. His teeth were very white in his dark, olive-skinned face. Alex hadn't seen him up this close before, and she now saw that he had a dimple in his right cheek.

"Well, we all have those days," he said and took the bags from her.

Alex smiled gratefully at him as she inserted the key into the lock. "You don't, I'll bet. At least, not that I've seen."

That confused Mike. "What?"

Alex could have kicked herself. It sounded like she was stalking him, then thought, wasn't she, though? "I go to the football games and I've seen you play. You have great footwork," she blurted.

Mike grinned. "Really? You come to the games? That's cool."

Mike played fullback for the Pinecrest Pistons, the local college team, and there were rumors that the NFL was courting him.

Alex opened the door and motioned for him to follow her. "Yeah. My dad was a high school football coach and our whole family is crazy about football."

"That's awesome," Mike said and put the bags on the table that stood in the middle of the large kitchen. Something smelled incredible. "You must bake a lot. It smells like cookies or something."

Alex watched his dark eyes light up at the thought of cookies and smiled. "I'm a caterer. Just small-scale stuff right now, but I plan to go full-time eventually." Shut up. He doesn't care. This hunk of a college kid doesn't care about your Suzie Homemaker lifestyle.

Mike's stomach rumbled as he kept inhaling the delicious aroma that lingered. He turned a megawatt smile on Alex. "I don't suppose you have any extra goodies around, huh?"

Alex was pleased that he asked, even if it was just a natural guy response to food.

"Uh, yeah, actually, I do." Something suddenly occurred to Alex. "Oh! You would be doing me a huge favor if you would try something new I tried. Cream cheese oatmeal raisin cookies. Are you up for it?"

Mike looked into Alex's beautiful green eyes and wasn't sure he could have denied her anything. She may be older than him by ten years or so, but she was a hottie. Besides, the cookies sounded great. "Yeah. Bring it on."

Alex pointed to a spot behind him. "Over there on the counter in that container. Have at it. I have to get some of this stuff in the fridge right away before it spoils."

Mike turned around, glancing at the rest of the kitchen. He'd never been in Alex's house before. It was a big room and he could see why it had to be. All of the kitchen equipment looked to be state of the art or commercial. He wouldn't know the difference, but did know that it didn't look like the type of refrigerator and freezers he'd grown up using.

There was a lot of counter space, which would certainly come in handy in Alex's type of work. He found the container she'd pointed out and opened the lid. Immediately, the scent of vanilla and cream cheese wafted up to his nostrils. The cookies were large, and they were moist judging by the one he picked up.

He took a big bite, going all in like he did with almost everything in life. His mouth was flooded with one of the most delicious flavors he'd ever tasted. Closing his eyes, Mike chewed, noticing that the cookie was definitely sweet, but that the raisins were slightly tart, a great combination. He finished that bite and stuffed the rest of the cookie in his mouth and chewed it quickly.

When he opened his eyes, Alex stood right by him. Startled, Mike jumped a little. Alex seemed not to notice.

"So? What did you think?" she asked eagerly.

Mike laughed. "Didn't know you were right there. Uh, well, they're ok," he said with a shrug.

He almost laughed when Alex's face fell and her pretty mouth turned down. "Ok? Just ok? Really?"

"Hell, no!" Mike burst out. "They're fucking awesome! Are you kidding me? I've never had a cookie so good. If you tell my mom, I'll deny it, but they're the best I've ever had."

Alex laughed so hard she had tears in her eyes. "You had me, you really did. You're such a shit," she said. "I thought they sucked."

"Sorry, I couldn't help it. I'm a natural-born smart ass or so my mother tells me." Mike laughed. "Seriously, though, these are amazing. Can I have a couple to take home?" he asked.

Alex suddenly grew conscious of the fact that Mike's bare chest was at her eye level. And what a nice chest it is, she thought. He was ripped, that was for sure. Her gaze traveled over his big shoulders and further up until it reached his eyes, which held amusement.

His words registered with her a moment later. "Oh, yeah. Definitely. I have to pay you for helping me out somehow."

Mike looked over her shapely form. She was about five-foot-three, he judged. The jeans shorts Alex wore showed off her tanned, sexy legs and slim hips. Her red, spaghetti strap top let him see some cleavage from his height and it looked great. Mike could definitely think of a way Alex could express her gratitude to him.

He nodded and said, "Cool. Well, I gotta get back to work or my dad will have my ass." Mike grabbed two more cookies from the container and headed for the door. "See ya later."

"Bye," Alex said and watched him leave.

She sighed and sank back against the fridge. "You should not be lusting after a college kid, Alex," she said. But Mike wasn't just any other college kid. He was a very hot young Latino man, and that fact was hard to ignore no matter what age.

His short dark hair, rich brown eyes and flashing dimple didn't make it any easier, either. Alex thought he was even better looking up close. And those hard, sweaty muscles? Yeah, she would happily dig her nails into him, she mused as she set about making her cake.

She glanced out her window from time to time, watching Mike work. The kitchen just got hotter and hotter and not entirely from the oven. Finally, Alex decided that she needed to go out on a date. She called her friend Monica who'd said she had the perfect guy for her.

Seven that night saw one Jeff Carstairs picking Alex up. Mike had just finished his work for the night when the guy drove up in a Mercedes. He watched the guy get out of the car, all dressed up, and ring Alex's front door bell. So, maybe Alex had a boyfriend, Mike thought. He didn't know that Alex was seeing anyone, but then again, why should he? It wasn't like he kept tabs on the woman.

He turned and entered his house, intent on getting showered up and heading out to hang with the guys. Something kept niggling at him, but he didn't know what bothered him.

Shrugging it off, Mike got on with his evening.

"Man, would you look at that?" Jimmy Harner said. "She is fucking hot. How come you're living next door to her and not hitting that?"

Mike's friend had been watching Alex hang laundry out as he and another friend, Tom, helped Mike dig out the old cement from a set of stairs by their back porch.

Mike laughed and shook his head. "She has a boyfriend, man."

"So what? It's not that she doesn't look at you that way," Jimmy said. "I've seen her. How 'bout you, T?"

Tom nodded, his blonde locks bouncing. "Yeah. She does, Mike."

"Yeah, maybe, but I don't horn in on someone else's action. Not my thing," Mike said and shoved his shovel into the ground.

Alex used the clothes she was hanging as a shield so she could watch Mike work without being noticed. She gazed on as his muscles bunched and strained as he dug up more concrete and threw it off to the side. His powerful legs propelled him forward as he went for another shovelful.

She'd stopped with her hand above the clothesline as she watched Mike. Suddenly, she noticed that one of his friends was watching her and grinning. She gave him a little wave and decided to cover by offering them some drinks.

Walking across the yard, she said, "Hi, guys! You look like you're working up a sweat there. Can I get you some iced tea or something?"

Mike stopped shoveling and wiped his forehead with his forearm. Alex looked so damn sexy in a short little sundress that Mike wanted to throw her down right there and fuck her brains out. Her blonde hair was drawn back in a ponytail, emphasizing her pretty neck.

"Yeah, that'd be great." He turned that megawatt smile on her. "You got any more of those cookies?"

Alex smiled. "Not only do I still have some of those, I have another new flavor if you're game to try them."

"Game on!" Mike said and thrust his shovel into the ground. "Lead on," he told Alex.

Tom and Jimmy exchanged glances and laughed as they followed Mike and Alex to her house. They all trooped inside, and Alex had them sit at the table. She poured them big glasses of sweet tea and put together a nice plate of cookies. Turning back to the table, she explained about the cookies.

"Now, uh, I don't know your names," she said, feeling lame.

"Sorry. I guess I didn't introduce you guys," Mike said. "My bad. This is Tom," he said indicating the tall young man with unruly blond hair. "And this is Jimmy," Mike told her as he motioned towards a very handsome young black man.

"Nice to meet you," Jimmy said.

"Yeah," Tom said.

"Nice to meet you, too. Now, these are cream cheese oatmeal raisin, and these are chocolate mocha chunk," Alex told them as she pointed out which was which.

"I gotta try that new one," Mike said. "I wanna see if it's as good as the oatmeal one."

He picked up a chocolate cookie and bit off half of it. His dark eyes got big and settled on Alex as he chewed. He gave her a double thumbs up and then covered his heart with both hands. Once he'd swallowed he said, "Damn, those are phenomenal!"

Tom and Jimmy concurred, and the room grew quiet as they set about devouring the whole tray. Alex smiled. She enjoyed cooking and baking for other people and liked watching them enjoy her food. Since she lived alone, she didn't always have the pleasure of cooking for others. This was as much a treat for her as it was for them.

Mike finished his last cookie and drained his glass of iced tea. He smacked his lips in appreciation and grinned. "Alex, you make fantastic cookies. How is it that you don't have a store or something?"

"That's what I'm working on. I'm saving up money for a down payment," Alex answered.

Tom said, "Do you have a business card or a website?"

"I have a business card, but I don't have a website yet," Alex said. She went to the counter and pulled out a drawer. She came back with one and handed it to him.

"Sweet. I'll give this to my mom. She hates cooking for Dad's dinner parties. She'll be glad to have someone do it for her," Tom said with a big smile.

Alex laughed. "I'll be happy to do it for her."

Jimmy finished chewing and said, "You don't have a website? You gotta have a website. Give me one of those cards. I'm a web designer. I'll make you an awesome site."

Alex gave him a card. "Let me know how much I owe you then."

"Nah. You can just pay me in food." Jimmy's smile lit up his face. He obviously liked that idea.

"Deal," Alex said.

"I'll help drive traffic to your site once it's up," Mike said. "C'mon, guys. We gotta get the rest of those stairs out today or my dad's gonna have a fit."

All of them thanked Alex for the refreshments and left. Alex cleaned up, smiling as she went. The three guys were fun and it had actually been a profitable time businesswise, too. Plus, she'd had some good opportunities to really ogle Mike. She just couldn't help herself.

Late the next night, Alex sat at her kitchen table with her laptop working on some recipes when someone knocked on her kitchen door making her jump. She looked up and saw Mike peering in the door's window. Her heart did a funny little jig.

"Hi," she said when she answered the door. "What's up?" He looked really cute in a pair of jeans and red polo shirt.

"Can I come in?" Mike asked.

He looked serious to Alex. "Yeah. Sure. What's wrong?"

Mike crossed his arms over his chest. He was nervous and wasn't sure how to start the conversation. "You know that guy you were out with a couple nights ago?"

"How do you know about that?" Alex asked.

"I was just finishing up with my work, and I saw you guys leave, that's all." Mike shifted and didn't make eye contact for a moment. "Look, I was at the Wild Pony with the guys tonight and I saw him there. He wasn't alone. He and this chick were getting awful tight, if you get my drift."

Alex looked into his serious dark eyes and thought him incredibly sweet for looking after her. She smiled and laid her hand on his arm. "Thank you for watching out for me. It means a lot, but that was the first time I was ever out with him, and we didn't hit it off, so it's ok."

Mike felt like an ass. "Oh, well, good. I mean good that you weren't like, a couple or anything, not that you didn't hit it off." Her touch felt so good and Mike became centered on the contact with her.

Alex tried not to giggle, but she couldn't help it. He was so earnest, and now he was flustered. She tightened her grip on his arm a little. "It's ok. Really. Thank you. You are so sweet."

Mike smiled, the dimple flashing and entrancing Alex. She couldn't take her eyes off his sensual mouth. It was a very pretty male mouth, and she couldn't help but want to kiss it. Now, it was her turn to become flustered.

Mike noticed her glance and gave her one of his own. The air became charged between them, and Alex cleared her throat nervously.

Mike decided to jump into the situation head first. "Alex, do you like me?"

Alex smiled and looked into his eyes. "Of course I like you. I don't just give my cookies to anyone," she joked.

He smiled, too. "You know what I mean. I see you watching me and so have the guys."

Alex felt her face growing hot and looked down.

"It's ok if you do, you know. It's not like I don't watch you, either. What's wrong with that?" he wanted to know.

Alex closed her eyes for a moment then opened them. "Yes. I like you. I like you a lot. Too much. You're what? Twenty? I'm thirty, Mike. I'm too old for you."

Mike looked into her beautiful green eyes. "You're thirty? I thought you were like, twenty-five or something."

Alex grinned. "Really? You just made my night."

Mike slid an arm around her waist. "I'd rather do something else to make your night."

Alex looked up at him. "That's not a good idea."

"Tell you what; kiss me once and if you don't like it, I'll leave and we'll never talk about it again. If you like it, I get to stay," Mike said.

Knowing she was crazy for agreeing, Alex nonetheless found herself agreeing to his terms. "All right."

Mike didn't delay in pressing his advantage.

He dipped his head and captured her mouth at the same place pulling her slowly against him. Her breasts felt so good against him. She was soft and toned at the same time. Womanly, he guessed you'd call it.

Alex seemed of the same mind and opened her mouth to him quickly. Mike's tongue touched hers, and she sighed and opened further. Mike angled his head to gain better access and felt a heat build in his loins. She tasted sweet, and her mouth was warm and soft.

His other powerful arm came around to pull her even closer. Alex's hands slid up under his shirt, her fingertips tracing the outlines of his six-pack abs and pecs. Mike shivered a little when her hand brushed his right nipple.

Alex broke off the kiss and stood looking at Mike for a moment.

"What? What's wrong?" Mike asked, worrying evident in his eyes.

"Fuck it!" she said and grabbed his hand. "Come with me," she said and led him through the kitchen.

Mike grinned and followed her up the stairs and down the hall. They entered her bedroom, and Mike barely had time to look around before she was on him. She practically ripped his clothes off and didn't waste time with hers, either.

"You're right," she said as she undid his jeans. "I've been watching you ever since you guys bought the house next door six months ago. I can't help it. You're so fucking sexy and young and hot and if you want me, I'm going to just go with it."

"Fine with me," Mike said. "I'm not complaining, if you hadn't noticed."

Alex pulled his jeans down. His cock was already at half-mast when she freed it from his underwear. "Oh, damn, that's beautiful," she said.

Mike laughed. "Really? I'm glad you like it. I'm gonna do all kinds of stuff to you with it."

"Damn straight you are," Alex agreed and pulled off her tank top. Her jeans shorts were next.

Once they were naked, Mike reached for Alex. It felt so good to be naked with her, to touch her soft skin and inhale her scent. She had a tight little body, even better than a lot of the college girls he'd been with. He bent down and sucked on a nipple. Her tits weren't big, but they were so pretty.

He picked her up and fell backward onto the bed with her. They laughed together and Alex wiggled around on top of him. Mike rolled over, putting Alex on the bottom this time. He kissed her neck and licked her ear, then blew in it. Alex jerked at the hot sensations he created in her.

He kissed his way down to her breasts and sucked each nipple in turn. Alex squirmed underneath him and moaned. She ran her hands through his thick hair and moved her hips as hot jolts of sensation shot through her lower abdomen. The boy definitely knew what he was doing, that was for sure.

Mike loved her tits. They were driving him crazy. His dick was getting incredibly hard as he sucked and played with her nipples. Then he licked his way down her luscious little body until he reached her shaved pussy. It was smooth and soft. Mike kissed all around her lips and the mound of her sex, exciting her and him.

Alex burned for Mike. She'd been watching him for so long and lusting after him and now that he was here with her like this she was extremely excited. She spread her legs and urged him on.

"Lick my pussy, Mike. Please."

Mike looked up into her bottle-green eyes and smiled as he lapped at her.

Alex giggled and said, "That feels so good."

Mike licked a little harder and faster.

"Oooh, yeah." Alex played with one of her nipples as Mike began to flick his tongue over her clit rapidly.

Mike watched her as he ate her, thinking that it was incredibly sexy that she would play with her tits while he licked her. His dick throbbed and he groaned. The taste of her excited him even more. Alex's hips began moving and Mike moved with her, licking faster.

Fisting her hands in the sheets, Alex threw her head back. She couldn't believe how fast she was ready to cum. "Mike, don't stop. I'm gonna cum."

Sensing that she was only moments away from an orgasm, Mike didn't answer and just kept going. Alex gasped and looked down at Mike. She loved watching him eating her cunt. He did it so well. Mike might be young, but he was obviously experienced and it showed.

Alex felt the spasms start deep inside and whimpered. She threw her head back and cried out as she came. It was intense, and Alex couldn't do anything but moan and pull at the sheets. "Oh, God! Mike, it's so good!"

Mike's laugh rumbled against her pussy.

Alex began to relax as her climax ebbed. Then she sat up and looked at Mike as he looked up at her. Crooking her finger at him, she slid further up on the bed. She lay down on her back.

"Come up here really close. I want you to feed me that cock. My, you are a big boy," she said.

Mike's cock was indeed large and thick. Alex wanted to taste him. Mike did as she directed, straddling her chest and pointing his dick down at her mouth. Alex ran her fingers lightly up and down his hard dick, loving the way he felt in her hand. Then she guided him into her mouth, running her tongue around the head of his cock.

"Mmmm," she said. "You taste so good."

Mike smiled. "I'm glad you approve."

He closed his eyes as she began sucking on him, giving himself over to sensation. He reached behind him and found her pussy. Slipping his finger inside her, he found her clit and stroked it.

Alex moaned and moved her hips. She kept going, however, sucking harder and working his base faster. Mike couldn't help but move his hips as heat built in his groin. He stopped teasing Alex and concentrated on what she was doing to him. She was driving him towards an orgasm.

Knowing that if she kept on, Mike was going to cum, Alex stopped and grabbed a condom from her bedside stand and opened it. Mike watched her roll the condom down his dick and understood that it was time. That was just fine with him.

He wanted to ride her in the worst way. When she was finished, Mike spread Alex's leg wide and threw them over his shoulders. Her green eyes were smoldering with desire for him, and it turned him on no end to know that she wanted him to fuck her.

Her pussy was slick, and he got his dick lubed up before entering her. He found Alex so tight and hot he had to clamp down on his desire to cum. He pressed all the way in, watching for any sign that she was uncomfortable. Seeing none, he drew out and thrust in hard.

Alex opened her mouth and whimpered in pleasure. "Yeah! Give it to me!" she said.

Mike went to work then, thrusting and rolling his hips as he did so that he could hit her clit from a different angle and involve both body parts for her. He grasped her thighs tight and pounded in her. She reached up and grabbed the headboard, holding on for dear life.

"Shit! Yes! Pound my pussy! Oh, yeah!" she said.

"That's right. I'm gonna pound the shit out of it, bitch!" Mike said then regretted calling her that name.

Alex laughed. "I love it! Say it again." She liked it rough and a little nasty sometimes.

"I'm gonna fuck you silly, bitch," Mike said with a small laugh at the end.

He moved even harder, watching his dick

disappear into her cunt. Damn, it looked so erotic. "How's that feel, you little whore?"

"Fantastic, you horny bastard! I love the way you fuck that little pink pussy," Alex told him, really getting into the role. And she did love the way he fucked her. He ground on her as well as thrusting and it was a completely different feeling, more intense.

"Where'd you learn that?" she asked.

"You mean this?" he asked and demonstrated.

"Yeah, that."

"A men's magazine," he said with a grin and pumped faster.

Alex moaned and moved with him and the sheer sensation blew her away. She rocketed into an orgasm and shouted his name.

"Mike! Mike! Oh shit, oh shit, oh SHIT!"

Somehow, Mike hadn't expected her to be a screamer, but he was enjoying the fact that she was. He couldn't contain his own orgasm any longer. She was so tight and wet and felt so good.

"Alex?"

"Yeah?"

"I'm gonna cum, baby," he said.

"Yeah, cum, Mike. I want to make you feel good," Alex said.

"You are. Trust me, you are!" Mike felt his climax begin and he growled as he came, pumping into her for all he was worth. "Oh, God, Alex! Shit, yeah!"

His movements eventually slowed then stopped altogether. He kneeled between her legs feeling like he'd just finished a football practice. Giving Alex a big smile, he said,

"Damn, girl. You got me out of breath like I just ran the five hundred yard dash."

Alex giggled as he slid out of her and put her legs down. "I know the feeling."

"I'll be right back," Mike said and left her room.

Alex knew he'd gone to find her bathroom. He was back in a matter of a few minutes. He crawled on the bed with her and lay down next to her.

Alex turned on her side and laid her head on his muscular chest.

"I'm twenty-one, you know," Mike said into her messed up hair.

"Good to know," Alex said.

"I'm not a kid," he said.

Raising her head to look him in the eye, Alex replied, "I know you're not. It's just that you're at a different stage in your life than I am, that's all."

Mike kneaded the muscles in her back. "Seems to me that you're starting something new, too."

"Yeah, I am. What are you getting at, Mike?" Alex could tell that he had something on his mind.

Mike looked up at the ceiling for a moment then said, "I'd like to take you on a date. I know that that would be doing things kind of backwards, but that's what I want."

Alex didn't know what to say for a moment. What would people say? She was ten years his senior. Tongues would wag, that was for sure. And what about his parents? She wasn't Mexican. Would that fact and her age count against her? Then she thought, why is it ok for older guys to date younger women but not the other way around? Screw society. I like Mike and he likes me. Why shouldn't we have some fun?

Mike grew nervous as Alex mulled things over. Maybe, he shouldn't have said that right at that moment, but he always followed his impulses and they rarely steered him wrong.

Alex made her decision. "I'd love to go out with you. Why not?"

Mike got a big grin on his face. "Awesome! How about Friday? I have plans the next couple of nights. Does Friday work for you?"

"Great," Alex said. "I'm really looking forward to it."

"I'll see you about seven, ok?" Mike asked.

"Sounds good."

Mike's smile faded. "I hate to, but I'd better go. My mom always freaks out when I stay out all night. It's one of the curses of living at home to save money."

Alex smiled. "I understand. It's ok."

Mike gave Alex a long, lingering kiss. "See ya later," he told her and got out of bed and started to dress.

His strong, muscular body fascinated Alex. She was getting horny just watching him pull his clothes on. Once Mike was dressed, Mike came to give her a last kiss and then left.

Alex panted as she worked out, sweating to an aerobic DVD. She pushed herself hard, as always, since she had to taste so much food for her career. It was necessary to burn off the high amount of calories she consumed on a daily basis if she didn't want to start resembling a beached whale. Just as she was heading into the most intense part of the DVD, a knock sounded on her door.

"Shit! Who the hell is that?" she said as she paused the DVD and grabbed the towel she'd laid out. Alex patted the sweat from her face and neck as she walked to the door. When she opened it, Mike stood on the stoop with a big smile on his face.

"Hi," he said. "Are you busy?"

"Uh, well, I was just working out," Alex answered. Her gaze roamed over his broad shoulders and chest. He wore a pair of nice jeans and a button down shirt and looked delicious.

"Perfect. I'll help you finish," Mike said with a wicked gleam in his eyes.

Alex laughed. "Somehow I don't think you mean working out to a DVD."

Mike brought out the hand he'd been holding behind his back. He held a fresh bouquet of summer flowers. "Pretty flowers for a pretty lady," he said.

Alex's heart melted a little. It had been a long time since a man had given her flowers and she was very touched by the gesture.

"They're lovely," she said. "Come in and we'll put them in a vase."

Mike crossed the threshold, closed the door and snaked an arm around her waist. He pulled her against him and planted a bold, searing kiss on her lips. His kiss was possessive and deep, and Alex moaned against his mouth as his tongue teased hers. After groping each other for several minutes, Mike pulled back a little.

"Go get changed and dressed. We're going out," he said.

"Really? You wind me up and then just cut me off like that?" she said with a laugh.

Mike's dimples flashed. "That was just a preview of coming attractions."

"Ok," Alex said and kissed his nose. "I'll be back in a jiffy." She went into the kitchen and got a vase out of the cupboard. She put water in it and arranged the flowers in it. Placing them on the dining room table, Alex said, "Going to get freshened up. Be down soon."

"All right. I'll just sit in the living room," Mike told her.

An hour later, Mike and Alex were seated at a favorite mid-class restaurant in town, eating seafood dinners. They attracted a few stares, but other than that, no one seemed to notice them. Alex was surprised at how much she and Mike had to talk about. Football was only one topic they touched on. They discussed how Alex might market her business better and whether or not she could acquire a loan for a delivery van.

Mike had good ideas, which showed Alex that he was much more than just a hunky football player. NFL teams might be courting him, but he planned on finishing his business degree to have something to fall back on.

Dinner concluded after a lot of laughter. Mike had also kept Alex entertained with stories about exploits with Jimmy and Tom. The three of them liked to play pranks on people and Alex got a kick out of some of the stunts they'd pulled.

When they got in the car and started out, Mike didn't head for home. Instead, he turned the car in the direction of the college and then pulled in at the football field. Mike got out and ran around to her side of his car and opened the door.

"Come on," he said grabbing her hand and tugging her from the seat.

Alex laughed. "What are we doing here?"

Mike sent her a grin. "You'll see."

Realizing that Mike wasn't going to tell her, Alex let him lead her into the field house. "You ever do it in a locker room?" he asked her.

"No," Alex said with a laugh.

Mike's laughed joined hers. "Well, then it's time you did."

"No! We can't do that. What if someone comes around?" Alex said.

"Don't worry. No one's going to come around. It's not football season so no one hardly comes here," he assured her. He drew her against him and kissed her ear.

Goosebumps immediately peppered her arms, and Alex felt her nipples harden in response to the touch of his lips. Her intense physical reaction to him shouldn't come as a surprise, yet she was amazed that he had that kind of effect on her. She shivered as his mouth found her neck, and he trailed hot kisses down it until he reached the base and bit her lightly.

Alex giggled and brought her hands up to rest against Mike's chest. She found his nipples through his shirt and teased them.

Mike gave a low moan and slanted his mouth over hers, coaxing her to open to him. Alex granted him access and met his tongue, twirling hers around his and drawing it further into her mouth.

She felt Mike's hands slide up her bare thighs and up under her dress. He cupped her ass, and she felt his cock as he ground against her. Suddenly, she was intensely aroused. Maybe, it was the unfamiliar, slightly risky place they were in. Alex didn't know what it was, but she did know that she wanted him right then.

Grasping his belt buckle, Alex undid it swiftly and unzipped them. Slipping her hands inside, she began playing with Mike's dick, enjoying the contrast between the soft skin and growing hardness of it. Mike kept kissing her as she stroked him and worked his cock. He unzipped her dress and pulled the top down to reveal a bra that Mike was sure had come from Victoria's Secret. It was satiny black with a lacy fringe and it drove him crazy. Always a sucker for sexy lingerie, Mike bit Alex's breast through the tantalizing garment.

Alex gasped when she felt his teeth close around her nipple. Thin shoots of fire burned along her veins as Mike sucked on the turgid peak. He had grown very hard in her hands, and her pussy was getting wet from him sucking her nipples. Mike groaned and pulled her bra straps down over her shoulders then bared her tits to his gaze. They were so perfect, so beautiful, and he knew how good they tasted.

Letting go of his cock, Alex slid her hands up over his arms and then around the back of Mike's neck. "Suck my tits, baby," she half-ordered. "Suck them hard."

Mike's dark eyes filled with a smoldering passion as he held her gaze. In that instant, Alex could see the man Mike would become. He was entrancing now, but give it five years or so and he would be devastatingly handsome. As he bent his head to do her bidding, Alex's hand tightened on his neck and she arched her back, raising her breasts towards his mouth.

Mike grasped her right tit and covered her nipple with his hot mouth and sucked it hard, as she'd told him. Alex's cry of pleasure bounced off the painted concrete block walls and she writhed against him.

"Shit, yeah, Mike!" she shouted.

With a growl, Mike slid one of his hands up her dress and ripped her panties off. Then he delved a finger into her slick pussy and stroked her hard. He had to hold her tightly with his other arm because she sagged a little as sensations of bliss enveloped her. Alex whimpered and bit Mike's neck as she came. Her pussy juice dripped onto his palm and Mike wanted to lick it off.

Withdrawing his hand from her, Mike did just that with Alex looking on. The sight of him lapping away at the wetness on his hand did dirty things to Alex, and she wanted him more than she'd ever wanted anyone. Mike disentangled himself from Alex and began to strip. Soon, he stood before her in his virile nakedness with a raging hard-on.

"Get naked," he told her and disappeared for a few moments. As she did what Mike told her, Alex could hear water being turned on and wondered what Mike was up to. She'd barely folded her dress and put it on a bench when she found out. Mike grabbed her and swung her off her feet, making her squeal in surprise.

"What are you doing?" she asked with a laugh.

"You'll see," Mike said.

He carried her around a corner. The doorway opened onto a large communal shower room. Mike had turned on all of the jets and hot water spurted everywhere. It was like their own private water park, Alex thought with giddy wonder. Mike walked forward right into the spray and Alex laughed as the water hit her from all directions. Mike laughed, too, and then twirled her around, sure-footed even on the slippery floor.

Alex clung to his neck and kissed him when he stopped. Their tongues played together, water seeping into their mouths so that their kisses were very slippery and wet. Mike shifted Alex around so that she could wrap her legs around his waist and then plunged inside her hot pussy. Alex's nails bit into Mike's shoulders as she hung onto him while he quickly filled her. Exquisite pressure made her gasp and moan. The water jets hit her in the ass, back, and shoulders. They felt so good.

Mike walked over to where he'd spread a couple of towels on the shower floor and lowered her into it. Water poured over them as

Mike thrust inside her over and over. Alex's cunt clenched around him in an orgasm, and Mike had to hold back since he wasn't wearing a condom. He pulled out as he felt the spasms pass. Snatching a condom out from under the towels, Mike quickly put it on and got Alex to turn over and get on her knees.

Entering her from behind, Mike used the slipperiness of the towels against the floor to slide Alex forward and back as he pumped his cock into her. Alex giggled and moaned alternately at the wild ride. She thoroughly enjoyed Mike's playful side, and they laughed and panted together as he pushed her to another incredible orgasm.

As she relaxed, Mike laid down on the shower floor next to her. Alex turned to him and kissed him, then she rose up on her knees and took the condom off him. Taking his hard dick in her hand, she stroked it and kissed the head. His cock had a different taste with all the water on it and Alex liked it. She tickled the underside of the head with the tip of her tongue and did the same to the little hole in its tip.

Mike sucked in a breath as he snaked a hand through her wet hair and held it back from her face for her. Alex ran her tongue down his thick shaft and back up again. She repeated this maneuver several times, and Mike's dick throbbed in response. Hot water poured over them, adding a sensual level to their sex play.

When Alex took Mike's cock deep into her mouth, Mike groaned and his hips thrust upwards. She created suction and pulled back, swirling her tongue at the same time. It was something that some women couldn't master, but Alex enjoyed oral sex and had practiced a lot. Mike was amazed at her skill and the fact that she was enjoying herself.

Then Alex started working him in earnest, bobbing her head up and down and keeping a constant suction. It felt incredible to Mike, and he could tell that it wasn't going to take him long to cum. Playing with Mike's balls, Alex moaned her enjoyment, both over the feel of his firm balls and the taste of his dick as she sucked it.

Mike felt like he was going to burn up despite the water cascading over their heated bodies. The sweet pressure was building in his loins and he groaned.

"Oh, shit, baby," he said, "That feels so fucking good. You're gonna make me cum."

All Alex said was, "Mmm hmm," and kept on with his blowjob.

Watching his dick disappear repeatedly into Alex's mouth was hypnotic and ratcheted up his excitement even higher. His cock pulsed and he felt his ball sac tighten.

"Fuck! Alex, I'm coming!" he shouted and then moaned as his hot cum shot from him.

Alex took him deep, letting his cum run down her throat while she stroked his balls. As his orgasm ended, Mike slumped onto the shower floor. Alex released his cock and smiled as she watched Mike's muscular chest heaving under the hot water spray. He looked up at her and grinned.

"Damn, Alex! That was phenomenal," he said.

Nodding, Alex said, "I know," as she slid over to him and sat next to him. "This was really fun. I've never done anything like it."

Mike stroked her cheek and said, "I'm glad you had a good time. I know I sure did." How beautiful she was even with her hair wet and no makeup. Alex was one of those women who had such natural beauty that they didn't need any enhancement.

He sat up and kissed her. "We better get out of here. I paid Fred to go for an hour long walk."

Alex's brow puckered. "Who's Fred?"

"The security guard," Mike said matter-of-factly.

Alex had a good laugh at that. "You paid off the security guard?"

Mike shrugged and said, "He knows me and knows I'm not going to cause any damage."

"You're too much. C'mon, let's get out of here before he gets back," Alex said and stood up.

Fifteen minutes later, Mike and Alex left the locker room hand in hand. During their time together, Alex had started to realize that their ages had little to do with the way they related to one another. She pondered this on the way home, too. Mike kissed her goodnight at her door, and she watched his broad back walk away, thinking that maybe they really had something.

For the next two weeks, Alex and Mike went

out several times, but kept things quiet. It was starting to grate on Alex's nerves. Mike had wanted to be public about their dating, but Alex had insisted on being discreet at first. It quickly got to her that she had to act like there was nothing between them when other people were around or that they were just friends.

They were so much more than friends, and Alex was amazed by how quickly she'd developed feelings for Mike. Not only was her Latino lover amazing in bed, but out of it as well. He treated her like a lady, something that was rare for guys his age, and was supportive of her business venture.

Mike and his buddies had created a very comprehensive website and merchant account so that Alex could process credit card payments if necessary. Jimmy also showed her how to use accounting software to keep track of her finances. She knew that without Mike, the two young men wouldn't have even noticed her.

She decided that she wanted to give a relationship with Mike a real shot, as long as he still felt the same way. That night, when Mike knocked on her kitchen door, Alex pulled him inside and sat him at the table. She sat on his lap and looked down into his beautiful dark eyes.

"Hi," she said.

"Hi," Mike replied with a curious look on his face. "What's up?"

"I want to talk to you," she said.

"Ok." Mike circled her waist with his strong arms. "Shoot."

Alex took a deep breath and then began. "Do you remember how you wanted to date openly?"

"Yeah."

Alex's green eyes never wavered from his as she asked, "Do you still want to try it?"

"You know I do," Mike answered.

"Then let's do it."

Mike blinked a few times, sure that he'd heard her wrong. "Really?"

Alex nodded. "You and I have this connection going on, despite our age difference. I've never experienced anything like it with anyone before and I want to explore it."

A huge grin lit Mike's face, and he stood up with her in his arms and whirled her around in a fast circle. Alex laughed and clung to his neck. Then he was kissing her, and his hands were all over her body, igniting such a passion in her that it left her breathless.

"I guess that makes you happy or something," Alex quipped.

"You bet your sweet ass, it does!" Mike answered as he pulled her to the floor and started taking off his shirt. "We're gonna do it right here to commemorate the spot where our relationship first took the next step," he said.

Alex grinned. "Bring it, big man," she said.

And he did, in breathtaking fashion, showing her and telling her how he felt about her. When they were finished, Alex knew she would never look at that spot on the kitchen floor without thinking of that moment.

4 SERVICE WITH A SMILE

The ocean breeze lifted tendrils of Bree's vivid red hair as she stood out on the balcony attached to her room at the Harrah Hotel. She was finding the coast of North Carolina very beautiful and she felt that this was the perfect place to have come to recover from the debacle of being left at the altar.

Her groom-to-be, Greg, had completely stood her up, not even bothering to call her. She didn't realize that Greg was such a coward. All through the wedding plans, he'd been right by her side, helping make decisions and seeming so excited about the ceremony. Bree guessed that he choked at the last minute and couldn't face her. Coward.

Her sister, Rachel, was right; she was better off without him. If he couldn't handle a wedding, how would he handle kids or any other major occurrence in their life together?

No, it was better that she'd found out now what kind of man Greg really was then later on down the road.

Now she needed some rest and relaxation. As an heiress, she had plenty of money at her disposal and she could stay as long as she wanted. Rachel had come here the year before with her boyfriend Nick and said that it was gorgeous. Rachel had been right. It was beautiful here, and the Cherokees were fascinating.

Someone knocked on her door. When she opened it, the Native American bellhop who stood on the other side of the threshold captivated Bree. He was around six-foot-two and his uniform couldn't hide the fact that he was very well built. Bree found her pulse slightly picking up speed as her eyes roamed over him.

"Hi," she said.

"Hi," he responded. "I have your luggage." His dark eyes roamed over her lush figure, which her blue shorts and white halter-top showed off well. Sean hadn't missed the way Bree had looked him over, and he did the same in return. He figured it was only fair. He liked what he saw very much.

Bree smiled at him. "Great. You can just put it on the bed." You can put yourself on the bed, while you're at it, she thought.

Sean hefted the two large suitcases with ease, placing them where she'd indicated. Then he returned to the hallway to retrieve her two smaller bags.

"Looks like you're gonna be here for a while, huh?" Sean said. He put the bags on the bed beside the suitcases.

"Yes. That's right. I need a nice long vacation. I need the sea, the sun, and lots of fun," she said as she looked at him suggestively.

Sean cocked a dark brow at her. "Really?" He read her signals loud and clear. With his dark, exotic good looks, Sean was used to women coming on to him. It was one of the reasons that he loved working at the Harrah. He pretty much had his pick of the hot women who came there. "What kind of fun are you looking for?"

Bree reached out to finger the lapel of his uniform, running her hand over his chest a little. "Why don't you come back tonight and I'll show you?"

Sean caught her hand and held it still, running his thumb over her palm. "It might be late. My shift isn't over until eleven," he told her.

"Mmmm," Bree said, enjoying his touch. "It doesn't matter what time it is. I'm just going to have dinner downstairs and then come up to read. I'll be here," Bree said.

"Ok. I'll see you tonight then," Sean said and let go of her hand.

"Yes. See you," Bree said as Sean left.

She hugged herself as she thought about all the things she wanted to do to the delicious bellhop. Bree took a leisurely bath and then headed down to dinner, erotic images playing through her mind.

Sean whistled as he stripped down and got in the shower. His shift was done and he was glad. It had been a really busy night and he'd been run ragged all over the hotel. The uniforms they wore were hot and scratchy, especially in the hot weather, and Sean didn't want to show up at Bree's room with bad B.O.

Fifteen minutes later, he'd shaved and dressed in jeans and a Pink Floyd T-shirt. His uncle had gotten him into the band when he was a kid and he still loved them. He thought about the woman he was going to see. She was just the kind he liked: beautiful, rich, and lonely. His ancestral wolf spirit seemed to help him sniff out this kind of woman and Sean was only too happy to take advantage of this ability.

He ascended the back stairs to Bree's floor, careful not to run into any of the hotel's personnel since it was against the rules to fraternize with the guests. So many of them did it, that if the hotel ever found out, about a quarter of all their help would be fired. Sean thought the rule was ridiculous and didn't adhere to it.

After knocking on her door, Sean stood back a little so she could see him through the peephole and know that it wasn't some creep out to hurt her. The lock turned and the door opened and Sean was rendered speechless at the sight that greeted him.

Bree stood before him in a white, lacy baby doll number that hid enough to whet his appetite and yet revealed enough to give him a good idea of what he was in for. Bree's long, wavy red hair had been let loose and poured over her shoulders in a river of silky flame.

"Come on in," she said and stood back.

"Thanks," Sean said as he slid by her

making sure to brush against her. She smelled incredible and he figured that she had on some five hundred dollar perfume of which he couldn't pronounce the name. As he moved past, Bree took notice of the way he filled out his jeans and T-shirt. It looked like he had muscles in all the right places and Bree was impatient to see him naked. She kept herself in check, however, intending to make the most of the night.

Sean noticed that Bree had ordered champagne and strawberries. He smiled, thinking that he knew some ways they could enjoy them. Bree came to stand beside him and looked up at him with her huge blue eyes. Sean could almost feel himself getting lost in those eyes and had to blink a couple of times to shake the sensation.

Bree lifted the champagne from the ice bucket. "Will you open it, please?" she asked.

Sean smiled. "Sure." Expertly he popped the cork and poured each of them a glass. It wasn't his favorite drink, but he liked it from time to time.

Bree's stomach was fluttering a little with nerves, but she figured that the bubbly would ease that. She watched Sean's strong, well-made hands as he poured their drinks and then handed her a glass. His black eyes traveled over her face and body appreciatively and Bree felt a thrill steal through her abdomen.

She could well imagine him as a wild brave about to make a conquest of her. Was it a conquest when your prey was willing, though, she wondered? His thick hair was just short of being black, she could see. He wore it short in a haphazard style that drew attention to his chiseled cheekbones and strong jaw.

His mouth was sensual and his teeth white, even when he smiled at her. She took a swallow of her champagne and let the sweet liquid trickle down her throat as she watched Sean do the same.

Sean thought he'd never seen any woman as sexy as Bree. Her creamy skin invited his hands to stroke it, and her pouty lips begged to be kissed. He wanted to get her steamed up and knew just how to do it. He set his drink down and crossed to the window. Sean drew the drapes and then turned back to Bree.

She smiled at him. "A little shy, huh?"

"Not at all," Sean said. "But this is a private show just for you." He took his cell phone from his jeans and pulled up his music player. All of the rooms were equipped with CD players. Sean connected his phone to the player.

"Sit down and enjoy," Sean instructed Bree.

Bree did as he said and sat on the bed. Sean hit the play button and a song Bree didn't recognize started pumping out of the speakers. It had a great beat, low sexy bass lines, and hot sax solos. There were no words, but words weren't needed as Sean treated her to a blistering strip show.

She couldn't take her eyes from him as he gyrated his hips in smooth, graceful movements. When he peeled off his T-shirt to reveal sleek brown skin and rippling muscles, Bree wanted nothing more than to touch and taste him. Sean threw the shirt onto a chair and then came over to Bree.

He bent, and cupping her chin, proceeded to kiss her teasingly, not melding their mouths together, but brushing his lips over hers. Then he straightened back up and danced away from her. Bree thought she was going to die from anticipation as Sean slowly undid the button and zipper of his jeans.

Bree spread her legs and began rubbing her pussy through her panties. Sean's eyes widened as he watched her touch herself. He felt a tightening of his loins as his cock started standing at attention. Soon the jeans and briefs were gone and Sean stood before her like a proud Indian warrior.

Slowly Sean began stroking his cock, which was becoming very hard as he watched Bree slip a hand down her panties and play with her clit. She moaned and spread her legs further apart. Sean wanted to rip her panties off so he could see her pussy and what she was doing with it.

"No fair," he said. "I showed you mine, now you show me yours," he insisted.

Bree liked that she was having such a strong effect on him. She was glad that he found her exciting and beautiful. She raised her legs and slid the panties off, letting them drop to the floor. Spreading her legs again, she leaned back and resumed her stroking. She could tell it was really turning Sean on to watch her.

Sean almost salivated as he watched her fingers delve into her pussy and play with her clit. She had one of the prettiest cunts he'd ever seen. Her pale skin made the perfect foil for the light pink inside of her pussy. He could tell by the wet sheen on the skin of her pussy that she was wet.

Hungrily, Bree watched Sean work his big cock. She stroked her clit faster and moaned as she grew closer to cumming. She was so excited that it didn't take her long. Her head fell back as the orgasm suddenly gripped her and she whimpered and shook as she came.

Sean growled as he watched her cum. He walked over and knelt by the bed between her legs and grabbed her hand. Sean sucked the fingers she'd used on herself and enjoyed the heady taste of her.

Then he cupped her face in his hands and brought his mouth down on hers roughly. Bree was ready and met his lips eagerly, opening to him right away. She wanted it hard and hot and didn't mind if things got rough.

Their tongues danced in a swordplay that heightened their desire and made their breathing ragged. Bree reached between them to lightly grasp Sean's penis. It was hot and smooth and hard and she loved the feel of it between her fingers. She stroked him and he gasped against her mouth.

Bree squealed in surprise when Sean ripped the bra part of her lingerie apart and shoved it from her shoulders. In a frenzy, Sean took the pink nipple of her full right breast in his mouth, lapped it rapidly with his tongue and then sucked it hard.

With a loud cry of approval, Bree ran her fingers through his silky, dark hair and pressed his face harder against her breast.

"Oh, Sean, that feels so good. I want you to

fuck me hard. Don't be gentle. I won't break," she said. Her fiancé had always acted like she was too fragile to make rough love and she wanted to get crazy.

Sean had no problem with that. In fact, he wasn't sure he would be able to hold back and be very gentle. There was something about this woman that just drove him crazy, and fucking her hard was not going to be a problem.

He switched to her other breast, drawing her sweet-tasting nipple into his mouth and biting it a little. Bree gasped at the pleasure-pain and her hips moved forward. She stroked his dick a little faster and Sean moaned with pleasure.

Sean let her tit go and pushed her back roughly on the bed. Bree giggled as she bounced on the mattress. Sean grabbed her under her arms and pushed her over farther on the bed. His authoritative treatment excited Bree further and she was burning for him.

Once he'd spread Bree's legs apart, Sean launched an assault on Bree's pussy, licking and sucking the tangy flesh there. Bree had never been treated like this and she loved every second of it. Sean's masterful tongue strokes sent her higher and higher and she couldn't help but move her hips.

Sean held her legs still with his strong arms, and shook his head back and forth, applying a different pressure to Bree's clit. Bree cried out and came up off the bed.

"Yeah, suck that pussy!" she ordered as Sean did just that. "I'm gonna cum," she told him.

Sean's response was to lick faster. Bree came then, shouting her bliss and shimmying against Sean's mouth. He held her fast and kept licking, not giving her a break, ruthlessly driving her on. Amazingly, Bree felt another orgasm looming and with a sense of wonder, came again a moment later.

"Oh, fuck! Mmmmmm!" was all that Bree could manage to say as the intense climax rocked her.

Sean let her come down from the high for a few moments before he moved up and straddled her torso. "Suck it," he ordered, stroking his dick in her face.

Bree took his cock gladly, and licked his shaft. He tasted so good and was so hard and big. She ran her tongue around the engorged head and paid attention to his little hole. Sean groaned and gripped her head, threading his fingers through her soft hair.

When Bree put his cock in her mouth and began sucking in earnest, Sean moaned and his hips thrust forward. Bree worked his shaft and sucked harder. She played with his ball sac and felt it tighten. Sean fisted a hand in Bree's hair and pulled back slightly on it. Bree released his cock and looked up at him. The sharp angles of his sexy face stood out and his dark eyes blazed with passion.

Swiftly, Sean knelt between her legs and pushed into her pussy. He found her tight and moved forward slowly so he didn't hurt her. He wanted to possess her, to be rough, but not so rough as to bring her real pain. Bree reached around to his ass and pulled him forward.

"Fuck the shit out my cunt, baby," she said through clenched teeth. She was wild for him, ready for him, and needed him.

Sean took her at her word and plunged in as far as she would take him and then pulled back.

"Yeah! Do it!" Bree said.

"You asked for it," Sean said and plowed full speed ahead.

Bree felt him fill her and relished the sensations. He pounded at her, drove her to the brink over and over. Her pussy was so slick, so hot, and so tight that Sean had a hard time not cumming too quickly. They were both sweaty and panting and loving it all. Sean gyrated his hips, applying a different stroke and kept hitting Bree's G-spot.

She felt the sweet tension build up as he moved faster and faster.

"I'm gonna cum, baby. Oh yeah! Just like that!" And then she had the mother of all orgasms. She practically screamed as it ripped through her and she shuddered against Sean. He couldn't hold back any longer and his shouts of ecstasy filled the room as his hot cum filled her cunt.

Bree reveled in the feel of his sperm spurting inside her, and she loved seeing the pleasure on his face and knowing that she was responsible for it. His orgasm lasted for several moments and Bree enjoyed every second. He pulsed inside her and made little thrusts that felt good.

When the pleasure began to subside, Sean withdrew from Bree and knelt panting above her. He grinned and shook his head.

"Holy shit," he said. "That was off the chart."

Bree laughed. "You're not kidding. I didn't know who I was there at the end," she said.

"I know the feeling," he said as he lay down next to her and kissed her softly.

Bree laid a hand on his strong jaw and said, "That's what I call service with a smile."

Sean's laughed filled the room. "How long are you going to be here?"

Bree gave him a coy smile. "Long enough to have lots of romps like this."

"Glad to hear it. And every time I service you, I'll certainly be smiling," Sean said with a big grin.

Content, Bree snuggled against him, and was already looking forward to the next time.

5 DUSTY ROSE

Sweat slid down the sun-browned skin of Wade Kincaid's back and dripped down onto the dusty ground of the corral. He was installing a new fence post and wanted to get it finished before the day was through.

It was a hard work digging in the packed, rocky soil, and his muscles strained as he shoveled. The thought of a fried chicken dinner and homemade apple pie spurred him on. That's what Dusty was serving tonight, and Wade couldn't wait.

Wade let his thoughts linger on Dusty. If ever a woman was made for loving, it was her. The pretty dresses she wore showed off her lovely figure to perfection. Strawberry-blonde hair and big blue eyes drew a man's attention like a kitten to yarn.

He thanked whatever powers had led him to Dusty's boarding house upon his arrival in

Westfield. It was a booming town and living space was at a premium. The one friend he'd made in town, Joshua Thomas, a card dealer at a saloon, had put him on to Dusty's place.

Now, as he thought about it, what Wade really wanted was a nice big slice of Dusty pie. He wondered if her pussy was covered in golden or dark curls. Wade used the desire these thoughts created as impetus to get the job done. A half-hour later, he was through. He put his tools away and headed inside to clean up.

He climbed the stairs to the second floor and bumped into Dusty at the top landing.

"Oh! I'm sorry," Dusty said.

"No, I'm the one who should be sorry," Wade said with a smile.

Dusty looked up into his ruggedly handsome face and brown eyes, and then her gaze lowered to his sensual mouth. She wanted nothing more than to kiss him. She could see that he was sweaty and dirty, but she didn't care. Dusty would have been happy to spread her legs for him right then.

She shifted slightly at the slight ache that started between her thighs. Wade saw her pupils dilate and the way she watched his mouth and knew that she wanted him. Only the fact that he would mess up her dress if he grabbed her and kissed her prevented him from doing just that.

He moved to one side and said, "I'm on my way to clean up for supper. Can't come to a nice dinner like you're making looking like I do."

Wade smiled and Dusty thought her heart

was going to stop. The lines that formed at the corners only enhanced his appearance. She judged that he was somewhere in his late thirties, which meant he was experienced in the ways of women. In her twenty-nine years, she'd only ever been with a man a handful of times and only a couple of those had been enjoyable.

Wade exuded raw sensuality, the kind that made women swoon and men jealous. He had excellent manners and a sharp sense of humor. It was all a dangerous combination.

Dusty smiled at him. "I appreciate your thoughtfulness. Dinner will be ready in fifteen minutes."

Wade said, "I won't be late. That fence post is in and the rest of the fence mended, too."

"Thank you so much," Dusty said. She'd watched him working and hadn't been able to take her eyes off of him for a long time. "You didn't have to do that."

"Sure I did. You do so much for us around here, that I wanted to return the favor," he said. "Well, I'd better get cleaned up. I'm sure I stink."

Dusty stepped around him. "I hadn't noticed," she said. "See you at dinner."

Wade used all of the water in the pitcher in his room and cleaned up thoroughly, removing all traces of dirt and grime. Then he dressed in a white shirt and dark pants and wore his good boots.

When he looked in the mirror, Wade saw a six-foot tall man with black hair and deep brown eyes: throwbacks to his maternal Indian heritage. Broad shoulders and chest filled out the shirt nicely. With his trim stomach and lean hips, Wade knew that he made a nice picture for the ladies.

He'd been told how good-looking he was from the time he was fourteen, but even though he knew it, he didn't get overly cocky about it. Wade wasn't above using his sexuality when he wanted something, but he'd never been mean or hurtful with it.

Satisfied with his appearance, Wade went down to dinner. Dusty was just sitting down and he helped her with her chair.

"Thank you, Mr. Kincaid," she said with a pleased smile.

"You're very welcome, Miss Rose," Wade returned and took one of the empty seats.

His chair was between Mr. Eliot Hanson, a retired schoolteacher, and Tom Stanton, another cowboy who was working in town to make enough money to move on again. Eliot smiled at Wade while Tom just scowled at him. Wade knew that Tom had a thing for Dusty, but Wade could tell that Dusty didn't return those feelings.

Tom wasn't smart enough or willing enough to see it, though. Poor guy, Wade thought.

Dinner was delicious. The chicken was tender and tasty, the mashed potatoes fluffy, and the corn sweet. Dusty's apple pie practically melted on Wade's tongue, and he thought that the only thing sweeter was Dusty herself. The meal had definitely been worth the hard work he'd put in that afternoon.

Dusty's two kitchen girls cleaned up, and Wade left for the Sun Down Saloon where his friend Josh worked. He'd looked at his funds that afternoon and decided that a little cash infusion was in order. When he walked through the door, he found the place getting crowded already.

He headed for Josh's table. Josh usually dealt blackjack, and Wade figured he could make good money playing the game.

"Hey there, Wade," Josh greeted him, his blue eyes shining with a devilish light. "How are you?"

"Doing all right. How 'bout yourself?" Wade asked with a smile.

"Can't complain. You gonna play?" Josh said getting his cards ready.

"What the hell do you think I'm here for?" Wade ribbed his friend.

Josh laughed. "Ok. Let's get it going then."

Wade played blackjack for the next two hours and won four hundred dollars. Nothing to sneeze at, he thought. After saying goodnight to Josh, Wade left the saloon and headed home. He'd had a couple of whiskies and was feeling pretty good. He entered the boarding house and went upstairs. As he walked to his room, a door further down the hall opened, and Dusty came out wearing a pretty pink nightgown.

Wade's hormones starting acting up instantly. His mouth watered at the sight of her luscious mouth, and his hands itched to trace her body through her nightgown.

"Evening, Miss Rose. How are you?" he said.

She smiled at him. "I'm fine, thank you. A bit lonely, perhaps. I was wondering if you'd like to come sit for a spell," she said. She took in his fine, masculine form in his nice pants and shirt. He looked a little rumpled and sexy as hell.

Wade was surprised but pleased. "I'd like that very much," he said with a smile.

Dusty stepped back into her room and closed the door when Wade had passed through. He seemed to fill up the space and make the room smaller. It was foreign to Dusty to have a man in her rooms.

"Would you like a drink?" she asked Wade. Her heart was thumping in her chest.

"Sure. Whatever you have is fine," he answered.

"Scotch?" she asked.

"Yeah." He watched her pretty hands pour the drink and imagined the way they'd feel on his body. Things were happening below his belt, and he had a hard time sitting still.

She brought his drink to him and settled in the chair next to him. Smiling, she asked, "Did you have much luck tonight at the tables?"

"Actually, I did. I think it was some lady luck I took with me that helped," he said with a flirtatious grin.

Dusty flushed and said, "You're a charmer, I see, Mr. Kincaid."

"You got me pegged. Please, call me Wade, if you like," he said.

"All right, Wade. You may call me Dusty," she said. Dusty didn't miss the way his brown eyes looked her over. She could tell that he desired her and that suited her just fine. "So tell me how a cowboy like you has such nice manners?"

Wade laughed. "Well, I wasn't always a cowboy. My family was actually fairly well off until the market crashed and things went south. Then we hit rock bottom, and I had to take any job I could get to help out. Thing was, I made more money gambling and training horses, so that's what I started to do. I travel around and play the tables and break horses. That's pretty much my life story."

Dusty's blue eyes regarded him seriously. "I'm so sorry, but I'm glad you're here," she said. She wasn't normally so forward, but felt secure in saying such a thing to him.

"Why thank you. It's nice of you to say so. I'm glad I'm here, too," he said with sincerity. Lord, how he wanted the woman. He reached out and took her hand.

Dusty was surprised but didn't pull away. Wade rubbed the back of her hand with his thumb, and Dusty felt tingles of awareness spread through her body. She looked him in the eyes, registering the smoldering desire she saw there. She answered that desire by squeezing his hand back.

Wade lifted her hand to his mouth and kissed her knuckles. Her sharp intake of breath sounded in the room, and Wade knew then the effect he was having on her. He stood up and came to stand in front of her. Her eyes never wavered from his as he bent and brushed his lips against hers. She gave a small moan and moved her mouth against his.

Kneeling down between her legs, Wade took her in his arms and kissed her savagely, giving in to the hot feelings she instilled in him. Dusty came alive in his embrace, ran her hands over his back, and opened her mouth to him.

Wade plundered her mouth, teasing her tongue with his and running it over her pretty, white teeth. Her breasts rubbed against his chest and Wade started to burn. Dusty felt his waist rubbing against her sex, and she couldn't help but to move her hips. Wade felt the movement and smile against her mouth.

"Looks like I'm not the only one who's really horny. Pardon the crude language, but I call it like I see it," he said.

Dusty laughed a little. "I can't help it. I've wanted this since you came here, and I hope you don't mind me being so forward."

"Mind? Hell, I'm glad. I've wanted you, too. I'm gonna make this so good," Wade said and kissed her again, long and deep.

He wrapped his arms around her waist and brought her pussy in contact with his body again. Dusty moaned and moved her hips. The contact hit her clit, and she ached inside. She thrust again and fiery sensations jumped along her legs and into her pussy. She needed that release, and Wade seemed to have no problem with that.

Wade let her grind on him a little and then scooted back a little. He grabbed the hem of her nightgown and shoved it up revealing her underthings. Wade was wild for her at this point. He wanted to taste her so badly that he simply ripped her underthings so he could get to her faster.

"I'll buy you new ones," he told her as he rid her of them.

He stopped at the sight of her pussy.

Golden down covered it. He put each of her legs over an arm of the chair and watched as her pussy lips spread open for him. He tickled her with his fingers, and she whimpered and moved against his hand. The fact that she was so hot for him made his dick incredibly hard. His pants were tight, but he ignored it for the time being.

Starting at the bottom of her pussy where her entrance was, Wade ran his tongue up her slit, getting the flavor and scent of her. She was delicious. Her clit was swollen and ready for him. He flicked his tongue over it and Dusty jerked.

"Oh, Wade. More, please," she said and moaned.

Wade set at the task earnestly, and his tongue stroked her clit with amazing speed. Dusty couldn't stop her hips from moving, but Wade held her still enough so that he didn't lose his place. His sweet torture was driving Dusty crazy. She panted as the blissful tension rose inside, and she knew she was moments away from an orgasm.

Dusty wanted it so badly, needed it so badly. Wade increased the pressure a little, and Dusty cried out as she was almost there. She hung on the edge for a moment and then her climax broke over her. She grabbed Wades head and pressed him harder against her cunt as she rode the ripples of pleasure.

Wade made her orgasm last as long as possible. But he couldn't wait any longer; he undid his pants and shoved them and his underwear down. His dick was hard and throbbing, and he needed to fuck her right then.

Dusty saw what he meant to do and welcomed it. Her eyes widened when she saw the size of his cock, and she was hungry to feel it inside her. She slid into the chair a little and spread her legs wider.

Wade noticed and smiled. "You want this, huh?" he said as he grasped his cock and rubbed it against her pussy, making sure to hit her clit.

Dusty nodded. "Oh, yes, Wade. I want your... cock."

"I'm gonna give it to you," he promised and got the head of his cock wet from her pussy juice.

Then he slid inside her and thrust hard. Dusty threw her head back and moved her hips to meet him. Wade grasped her around the waist and slid her to the floor, still joined. The nightgown was in the way, so he ripped it up the middle and Dusty removed it from her arms. She lay naked under him now. He thought her breasts were the prettiest he'd ever seen.

They were full, and the pink nipples drew his mouth like bees to nectar. They were sweet and warm, and Wade would have gladly sucked them all day. Dusty wrapped her legs around Wade's waist and thrust upwards. Wade responded by plunging inside her cunt hard.

"Yes, oh, yes!" she shouted. "Hard, like that."

Wade willingly complied with her request and began pumping a hard, fast rhythm, driving into her pussy over and over. He sucked on one of her breasts at the same time, and Dusty went crazy as jolts of pleasure shot straight to her cunt. She whimpered and mewled, and her nails scored his back.

Shifting his weight slightly, Wade grasped her hips and held her firmly while his hips hammered away at her. She was hot, wet, and tight, and he thought he'd never been inside such a wonderful pussy. Suddenly, he felt Dusty clench around him, an intense orgasm shaking her body.

Wade pumped harder as he started to cum. Hot spurts of semen shot from him, filling Dusty's cunt. His release was hot and so strong that he couldn't think for a moment. He was lost in the sensation. His hoarse cry of pleasure joined Dusty's loud moans. Their duel orgasms left them spent and sated.

Slowly, Wade lowered himself onto Dusty, and she relished the weight of him on top of her. She stroked his back while her breathing slowly. Presently, Wade rolled onto his side, smiling at her.

"I'm sorry, I sort of attacked you there, Dusty, but there's only so much a man can take," he said.

Dusty laughed, the motion shaking her breasts. "You didn't hear me complaining any, did you?"

Wade chuckled. "Well, no, I didn't. Lord, woman, what you do to me."

"I feel the same way. That was very... intense," Dusty said. She trailed a hand over his chest and wished he could have stayed the night, but it wouldn't look right in front of the other guests.

As if reading her thoughts, Wade said, "I really hate to leave you, but I guess I should."

"I don't want you to leave, but it would look improper. Not that what we did here tonight wasn't, but you understand," Dusty said.

Wade laughed. "Don't worry. I'm not offended. I don't want to do anything to soil your reputation." He gave her a brief kiss and helped her stand up. "Next time, it won't be so rushed, though."

Dusty's heart started beating faster again at this pronouncement. "There's going to be a next time?"

"I sure hope so," Wade said. "I want to do better by you," he said looking at the ruined garments on the floor. He pulled his pants back up and fastened them. Then he took out his wallet and gave her some money. "Will this cover your nightgown and such?"

Dusty shook her head. "That's not necessary, Wade. I made no protest."

"Yes, it is. Please, take it," Wade said.

Reluctantly, Dusty took the money, figuring that she would buy some very nice lingerie in a shop a few towns over where she wasn't known. "All right."

Wade tipped her chin up so he could give her a long lingering kiss. "Night, Miss Rose."

She smiled at his mock formality. "Goodnight, Mr. Kincaid."

Wade peeked out her door, making sure no one was around and then slipped into the hallway. Quickly, he went to his room and went inside. No one was the wiser for what had taken place in Dusty's room and that was just fine.

Three days later, Wade found himself doing more work for Dusty. This time, he was fixing a stall door in the barn, so at least he was out of the hot Arizona sun. The old door had rotted through at the hinges and was very loose. Wade had constructed a new door and was installing it now.

"Hello, Mr. Kincaid," he heard Dusty say from behind him.

She had been standing there for a few minutes, admiring his ass and the curve of his back as he hammered the lower hinge into place. Now, as he straightened and locked in on her with a come-hither-smile and those coffee-brown eyes of his, her breath caught in her throat.

"Why, hello, Miss Rose. How are you this fine afternoon?" he asked stepping towards her.

She looked delicious in a green gingham dress with a lace collar. He well remembered the way her high, full breasts had looked a few nights ago. He remembered the way her nipples had tasted in his mouth and the way her tight pussy had felt around his cock.

"I'm fine, thank you for asking," she responded. Her full mouth turned up at the corners. "I appreciate the work you do around here. Would you like some mint tea? I made some fresh this morning, especially figuring that you were going to be working in this heat and that it would refresh you."

"You're quite welcome. I don't mind the work, ma'am. It keeps me out of trouble," he said with a sexy twinkle in his eyes.

Dusty blushed, remembering the trouble they'd gotten into three nights prior. "Yes, well, the tea is up at the house."

"Be right there," Wade said and set about putting away his tools.

Dusty hurried to the house and got everything ready out on the back porch. It overlooked a flower garden that she spent a lot of time watering so that the flowers bloomed nicely. It was hard growing the flowers because of the arid whether in their part of the state. There also were a couple of oak trees that provided some shade from the merciless sun.

Dusty arranged the tea and some sandwiches nicely on a small table that sat between two chairs. When Wade arrived, he had cleaned up and looked so handsome that Dusty felt her nipples tighten in response. His brown eyes roved over her with a hungry gleam, and Dusty had to concentrate on pouring the tea into tall glasses to keep from jumping Wade.

"This looks delicious," Wade said but kept his eyes on Dusty.

"Thank you," she said. Dusty handed him a glass and then took a sip of her own drink hoping that it would quench the fire building inside her a little. It didn't.

"You didn't have to do this, you know," Wade said. "I don't think it falls under your services."

Dusty gave him a wry smile. "Neither does what happened the other night. I don't do anything I don't want to do, so don't worry."

Wade nodded acknowledging her response.

"All right. As long as you're sure."

"I'm sure."

Wade bit into a sandwich, and the excellent chicken salad filled his mouth with savory flavor. As good as it was, he still craved a different flavor. "Very good," he said once he'd swallowed.

"Thank you. I'm glad you're enjoying it. Was the stall door hard to fix?" Dusty asked.

"Nope. It was easier just to make another rather than work with that rotting wood. You've got a section of roof that's going to need repairing. I'm afraid that's not my expertise, but I can look around to find someone to do it," Wade told her.

"That sounds good. Thank you," Dusty finished a sandwich and drank some tea.

Wade was hungry and finished off another sandwich and then downed his tea. He looked at Dusty. She had her hair up in a French twist, and while it looked lovely, he wanted nothing more than to take it down and spread it over her shoulders.

"Where's everyone else?" he asked her.

"In town."

"Are you finished?"

"Yes. Why?" Dusty asked.

Wade's response was to rise out of his chair and hold out a hand to her. Her eyes widened and she gave him a questioning look. He held his hand closer and raised an eyebrow at her. Dusty took his work-roughened hand and let him tug her out of her chair. Quick as a cat, he hooked a hand around her waist and pulled her against him.

His mouth lowered, capturing her open

mouth and plundering it with his agile tongue. She wrapped her arms around his neck and kissed him back until they were both breathless. Then he broke the kiss and led her upstairs to her room.

Once inside, he closed her door and locked it. Wade had no intention of them being disturbed. Slowly, he removed her clothes, kissing her smooth flesh as it was exposed. Dusty was amazed at how gentle he was and the fire she had felt downstairs flared into a blaze with each touch of his lips. By the time she was naked, Dusty was burning for the man.

She returned the favor, taking her time undressing him even though she wanted to rip his clothes off the way he'd ripped hers off the other night. When his broad chest was exposed, she ran her fingertips over his nipples, the feel of them under the pads of her fingers exciting and foreign.

Wade groaned as pleasurable sensations ran through his body at the contact. Then she undid his pants and slid her hands down his underwear, cupping his cock and balls, and Wade felt such a jolt of desire that he felt his dick harden rapidly at her touch.

The feel of him hardening in her hand excited Dusty. She took his cock in her hand and began pumping him until he was fully erect. Dusty released him so she could get rid of his pants and boots. He stood before her in all his male glory, and she had such a hunger for him that she couldn't keep her mouth off him any longer.

She licked his nipples and sucked on them,

then bit and licked her way down his stomach to his cock. Dusty backed him up to the bed and had him sit on it while she kneeled between his legs.

Wade wanted what she was going to do to him, but was surprised that she knew what she was doing. Evidently, she had some experience in this area. Wade didn't question it, just thanked whoever had taught her such things.

Dusty's pretty pink tongue flicked out over the head of his cock and Wade sucked in a breath and leaned back on the bed. She ran her tongue around the head and dipped into the little well at the tip of it. Dusty was rewarded by a small drip of his pre-cum and relished the taste.

She licked up and down his shaft, loving the feel of him throbbing in her hand. She played with his ball sack and sucked on it, Wade moaning much of the time. Her pussy was tingling by this point, and she knew she was going to be very wet by the time she was done with Wade.

Grasping the base of his dick, Dusty took him deep into her mouth and sucked. Wade cried out and jerked his hips, and she worked his cock and sucked and licked. She had an amazing tongue and knew the proper techniques for sure. Dusty continued for several minutes, loving the taste of him.

Wade could feel himself nearing orgasm, but he didn't want it to happen yet.

"Dusty, you gotta stop. I don't want it to be over yet," he told her gently.

Dusty released him and smiled up at him.

"Neither do I, but you taste so good that I didn't want to stop. And you feel so good, too," she said stroking him.

Wade patted the space up near the pillows. "Come here and lay down. It's your turn."

Dusty complied and sighed when Wade parted her legs. She knew what was going to happen and she was so ready for it.

Wade put her feet over his shoulder and positioned himself above her open, pink pussy. Her clit was swollen, and she glistened with moisture. Wade licked the juice from her opening and relished the slightly salty taste of it.

"Mmm. You taste incredible," he said in a husky voice.

"I'm glad," Dusty said.

Wade licked his tongue completely up her slit, hitting her clit over and over until Dusty thought she'd die if she didn't come soon. She whimpered when Wade got down to business and began licking back and forth over her clit. His tongue moved fast and hard and Dusty arched her back and grabbed the sheets.

Wade moved his tongue faster and inserted a finger into her slick pussy. He finger-fucked her while licking her clit. Dusty almost came up off the bed as her release overtook her and held her in paralyzing grip.

"Wade! Oh. My. God!" she cried out as she came.

"Mmm," Wade said as her pussy became even wetter. There were going to be spots on the sheets, he knew.

When the movements of Dusty's hips slowed, Wade stopped. He ran his hands over her body, keeping her excited while he let her rest a moment.

"On your knees, woman," he told her then. "Scoot back to the edge of the bed."

Dusty did so and shook her ass at him, laughing.

"Oh boy. Looks like my mare is in heat," Wade teased her.

"Oh yes. She is. What are you going to do about it?" She challenged him with a saucy look over her shoulder.

"Well, your stallion is going to mount you and fuck you silly, that's what," Wade responded.

"That's exactly what she needs," Dusty said with another shake of her delectable ass.

Wade readied his cock and thrust inside Dusty's tight pussy. She moaned and moved back so that they were pressed against each other. She wanted to take in all of him. Wade created smooth, expert strokes, and varied his angle and speed. He grabbed her hips and thrust into her hard, the sensation of her squeezing his cock and working it driving him crazy.

It felt so good having Wade pump into her repeatedly and fucked her hard. She whimpered and moaned and her pussy pulsed around his dick. Crying out his name, Dusty's orgasm ravaged her, coursing through her with shocking intensity. Wade loved hearing her cum, loved the high-pitched moans and the way she called his name again and again. His own climax neared, and he stroked harder and faster. He came hard, growling and moaning as he filled her with his cum.

Their expressions of pleasure mingled, telling one another of their pleasure and completion. Soon Wade's movements slowed and then stopped. He withdrew from her and stood panting. Dusty slid forward until she was lying down. Her breathing was ragged as well.

Wade slowly walked around the side of the bed and lay down beside her, rubbing her back. Then he pulled her up until her head was resting on the pillows next to his.

"You're so beautiful," he said looking into her sky-blue eyes. "And passionate. Lord, what you do to me, woman."

Dusty smiled back at him. "You do the same things to me, if you couldn't tell."

"Oh, I could tell. We definitely have great chemistry in the bedroom," he said with a grin.

Dusty laughed. "Yes, we do."

Wade grew serious. "Don't you think it's time that I started courting you proper?"

Dusty's expression grew troubled. "But you won't be around all that long. What would be the sense?" She hated to think of the time when she would be without him, but knew that she had to be practical and face it.

Wade stroked her cheek and said, "Dusty, I ain't had a reason to stay in one place, until now. I can see making a life here, as long as I had you."

Tears stung her eyes at his sweet words. "I can't ask you to do that. You're a free spirit and I won't tie you down and have you resent me later on."

"You're not asking me, I'm saying that

that's what I want. I want to be with you. It's not just this, either. I just enjoy our time together. I want to take you places and do special things together. Dusty, I want to be your man and I want you to be my woman. Will you please let me court you?"

The sincere light in his eyes and in his words moved Dusty. She wanted to be his so badly. She decided to take the jump, hope coming alive within her.

"Yes, I will. I want all of those things, too," she said as a tear ran down her cheek.

Wade wiped it away and kissed her softly. "Then we'll have them," he promised her. "Why don't you have a nap and I'll see you at dinner?" he suggested. "I have a little business in town to take care of."

She smiled sleepily. "All right. That sounds wonderful. I'll see you for dinner."

They kissed again and then Wade left her. Her eyes closed and visions of their future flitted through her mind. Love bloomed in her heart, and she now knew that it belonged to Wade. She couldn't wait for the day when she would tell him. Sleep claimed her as she dreamt of walking down the aisle in a white dress and having Wade put a ring on her finger.

6 WITNESS TO SEDUCTION

There's only so much that a man can take, Dex thought as he dealt with Meagan Bradshaw. The woman was by turns infuriating, entertaining, and alluring. Today, she'd started the day off by being infuriating. Again, she was arguing about going out in public. She was bored, she was feeling claustrophobic, and she was sick of seeing the same place for the past three days.

Dex couldn't say he blamed her, but the only way she was going to stay alive was to abide by the rules and stay out of sight. He kept reminding her that it was better to be bored than dead.

"Dex," she said now as she was shifting into entertainment mode. She'd abandoned using his official name, Marshall Hall, about five minutes after meeting him. "Aren't you bored? Wouldn't you like to get some fresh air? You shouldn't have to be cooped up any more than

I should have to be."

"Ms. Bradshaw, you know that we can't go anywhere. It's too risky. The trial is in two days. We can't jeopardize it," he told her in a cold tone of voice that he used when he was most angry.

Meagan had been after him for almost twenty minutes about going out somewhere and didn't show any signs of slowing up. "We're both too young and good-looking to be hidden away from the world," she said as she twirled around in a circle.

Dex couldn't resist a smile or looking at her breasts as they swayed with her movements. "Listen, you're right. I am bored being here so much, but it's all for a good reason and you know it. It won't be much longer, just a few days."

Meagan sighed, recognizing the firm tone of his that said he wasn't going to be swayed. Then an idea came to Meagan out of the blue. "Ok. Fine. But if we can't go out, we're going to have sex."

Dex said, "What?"

"You heard me," Meagan said. "If I can't be entertained by going out, then you're going to provide me with entertainment right here. You're not married or anything, right? Of course not. You're married to your work and don't have time to date as a result," she plowed on. "So this will be as good for you as it will be for me. You're a great-looking guy, and I'm a great-looking woman. There should be no problem."

Dex stared in shock at the beautiful woman before him. Her light brown hair hung straight over her shoulders. Bright blue eyes regarded him with no trace of humor at all. He let his eyes trail down over her large breasts, slim waist, and sweetly curving hips. She wore shorts and a T-shirt to bed, he knew, so Dex was aware that the woman had killer legs. *Yes, she was fine*, he admitted to himself.

He didn't know whether he was more irritated with her scathing remark about his lack of a love life or just assuming that he would sleep with her. Or maybe it was with himself because he was seriously considering it. Frankly, it had been a while since he'd been with anyone and the idea of sex with Meagan certainly had its merits.

Meagan watched Dex closely and saw his jaw tighten and his gray eyes become stormy. She decided to take matters into her own hands. She'd wanted Dex from the first time they met. He lived up to the tall, dark, and handsome image and was sexy as hell. Meagan was determined to have him even if it was only for a short time.

Quickly, before he could react, Meagan took off her sweater. She saw the shock and desire in Dex's eyes as he looked at her. She smiled and took a couple of steps towards him. He backed up in response.

"What's the matter, Dex? Are you scared of little ole me? I won't bite—unless you want me to," she said.

"Meagan, this isn't going to happen. I can't. Do you understand that?" Dex said in a rigid tone. He was trying hard to keep his desire off his face.

Meagan's answer was to undo the front

clasp of her bra and let it fall open. Her large breasts were high and firm; Dex could tell and his hands itched to touch them. Her nipples were pink and tightened even as he watched. He swallowed as a tingling started in his crotch in response to the lovely sight.

Meagan could see the effect she was having on him and decided to keep going. She ran her hands over her breasts and played with her nipples, keeping her eyes on Dex all the while. His eyes grew stormy and his hands clenched at his side. She smiled when he shifted restlessly where he stood. Hefting her right tit, Meagan turned the nipple up towards her face and licked it, running circles around the areola and then sucking it. It felt so good.

Then she looked at Dex again. His nostrils were flaring and his hands were still clenched. She could see that his chest was rising and falling a little rapidly. He followed her progress as she walked over to him.

"You want me, Dex. I can see it in your eyes. I know when a man wants me and you do. Why fight it?" she said, looking him in the eye.

"I can't. I'll lose my job," Dex told her.

Meagan laughed. "Dex, there's no one here but us, and you're not due to be relieved until tonight at seven. We've got a lot of time to kill and I can think of a lot of ways to kill it," she urged him.

Dex couldn't believe that he was considering it. Normally, he was a by-the-book kind of marshal and wouldn't think twice about breaking the rules. But Meagan was right: there was no one else around and it was a long time until his relief would arrive.

Meagan decided to press her advantage. She put her hand on Dex's crotch.

"Feels like someone might be getting excited," she quipped.

Before Dex knew what was happening, her deft hands had unzipped his pants and unbuckled his belt. She slid her hand down his briefs and cupped his balls. Dex gasped in surprise and jerked back a little.

"Don't fight it, Dex. I want you to fuck me and I know you want to. Your dick is getting hard just thinking about it. You can't deny it," she said as she grasped the shaft of his cock and stroked it.

Dex's control broke at that point. He ran a hand up the back of her neck and grabbed a fistful of hair. He yanked it so that her neck arched backwards and her face turned up to his. He crushed her mouth with his, thrusting his tongue between her lips, which she had voluntarily opened. She made a mewling sound and kept stroking him as he plundered her mouth.

Her attentions were making him incredibly hard and his dick pulsed in Meagan's hand. She broke the kiss and got down on her knees. After pulling his underwear down, she took him in her hand again and held him still while she licked the head of his cock. Dex growled and plowed his hands through her hair. Meagan licked all around the head and then took him in her mouth, looping her tongue around him.

Then she took him as deep as she could and sucked hard as she backed off. The sensation was exquisite for Dex and he groaned. Although Meagan's head moved rapidly, she was able to keep the right level of suction as she did so. Dex watched her as she sucked his dick, thinking how hot it looked from his vantage point. Meagan kept doing it until Dex was rock-hard and then she let his cock go and stand up.

Dex grabbed her and kissed her passionately until Meagan was breathless. She didn't think any man had ever kissed her like that, as if he was so hungry for her. Meagan steadied herself a moment by grabbing Dex's buff arms.

"Wow," she said. "You're the best kisser I've ever had."

Dex chuckled. "Thanks. You give fantastic head."

Meagan grinned. "I'm glad you enjoyed it."

She got rid of her bra, jeans, and panties. Dex's gaze devoured her hungrily. She was curvy and lush and he liked her trimmed bush. She was a little taller than average—around 5'8"—and her long legs were trim and shapely. Even her feet were pretty as Dex noted.

"Damn, you're gorgeous," Dex said as he shed his clothes.

Meagan blinked at what she saw. The man looked like he was carved out of granite. *He must have spent hours in the gym*, she thought. Dex was all broad shoulders, heavily muscled chest, and powerful arms. His eight-pack abs led down to finely developed oblique muscles and legs that looked strong enough to belong to Thor. His cock throbbed, moving up and down as she looked at him.

"Condom?" she asked.

Dex walked to his duffel bag and retrieved one. "You just never know," he said with a shrug.

Meagan laughed. "Just like a boy scout."

"Something like that," Dex agreed with a laugh. He came to stand before her, looking down at her. Then he picked her up and deposited her roughly on the bed. She bounced and giggled.

"That was fun," she told him.

Dex climbed on the bed and lay beside her.His mouth covered hers again and he sucked on Meagan's full bottom lip. *She tasted delicious*, Dex thought. Meagan ran her fingers through his short hair, scraping lightly with her nails. Dex could feel goose bumps rise along his back as a result.

Releasing her mouth, Dex concentrated on her ear, licking the delicate shell and running his tongue over the lobe before taking the lobe between his lips and sucking it. Meagan gasped and squirmed a little. Dex blew in her ear then and Meagan whimpered as the cooler air hit it. Her ears had always been very sensitive and somehow Dex had zeroed in on that fact.

He played with her tits, tracing rings around her nipples before squeezing them and rolling them between his fingers. Meagan's back arched as her pussy tingled and became damp. Dex took the nipple closest to him in his mouth and sucked hard while he slid a finger into her hot, wet cunt.

Meagan moaned and lifted her hips to give

him more access. Another one of Dex's fingers joined the first, and then he slid them deep inside her. Making trigger motions with them, he stroked her G-spot and Meagan felt a pulling tension beginning deep inside. She spread her legs and tightly gripped the bed sheets as Dex movements became faster.

He kept sucking on Meagan's nipple as he increased his pace, knowing that the sensation would only add to Meagan's pleasure. It had always been important to him to satisfy his sexual partners, and it was the same with Meagan.

Dex could tell that Meagan was going to come by her moans, which became higher in pitch the closer she got to an orgasm, and by the way her cunt was beginning to spasm. Her hips hitched up and down and her thigh muscles tightened.

"Dex! Yes! Oh God, yes!" she shouted as she came in a hot, shuddering climax that seemed to roll on and on.

Dex gave a low groan; she clenched tightly around his fingers as he kept moving them. Meagan rode the blissful wave of pleasure, relishing the ebb and flow of the sensation Dex had brought about. When she relaxed a little, Dex withdrew his fingers and lay back on the bed and put on the condom.

"Mount up, cowgirl," he said to Meagan in a fake western drawl.

Meagan rolled over and sat up, her big breasts swaying as she did. "All right, stud. Prepare to be mounted."

She swung a leg over Dex's ripped midsection and reached between her legs to take a hold of his cock. Guiding it to the entrance of her pussy, she sank down onto it slowly, enjoying the feel of him gradually filling her completely.

Meagan wasn't the only one enjoying the erotic experience. Dex watched his cock impale Meagan and became even more excited. He couldn't believe how hard she made him. As Meagan leaned back, taking him completely inside, he began caressing her breasts, squeezing them and flicking his thumbs over the nipples. She had such beautiful tits that he just couldn't keep his hands off them. He was sure he wasn't the only guy to ever feel that way about them.

Shivering in delight, Meagan began moving up and down as jolts of heat shot from her nipples to her pussy and back again. Dex grabbed her hips and supported her as she moved, thrusting up with his hips as she came down. Their movements became synchronized as they adjusted to each other's bodies and they set a fast rhythm. They were both so horny that they had needed little foreplay to get things rocking.

"You feel so good inside me, Dex, so hard," Meagan told him.

"And you're so tight and wet. It's incredible," Dex answered.

They rocked against one another, giving and taking, breathing hard and moaning. It was hot and fast, and both of them were soon lost to everything else. Their eyes met and locked then, as Meagan began to climax. It was powerful and shocking in its intensity, and Dex watched it all happen for Meagan and felt her clench tight around his throbbing dick.

"Oh, shit, Dex! Oh, oh, oh!" Meagan cried out.

"Yeah, that's it. Cum for me," Dex growled.

A moment later, he let himself go, loosened his control, and came. It was such a strong orgasm that he forgot to breathe for a few moments. His big body shook and his grasp on Meagan's hips tightened. She looked down at Dex, watching him cum, and smiled. She was so happy that she was able to make him feel that way.

Gradually, they both came down from their sensual highs and Meagan lay down on top of Dex.

"That was great," she said. "See? We should have done that days ago."

Dex laughed. "Yeah, it was. You wore me down. Seduced me."

Meagan cocked an eyebrow at him and asked, "Are you complaining?"

"Hell, no. Not complaining at all," Dex said.

Meagan rolled off him and scooted off the bed. "Good. Because later before the next shift arrives, we're going to do it again," she informed him as she went into the bathroom.

Dex laughed and relaxed. If any of his friends had witnessed his seduction, they would either laugh or be envious. Good thing for him that no one would ever know. He was still breathing hard, but he was already looking ahead to a few hours from then.

7 THEIR ANIMAL SIDE

Allie sighed and shook her head as her last patient and its owner left the exam room. The obese beagle was having breathing issues and it really was no wonder. Mrs. Janner just didn't understand that constantly giving the dog treats and table scraps were slowly killing poor Toby. She wished again that people would realize that there was more to taking care of their animal friends than giving them food and water.

Retiring to her office, Allie answered a few phone messages and emails. She was gathering up her purse and coat to leave when her assistant Jack poked his head in the door.

"Hey, Doc. We have an emergency. A guy found a dog on the side of the road and brought her in," he said.

"Oh, boy," Allie said with a sigh as she sagged in her office chair. She was tired and ready to go home to a bubble bath and a good book.

"She's already in the exam room," Jack said and then headed that way.

Allie straightened, squared her shoulders, and stood up. She followed Jack and they entered the exam room together. Two things struck Allie; the dog's horrible condition and how hot the man was who'd brought in the dog. She pushed away the latter thought and centered her attention on the dog.

"Hi. I'm Dr. Chen," she said holding out her hand.

The tall black man took it and her hand was swallowed by his.

"I'm Levon Haines," he said with a smile.

Allie took her hand back even though she'd really enjoyed his touch. She began to examine the dog. She looked to be a cross between about four breeds. Allie recognized features belonging to German shepherd, Husky, Lab, and something else she couldn't quite put her finger on. She was a large dog, about seventy pounds, Allie guessed.

"What happened?" she asked Levon.

"I was driving along Route Eleven and I noticed something in the snow along the shoulder. When I got closer, I saw the dog. So I stopped and I could tell that she was in bad shape. I've heard good things about you from my Aunt Betty, so I brought her here."

Allie knew she would need x-rays and an MRI to check for broken bones and internal bleeding. She was fairly certain that she detected a couple of cracked ribs. The dog's right front paw was also broken.

Allie liked the way that Levon kept stroking

the dog's head and talking to her while Allie examined her. At one point, the dog raised her head and gave Levon a weak lick. He smiled and kept murmuring to her.

As Allie finished, she had images of Levon's hands on her flesh and his full mouth kissing her skin.

"So what do you think, Dr. Chen?" Levon asked. He'd stood straight again and gave her a once over. She was a very attractive Asian woman. Long, dark lashes rimmed her exotic black eyes. Allie wore her long, luxurious black hair back in a simple ponytail, which showed off her delicate cheekbones and small, finely shaped ears.

Allie hauled her thoughts back to the dog.

"She's not in good shape, of course. Her right front leg is broken and she has a couple of cracked ribs. I'd say she's been on her own for some time since I see signs of malnutrition," Allie stroked the poor dog's flank softly as she looked Levon in the eyes. "I'm not going to lie to you, Mr. Haines. This dog is going to require a lot of care. I'll understand if you're not up for this."

A strong resolve entered Levon's eyes as he understood what she was telling him. He wasn't the kind of man who would abandon a helpless animal. "Dr. Chen, I'm willing to do whatever it takes to make this old girl well again. Don't worry about the cost, either. I know what it's like to be abandoned and underestimated. I'm not gonna do that to her."

Dr. Chen's happy smile flashed at him. "I was hoping you'd say that. She's going to need love as much as anything else."

Levon returned her smile thinking that she was one fine looking woman. "She'll have it."

"Good. We're going to get started with her treatment, but I'll call you tomorrow with an update on her condition," Allie said. "Just leave your information with Sandy out front, ok?"

"Ok. I'll look forward to it," Levon said. He was reluctant to leave both the dog and Dr. Chen. He'd like to get to know her better. "Thanks, Doc."

"Don't thank me yet. She's got a long road ahead of her," Allie warned him.

"I know, but I'm up to the challenge," Levon assured her. "Talk to you tomorrow, Doc."

He turned to leave and Allie was treated to a great view of his tight ass. She reined in her thoughts and got back to the poor creature on the exam table.

Three weeks passed, during which time, Levon named the dog he'd brought into Allie's clinic. He'd chosen "Xena" because she was such a fighter and had a scrappy personality. Allie was impressed by Levon's level of commitment concerning the dog. He came almost every day to see Xena. He petted her and talked to her, saying encouraging things to her.

Xena was firmly attached to Levon by this point, which concerned Allie. She didn't want the dog's heart broken when she went to a different home. She decided to talk to Levon about it.

The next day that he came in, Allie asked him to come to her office. Truth be told, Xena wasn't the only one attached to Levon. Allie had come to look forward to his visits and missed him when he didn't come in. She enjoyed Levon's sense of humor and the more she knew about the man, the more she liked him.

Allie's feelings weren't one sided. Levon wanted to see Xena, but he wanted to see Allie more. She was a beautiful, intelligent woman and he was very attracted to her.

Allie had Levon sit in the chair in front of her desk. Her serious expression concerned Levon.

"What's going on, Dr. Chen? Is something wrong with Xena?"

Allie shook her head. "No. In fact, she's doing great. She's come a long way and much of that has to do with you."

"Nah," Levon protested. "I haven't done much. You and your staff have done all the work."

"But you've given her the most important thing: love. Studies have shown that animals that are happy heal better. I think your visits have a lot to do with Xena's improvement. She's doing so well that she'll be able to go home in a couple of weeks."

Levon's face lit up in a grin and Allie's heart skittered a little. He was so handsome and sexy and Allie wanted him intensely.

"That's fantastic," he said.

"Yes, it is. The only question is where she'll go at that time."

Levon's smile disappeared to be replaced by a confused frown. "She goes home with me, Doc."

Allie was pleasantly surprised. "Oh! Good. We hadn't discussed that yet, so I didn't know," she stated with a smile.

"I'm sorry. I should have made that clear. I fell in love with that dog the first time she gave me a sloppy kiss with that big tongue of hers," Levon said.

Allie laughed. "Yeah, I can see how you feel about her. I think it's great."

"Me, too. She's going to be a lot of company for me since I live alone. I paid a deposit to my landlord for her and I've bought her a ton of stuff already." His smile was sheepish.

"Really? That's awesome." Allie was always happy when pets and people connected like Levon and Xena.

An idea occurred to Levon as he watched Allie's radiant smile. "Hey, Doc. Why don't you come over some night for dinner? I make a mean chicken Marsala," Levon said. Once the words were out, Levon became a little nervous, but he pressed on. "That way you could approve of her new home and maybe give me some advice about owning a dog. Plus, it would be my way of thanking you for all you've done for Xena."

Allie considered his offer, which greatly appealed to her. She wanted to make sure that Xena got a good home and while she was certain that Levon would be an excellent doggie dad, it would be nice to know where Xena was going. Spending more time with Levon on a personal level was even more tempting, she admitted to herself. What the heck? She really had nothing to lose.

"That sounds wonderful. I'd love to," Allie said.

"Great." Levon said, "You have my address already. How's Friday at eight?"

"I'll be there," Allie answered.

Levon left shortly after this exchange, buoyant with high expectations about their date.

Allie stood on the stoop of the house where Levon lived. It wasn't what she'd been expecting. Levon's house was large and very beautiful, the kind of place one expected to be owned, not rented. She could see that Levon took good care of it. The winter-brown lawn was well maintained and the flower beds were neat. Allie could imagine how pretty they must be in the spring.

She took a deep breath and rang the doorbell. A tingle of nerves ran through her. When Levon opened the door, she sucked in a breath as she saw how handsome he looked in a casual suit with a purple shirt. The top button was undone and Allie got a glimpse of a strong male collarbone. Allie wanted to skip the chicken dish and have Levon for dinner.

"Come on in. Welcome," Levon said with a smile.

Allie entered the foyer and looked around. The inside was as nice as the outside.

"Let me take your coat." Levon helped Allie

out of her black velour coat and hung it in the front closet.

"Thank you," Allie said.

"You look beautiful, Doc," Levon said as he took in her red sheath dress that emphasized her delicate curves and showed off her trim, toned ankles and knees. Her sleek black hair fell softly over her shoulders and back. She looked delicious.

"Thank you," Allie repeated shyly. "You look very handsome tonight."

"Yeah, I clean up okay, I guess," he teased. "Come into the dining room. Dinner's just about ready."

Allie followed him, thinking again that he had such a nice ass. Levon's table presentation impressed Allie. White candles and a fresh floral centerpiece created an intimate ambiance.

Levon pulled out a chair for her and helped her get seated.

"You are such a gentleman," Allie remarked. "That's very rare these days."

Levon smiled as he poured her a glass of white wine. "My mother taught my brothers and me how to show a woman appreciation. Even if she hadn't, I prefer to treat a lady well, especially such a gorgeous woman."

Allie blushed at his compliment and smiled. "You're a charmer, Levon. I didn't know that about you," she said.

Levon laughed. "There's a lot you don't know about me, Doc."

A timer sounded in the kitchen.

"There's our dinner. Be back in a flash," Levon promised as he left the room.

Allie sipped her wine and sat back in her chair, very content to be waited on after a rough day at the clinic.

Levon's chicken Marsala was all that he'd promised: flavorful, tender, and with just the right amount of spices. Allie finished hers and wiped her mouth, totally replete.

"Levon, how is it that you're not married? You're a fantastic cook, fun, good-looking, and you obviously have a kind, generous heart," Allie said.

Levon put up his index finger and got up from the table. He went out to the kitchen and returned with his cell phone. "Can you call my ex-wife and tell her what you just told me?"

Allie cracked up at his theatrics and Levon joined in. Allie's smile was so beautiful and her laugh entrancing. Levon loved her smile and wanted to see it all the time.

"You are so bad!" Allie accused.

"Now you're giving me mixed signals. First you say I'm good then you say I'm bad. Now, I'm no expert, but if I were a dog trainer, I'd say that your statements are counterproductive," Levon quipped.

Allie held her side while she laughed. "Stop it!" It had been a long time since she'd laughed like this.

"All right, all right. I'll give you a reprieve... for now." Levon stood. "How about I show you the rest of the place so that you can see Xena's new home?"

By the time the tour was over, Allie was very impressed with how prepared Levon was for Xena's homecoming in a couple of weeks. She thought it was sweet that he'd gone to such lengths to make the dog feels at home. Xena would be one happy dog.

A couple of times while Levon was pointing things out to Allie, they'd had moments in which strong sexual currents had passed between them. Allie wanted to kiss Levon, but wasn't sure how to initiate that.

Levon was feeling much the same way and wanted Allie intensely. He could tell that she was feeling much the same way and decided to press his luck a little.

"Allie, I'm so glad you came over tonight. Not just to see Xena's new home, but because I wanted to get to know you better as a woman," Levon told her frankly. "I've been attracted to you right from the beginning, but felt that I should keep it professional. But I've really come to like you, a lot."

As he spoke, Levon closed in on Allie, an intense light in his deep, dark eyes. They were beautiful eyes, Allie thought as she gazed into them.

"I'm glad you asked me to dinner. I appreciate you respecting our professional relationship, but I like you very much, as a man, and now that Xena's going to be discharged soon, I don't see any conflict of interest anymore," Allie stated.

Levon smiled. "Glad to hear it. I thought that you felt the same way. I picked up on it a couple of times. You are so beautiful, Allie. I want to kiss you. Can I kiss you?"

Allie's breath hitched a little in her chest and her voice came out a little husky.

"Yes. You can."

Levon's large hand slid gently around the

nape of her neck under her satiny hair to cup her head. His eyes didn't leave hers as he lowered her mouth to his. Allie's eyes closed when she felt his soft lips on hers. She laid her hands on his chest and enjoyed the feel of his hard, male muscles under them.

Levon deepened the kiss, testing the way she tasted and asking for entrance into her pretty mouth. Allie sighed and parted her lips at his gentle request. The sweetness of his kiss touched her deeply and excited her. She pressed against him and put her arms around him.

When Levon's tongue touched hers, Allie shivered and parried with her own tongue. Suddenly something snapped in them both and their gentle kissing turned into raging passion. Their hands were everywhere, caressing, squeezing, and teasing. Levon picked Allie up in his strong arms and carried her upstairs to his bedroom.

Setting her down, Levon slowly turned her around and began unzipping her dress. He followed the zippers progress with soft kisses on Allie's smooth skin. Her scent was tantalizing and Levon deeply inhaled it.

Allie felt another shiver run through her when she felt Levon's lips on her back. She offered no resistance when Levon drew her dress down her arms and turned her around. Her red lacy bra matched her dress. She realized that she'd put it and her matching panties on in the hopes that Levon might see them tonight.

Levon's gaze swept over her as Allie shimmied completely out of the dress. She was a sexy sight in her red lingerie. Her light golden skin was smooth and Levon couldn't wait to touch her. He ran his hands lightly up her arms making goose bumps break out along her flesh. Levon didn't miss the reaction and was encouraged that his touch had such an effect on Allie.

"You are so beautiful," Levon said.

Allie gave him a saucy look from under her long, dark lashes. "Thank you. It's not fair for me to stand here like this. I want to see you, too."

Levon laughed. "Your wish is my command," he said.

"That's what I want to hear. Just remember that," Allie teased.

"Why do I get the feeling that beneath that sweet exterior lies a tiger?" Levon asked as he unbuttoned his dress shirt.

Allie simply smiled as an answer.

Levon took the shirt off and let it drop to the floor. Allie's mouth practically watered as she watched his hard muscles ripple under his dark skin. Shit, but he is in fine shape, she thought. She couldn't take her eyes off him as he stripped out of his pants. His briefs bulged in the front and Allie could tell that something great was in that big package.

Allie loved the predatory gleam that entered his eyes as he came to stand before her. He grabbed her and pulled her against him. Levon's mouth closed on hers and Allie moaned and opened her mouth for him. She soon found that he was a talented kisser. He combined just the right amount of teasing and tasting with demanding thrusts.

Allie locked her arms around his neck and kissed him back for all she was worth. She hadn't been with anyone in a long time and she couldn't remember wanting anyone this much.

Levon had planned to take thing slower, to relish his first experience with Allie, but she seemed to have other ideas. Her urgency transmitted to him and soon his hands were roaming over her slim, supple body and unsnapping her bra. She helped him get it off her. Levon growled when he saw her pretty breasts with dusky nipples. He cupped them gently and took a nipple in his mouth.

Heat shot through Allie's loins. She ran her fingertips through Levon's short-cropped, springy hair and let her head fall back as Levon sucked harder. Levon swirled his tongue around her nipple, sucking and biting. With his other hand, he played with Allie's other nipple, squeezing it between his fingers.

Then he released her and slipped his hands under her panties, his fingers moving around to cup her ass and then remove the panties. Allie made quick work of Levon's underwear and freed his pulsing penis from its prison of cotton fabric. Grasping him lightly, Allie ran the pad of her thumb around the soft-skinned tip, marveling at its smoothness.

She looked up into Levon's midnight eyes and her breath caught at the intense light in them. They stared at each other for long seconds and then something snapped and their baser instincts kicked in again. Mouth met mouth and tongue met tongue. Their bodies collided and hands flew as they touched each other everywhere they could reach.

The back of Allie's knees hit the bed and she fell back with Levon on top of her. His weight was delicious and she squirmed underneath him, feeling his cock rubbing her leg. Levon knelt on the floor and dragged Allie back towards the edge of the bed. Spreading her legs, he gazed hungrily at her pink pussy, noting that Allie kept her pussy trimmed but not shaved.

Then he gently pulled the petals of her sex open and began a soft assault on her pussy, licking and sucking her clit. She tasted incredible, tangy, salty, and something else that was simply Allie's own taste. He smiled a little when Allie moaned and began moving beneath his mouth. Her heels rested on his back and he could feel her feet tensing along with her legs.

As his tongue swept over her, Allie felt her pussy tighten as she neared orgasm. She couldn't believe how quickly she was ready. Levon's talented tongue had a lot to do with that she realized. He was quick yet thorough in his movements and seemed to know just what she needed.

Levon's hands stroked their way up Allie's torso, skimming along her skin until they reached her breasts. His fingers found her nipples and squeezed and rolled them around. Allie thought she was going to explode as he caressed them. Her back arched and her head rolled to the side as she began quivering under his mouth.

Levon growled as he felt her reach the

brink. He stopped his circular motions and started a forceful back and forth stroke over her clit. Allie felt her orgasm begin and whimpered as the feelings intensified.

"Oh, Levon! That feels so good! Oh, yes!" Her words dissolved into cries of bliss as her climax continued to wash through her.

Wanting to draw it out, Levon kept up his attentions. He let up a little on the pressure he was using and slowed down slightly because he knew that her clit was bound to be very sensitive at that point. As her moans diminished, Levon slowed his stroked and then stopped. He gave her pussy a final kiss and looked up at her.

Allie's beautiful eyes opened and she smiled. "My, my, Mr. Haines. You are quite talented," she commented.

Levon chuckled. "Thank you and thank you for dessert."

"You're welcome," Allie said and pulled her legs from where they rested over his shoulders. She sat up and kissed him and tasted herself on his lips and tongue. It fired up her passion again. "Stand up," she told him.

He didn't question her, just did as she wanted. He stood in front of her, proud and one hundred percent male. Allie marveled at his hard cock. It was so smooth and nicely shaped and she wanted to taste him. She took him in her hands then, stroking him with feather light touches and caressed his ball sac.

Levon closed his eyes and gave himself up to her, enjoying what she was doing to him.

Then he felt her warm mouth close over him and he moaned in pleasure. Allie drew him in as far as she could and then applying gentle suction pulled back again. She swirled her tongue around the head of his cock and flicked it over the small hole in its tip. Allie almost smiled at Levon's sharp intake of breath but started sucking him in earnest.

Levon growled as he hardened even more as Allie licked and sucked and worked him with her hands. It felt incredible but Levon knew he would have to stop her soon or it would be over. He wasn't ready for that to happen yet. He wanted to give her more pleasure and he was in no hurry.

Allie stopped when Levon buried his hands in her silky hair and pulled slightly. Releasing him she looked up into his handsome face. He was smiling at her.

"That feels fantastic, but I've got more in store for you and I don't want it to end yet," he told her.

Allie grinned. "I'm so glad you said that. I don't want it to be over either."

Something passed between them, a connection that neither of them wanted to examine closer so soon, but that was there nonetheless.

Levon backed up to his dresser and opened a top drawer. He pulled out a condom and then came back to her. Expertly he put it on.

"On your knees, woman," he said with a

smile.

"Yes, sir," Allie said with a giggle and promptly presented him with her ass.

Levon kneaded her finely shaped ass cheeks and ran his hands up and down her back. Allie let her head fall forward and simply enjoyed his touch. Then Levon was rubbing her pussy and parting her lips. Levon found her cunt to be very wet and slipped two fingers inside of her. She was tight and hot. He began sawing his fingers in and out and placed his thumb on her clit.

Allie's hips moved of their own accord as instinct took over. She ceased to think, only felt. As Levon moved faster, Allie gave a feminine growl and tightened inside. Before she knew it, Allie was soaring over the edge into bliss.

"Levon! Oh, God, I'm cumming!" she shouted and brought her head back.

"Yeah, baby, that's it. You cum for me," Levon encouraged her. She was getting even wetter.

Allie's breathing was rapid as she came down from the high of her orgasm. She felt Levon shift behind her and then he was filling her with his cock and it was exquisite. Levon had to control himself as he slid deeper inside of her. He knew he was large and didn't want to give her more than she could handle. To his surprise, he didn't meet any resistance, even once he was completely inside her. That was a rare occurrence for him.

"Oh, baby, you're so deep inside me," Allie said in a voice that told Levon of her rapture.

"I know," he breathed. It felt so incredible,

so right.

When Allie squirmed a little, Levon took that as a sign that it was all right to start moving. He pulled out and pushed in and Allie whimpered and pressed back to meet him. Levon grasped Allie's slim hips and thrust forward again, burying his cock inside Allie more forcefully.

"Yes. Harder," Allie urged.

That was all the encouragement Levon needed to let loose. He plunged forward, deeper into her yielding flesh, groaning as her warm sheath enveloped him. Allie gasped as Levon's pace increased. Soon the sound of his body slapping against her backside sounded in the room. Levon slipped a hand around to Allie's front and he found her pussy.

Allie's clit was highly sensitive at this point and Levon's fingers only needed to brush against it to send her into an orgasm. Her pussy clenched repeatedly around Levon and he slowed down to enjoy the feeling. When the spasms stopped, he pulled out and flipped Allie over.

She laughed breathlessly as she bounced against the mattress. Allie flipped her hair back so she could see the smile that matched Levon's laugh as he crawled up the bed to her.

"That was fun," she said. "Sort of like an amusement park ride."

Levon's grin turned wicked and Allie's breathing quickened at the sight.

"You better hold on, then, 'cause I'm gonna take you on an even bigger, better ride," he told her and grasped her ankles.

He slung them over his shoulders, tipped

her ass up and impaled her with his cock. Allie submitted to him willingly, eagerly, wanting everything he would give her. She didn't have long to wait. Levon thrust again and again, speeding up then slowing down when he felt she was nearing the precipice.

Allie loved Levon's forceful strokes, the intense look on his face, and the way his strong hands held her hips. Levon was lost in blissful sensations as he drove into Allie again and again. He growled his pleasure and Allie replied with her own moans.

Levon held his climax back until he felt the first tremors of Allie's. As she came, Allie felt as if she were shattering, so intense was her orgasm. She called Levon's name repeatedly as her hands fisted in the sheets.

A powerful climax shook Levon and he shuddered as his seed poured forth. He couldn't think, only feel. They rode the rapids of their mutual ecstasy for long moments. It took them a long time to come down from the rapturous high.

Slowly Levon removed Allie's legs from around his shoulders and laid them on the bed. He moved off to one side and lay down next to Allie. Her eyes were closed but she was smiling.

Levon couldn't help but smile at the sight of her beautiful, happy face. Looking her naked body up and down, Levon concluded that everything about her was beautiful. Allie opened her passion-hazed eyes and rolled over to face him. She looked into his handsome face and then gave him a soft kiss.

"That was amazing," she said as her

breathing returned to normal.

Levon chuckled. "I think that's an understatement but I can't think of a word that's really accurate." He put an arm around her waist and drew her near.

Allie snuggled against him, content and happy. "This has been a wonderful night, Levon. Thank you for the beautiful dinner. I like a man who can cook."

"Mama always said that a man should be able to take care of himself and not depend on a woman to do everything for him around the house. She started teaching us when we were young and we each had to cook one night a week," Levon explained.

"I like your mother," Allie said and laughed.

Levon grinned. "Me, too. And she was right. It's a good way to impress the ladies."

Allie cocked an eyebrow at him. "Impress a lot of ladies, do you?"

"Nah. Not so many. But I impressed you and that's good enough for me," Levon replied.

"Yes, you did. In a lot of ways, not just dinner. You're a special man, Levon."

Levon could feel himself flushing at her words of praise. "Thank you." He liked the way he and Allie fit together. "Do you have to go or can you stay?" he asked.

Allie's heartstrings twanged a little at the hope in his voice. "I always carry a bag with fresh scrubs and stuff in my car. I spend a lot of time on the go and I never know when I'm going to need a change of clothes. I'd love to stay," she said.

"I'm so glad you said that," Levon said and slid out of bed. "I think we need a snack after that," he said.

Allie rose up on an elbow. She wanted to drink in Levon's chiseled physique.

"Where are you going?" she asked.

Levon laughed. "You'll see," he answered and did a little dance as he left the bedroom.

Allie giggled and lay back against the pillows to relive the evening as she waited to see what Levon had in store for her. Happiness filled her as she hoped this would be the first of many special nights they would spend together.

8 MONTANA JOY

It was going to storm. Cade stood in the doorway of his new residence, a small cabin on a Montana ranch, while lightning flashed outside. Thunder rumbled and rolled while he surveyed his small home. There wasn't a lot of room, but it would suit his needs just fine.

He liked the modern conveniences. There was a small kitchenette, complete with a microwave and a gas stove. There were several lamps in the living/bedroom area. A small TV occupied one corner of that space. A doorway off to the right led to a bathroom that was tiny, but at least had a working shower.

Cade was surprised to see another doorway. Crossing to it, he opened it to reveal a small closet. Empty hangers were ready for clothes to be hung on them. Three windows let in plenty of light and made it seem as if the cabin was a little bigger than it was.

Throwing his two duffel bags on the full-sized bed that was pushed against the wall opposite the bathroom, Cade ran his hand through his long black hair. His blue eyes roamed the room, taking in the nice western scenes that were hung on a couple of walls. The place certainly had seen a woman's touch, he thought.

He went back out to his truck to retrieve a couple of boxes. Those, his bags, laptop, and various computer equipment, were the extent of his worldly possessions. Traveling light was important to him since he'd spent the last year traveling around. Now, though, he hoped to stay in one place for at least a year.

It was one of the reasons he'd taken this job. Maddie Wilson, his new employer, had informed him that the job was his as long as he would stay. She needed someone reliable and who wouldn't leave after a month or two.

That suited Cade just fine. He was glad to have a stable job while he worked on his book. A closet author, he was in the process of writing his first novel. He'd been made fun of in the past for it. What was a traveling ranch hand doing writing a book?

Cade put his laptop and the box containing his other stuff that went to it on the kitchen table, which would be used as his desk. He'd have to ask Maddie if she had Wi-Fi capabilities.

He spent the next half hour putting away his things. It didn't take longer than that because he had so little. By this time, the storm had arrived and the lightning and thunder were in full force along with the rain.

The early June storm was needed and Cade was glad to see it come.

A boyish grin lit up his face. On impulse, he took off his shirt and pants and put on a pair of shorts. His half Chinook, half Irish heritage influenced his personality by giving him a playful fearlessness that sometimes led to trouble. He was a great prankster and enjoyed daring activities.

He went barefoot a lot, so his feet were toughened to the hard earth that he jumped out of the cabin onto. The warm rain instantly soaked him and that suited him just fine. His mother had taught him several Indian dances, and he started one that gave thanks to the god Neakanie for the storm.

Lightning streaked through the sky, but Cade simply rejoiced in it. He had very little fear of anything in life and didn't mind when people made fun of him as long as it wasn't overly malicious. He just figured that if they were picking on him, they were leaving someone else alone.

Maddie Wilson looked out her kitchen window at the storm with dismay. She'd hung laundry out on the line earlier that day and now it was getting soaked. She tried to hang it out whenever possible to save on the electricity bill. She hoped the storm passed quickly so that it could dry again.

She hadn't gotten to it because she'd been busy out in the barn tending to a sick calf. Plus, her new hand, Cade McAllister, had arrived and she'd seen to getting him settled in and brought up to speed on the routine of the ranch.

As she looked out the window, movement off to her right caught her attention. Maddie almost didn't believe what she was seeing. If she was correct, Cade was doing an Indian dance out in front of his cabin. With his long black hair, he did indeed look the part of a brave doing a war dance.

She was nearsighted and didn't always see things far off well, so she got her pair of binoculars and trained them on the dancing man. She sucked in a breath as the binoculars gave her a close up view of a spectacular chest, shoulders, and abdomen.

Then she trained her gaze upward and caught the look of sheer joy on Cade's finely sculpted face and couldn't resist smiling herself. His blue eyes were trained skyward and rain sluiced his tan body. She trailed her binoculars downward and sighed again as she saw the way his wet tan shorts molded to his package.

Abruptly ashamed of herself, she put the binoculars down. Then thought, hey, if he's gonna flaunt it, why shouldn't I enjoy it? She raised them again and watched Cade's joyful dance, admiring his dancing abilities. She could well imagine him doing a stint as a stripper. He'd do well with an Indian routine, she thought.

Cade finished his dance and stood still, just enjoying the cooling rain on his heated skin. He pushed his hair back and looked up at the main house. His vision was excellent and he could see someone watching him from a window. It looked like they had binoculars or something. He smiled and waved. The binoculars disappeared quickly and Cade laughed hoping that whoever it was enjoying the show.

He went into his cabin and got out of his wet shorts. He toweled off and put a pair of jeans on but left his chest bare. Cade wasn't ashamed of his body and had spent a lot of time running around almost naked as a youth.

Even though he wasn't supposed to start his duties until the next day, Cade decided to head out to the barn to get to know the horses and check out the cattle. Might as well be ahead of the game come the morning. Arriving at the horse barn, he saw Maddie go inside and followed her in.

"Hi," he said.

Maddie whirled around. She hadn't heard him at all. "Jesus! You scared the crap out of me!"

Cade didn't apologize, just grinned. "It's the bare feet. Very quiet," he said.

"Yeah, well, knock it off. Besides, you shouldn't be in your bare feet in the barn. That's how you get hurt. I don't need you starting off the job by getting your foot broken," she groused at him to hide the fact that she couldn't take her eyes off his bare chest. At least he'd put jeans on.

"I've been around horses all my life and I've never gotten stepped on. I'll be fine, I promise," Cade said. He'd noticed that she was flustered and it amused him.

He knew his affect on women and wasn't above using it. He stepped nearer to her and watched her big brown eyes widen a little. Her nostrils flared slightly, too. She wore her light brown hair in a ponytail. She took a step back.

Maddie swore in her mind. The man was doing crazy things to her body, and he hadn't even been there two hours. She'd noticed how hot he was as soon as she'd answered the door. The shoulder blade length, black hair, and deep blue eyes had entranced her on the spot. Watching him do his almost naked rain dance hadn't helped her any, either.

His bare chest was slick with rain. He'd changed but still walked over in the rain. Obviously, he was used to the elements. She realized that he was watching her closely and she was determined not to give up any more ground.

"That's great," she said, "but I prefer that my employees wear protective gear. I don't need my workman's comp premiums going up if at all possible."

Cade smiled again. "I'll wear boots tomorrow, but I was just getting the lay of the land right now. I wasn't going to do any real work," he told her.

"Oh. Yeah. Right." Damn! She had to get herself under control. "Just be careful," she said and turned and walked away from him.

Cade let her go, smiling as she went. He watched her killer ass move from side to side as she walked. Her back was straight and her ponytail switched while she moved. Oh yeah. He could definitely see himself riding that.

Then he remembered that she was his boss and laughed. There would be nothing like that with Maddie. Cade made it a habit to never get personally involved with bosses, especially female ones. Too much trouble lies that way, he knew.

True to his word, when Maddie entered the horse barn in the morning, Cade was wearing boots with his jeans and T-shirt. It boasted a Mickey Mouse print which she found amusing. She'd been expecting a hunk like Cade to be wearing a plaid short-sleeved western shirt or something similar.

"Good morning," she said.

Cade looked up from the rear hoof of a bay mare that he was cleaning. He gave her a broad smile that made her heart skip.

"Morning. You look pretty," he said. "Green suits you."

Maddie became flustered. Damn it, he was always throwing her off guard. "Thanks. Who assigned you Brown Betty?" she wanted to know.

"Me," Cade said simply. "I just started at one side of the barn and worked my way down."

She liked the fact that he was taking the initiative. Maddie hated it when she had to constantly keep track of what a ranch hand was doing and make sure they were actually working. It looked like she wasn't going to have to worry about that with Cade.

"Great! Keep up the good work," she said. Then she smiled as Betty Brown started leaning on Cade. Horses did that sometimes when their back hooves were being cleaned.

Cade grunted and then laughed. "Hey, you, knock it off," he said and gave Betty a gentle poke with an elbow. The mare straightened immediately.

"She does that all the time. She can be lazy," Maddie said stroking the horse's face affectionately.

"I'll remember that," Cade said. "Is there anything special you want me to do today?"

Maddie thought for a moment. "Well, some of the barbed wire in the south pasture needs attention. Have Luke show you the section," she said referring to her foreman.

Cade nodded. "Do you have Wi-Fi?"

"You have a computer?" Maddie asked. Somehow she just couldn't see him typing.

"Yeah. I need an Internet connection. Is that possible?" he asked.

Maddie said, "Yeah. I'll get you the network information by lunch, ok?"

"Sure. Sounds good," Cade answered.

"Well, I'm off to do some paperwork in the office," Maddie said and left him.

Cade fixed a toasted cheese sandwich for lunch. It was quick and easy. He had an hour for lunch and wanted to get the Wi-Fi connection set up. He was just sitting down to eat when Maddie knocked on the doorframe of his door. Cade preferred fresh air and just let his door stand open.

He looked up from his sandwich and smiled. "Hi. Come on in."

Maddie entered and looked around. There were a few things of Cade's around, but not much. It looked like he traveled light.

"Luke said you did a great job on that fence today," she said.

"Good."

Maddie was nervous in the close confines of the cabin. Cade seemed to fill the space even though he was sitting down. He was shirtless again.

"Do you always go without your shirt?" she asked. Irritation tinged her voice.

Cade frowned. It was the first time she'd seen that expression on his face and it looked fierce. "Is that a problem when I'm not working?" he said with a note of challenge. He rose from the table and came toward her. His height was imposing and his broad shoulders filled her line of vision.

She stood her ground, though, and looked up into eyes that were an icy blue at the moment. "No," she said. "It was merely an observation." She pulled a piece of paper from her jeans pocket. "Here's the Internet information you wanted."

Cade reached for the paper and their fingers touched. Maddie's gaze collided with his, and an awareness of each other as a man and a woman flowed between them. Cade didn't flinch, didn't look away. In that moment, as he looked into her beautiful brown eyes and looked at her full, sensual mouth, Cade knew he was going to lose the battle to not bed his boss.

There was something about her that drew him to her and he'd only known her for a day. Maybe it was the challenge she represented, but he didn't think so. Her chest rose and fell a little faster indicating that she was feeling much the same as he. He couldn't help but let his gaze drop to her breasts. He wanted to see them bare and suck on them.

Hot desire shot through him and he could have groaned. Cade didn't though. He pulled the paper slowly from her fingers and broke the physical connection. Maddie barely registered his movement as she let her gaze roam over his muscular chest and midsection, up over his to-die-for shoulders and his beautiful mouth. When her eyes met his again, she gave him a shy smile.

"Thanks," Cade said. "I appreciate it and you can take some money out of my pay to help with the costs of the Internet. It's only fair since I'm using it."

Maddie just stood there watching him for a moment before she could speak. "Oh, well, there's no need for that," she said. She could barely think. Maddie wanted to touch him so badly it scared her.

Cade saw her pupils dilate, a telltale sign that she was aroused. His cock had similar ideas and his loins tightened. The way her jeans fit her showed off her softly flaring hips and flat stomach. He wanted to bury his dick in her pussy, but Cade knew he had to move slowly so that he didn't scare her off.

Maddie was like a nervous filly that he had to be gentle and calm. "Are you sure? Because I'm happy to pay for access to it," he said. Slowly, he moved another couple of inches closer to her.

He looked down into her eyes, letting his desire show in his. Maddie opened her mouth to say something but nothing came out. He smelled so good, male, hot, and a little bit like horses. It was a heady combination and it whetted her appetite for him. She wondered what he tasted like and almost gulped.

Finally she said, "Don't worry about it." Her voice was husky and she cleared her throat. She saw it in his eyes that he wanted to kiss her and she wanted that so badly. She wanted him to claim her mouth, to thrust his tongue inside it.

Cade slowly slid a hand around to the small of her back and rubbed her softly through her shirt. He closed the gap between them and brushed his torso against her breasts. Maddie let out a little whimper. Cade let her get used to the feel of him and ran his other hand up her arm.

All of his movements were slow but purposeful. Maddie was entranced and couldn't move. His bare skin against her was hot. Either he waxed or he just didn't have a lot of body hair. Her fingers itched to run over that smooth brown skin. She didn't know if she dared because she knew that once she touched him it was all over.

Cade watched conflicting emotions flit across her face and knew that he needed to step it up before she backed away. He pressed harder against her and tipped her face up so that she had to meet his eyes. Cade didn't say anything; he communicated through action and body language.

Ever so slowly he lowered his head until his mouth met hers. He flicked his tongue over her mouth. She opened to him and he melded his lips with her and touched her tongue with his. Maddie moaned and put a hand against his chest. He'd won, she knew, but then felt that so had she.

His hot skin under her hand released all of her lust for him. She kissed him back with abandon, embracing his waist and leaning into him. Cade reached out and closed the cabin door then grabbed her hair and plunged his tongue deep into her mouth.

Suddenly, Maddie turned into a wildcat. Her hands were everywhere, over his back, up and down his chest, and then undoing his jeans and delving into his underwear. He wasn't complaining. Her touch ignited his desire and he made quick work of her shirt and bra. Cade stopped for a moment to admire her beauty. Her breasts were perfectly round with pale pink nipples that fascinated him. They hardened as he watched, and he bent his head and took one in his mouth. Circling her areola with his hot tongue, Cade pinched the other one at the same time.

"Oh, God!" Maddie said and grabbed his shoulders and clung tightly.

Cade moaned against her breast and sucked gently on her nipple. Maddie moved her hips against Cade's leg, and her pussy came in contact with his hard thigh. She was melting and was happy about it. She was so turned on she couldn't think.

That was exactly what Cade wanted. He wanted her hot and horny. But he also wanted to take his time, but could tell that he was going to have to slow her down a little. He straightened up again and undid her jeans and pushed them down quickly. He got rid of his and his underwear.

Maddie's breath caught at the sight of his big cock proudly jutting from his crotch. Damn how she wanted it. She squealed when Cade picked her up and deposited her playfully on the bed. He finished taking off her jeans and panties and quickly spread her legs apart.

She had such a pretty pussy. He could see that she was getting wet for him. He stood by the bed and hauled her ass up in the air, then bent over her pussy and went to work on her clit. Maddie kept from crying out, but just barely. Her mind registered the fact that there were people around and she didn't want them to know what was going on in Cade's cabin.

The way he was handling her was incredibly exciting. He put her legs over his shoulders and thrust his tongue inside her pussy and then flicked it over her clit with incredible speed. Most of her weight rested on her shoulder blades. It was a foreign position to her and she loved it.

Cade licked her delicious pussy, loving the way she moved and sounded. He was quiet, only letting out low moans or sighs as he lapped away at her cunt. Maddie squirmed and grabbed the sheets as he brought her closer to what she needed. Maddie could feel it on the way and snagged one of Cade's pillows.

She started coming and shuddered against Cade's mouth. Maddie put the pillow over her face to muffle her cries of ecstasy. It was a long, hard orgasm and Maddie had never experienced anything quite like it. Cade rode it out with her, licking and sucking as it crashed over her.

By the time her climax started to ebb, Maddie was panting. She threw the pillow from her and smiled up at Cade. He winked at her and eased her down onto the bed. He made a motion for her move over. Then Cade joined her on the bed and lay beside her.

He proceeded to kiss her languidly, savoring the taste of her mouth and tongue. Cade traced the outline of her lips with the tip of his tongue, making Maddie shiver in delight. Maddie didn't know how long it was, but they kissed slowly like that for quite a while. By the time Cade started to move on, her pussy ached again for him.

Cade licked her ear, using the tip of it to tickle each part of it and then he sucked on her lobe, which drove her crazy. Then he gently blew in her ear and Maddie gasped at the sensation. Cade chuckled in her ear then trailed kisses and little bites down her neck to her shoulders.

His palm skimmed over her nipples and Maddie squirmed. It felt so good. Her nipples were extremely sensitive and she loved having them played with. Cade seemed to sense this and began squeezing them and rolling them between his fingers. He kept doing it, varying the intensity and angle. Maddie could feel something happening in her pussy and looked at Cade in amazement.

He just gave her a wicked smile and

nodded. Maddie had never known someone who could communicate so much with gestures and facial expressions. Maddie thought, if I didn't know better, I'd swear I'm gonna cum. She kept looking at Cade who smiled at her. Then he squeezed harder and Maddie grabbed his shoulders, as her cunt seemed to come alive.

A sweet burning filled her and she was stunned when a soft release flowed through her. It was an orgasm like she'd never felt before. It was rich and full compared to intense and hard. Gentle spasms held her for a few moments before fading.

"Oh my God," she whispered. "I've never... that's, uh... new," she said.

Cade's rich chuckle sounded softly. "Glad to introduce you to something you've never experienced before."

Maddie wanted to touch him and started stroking his chest. His skin was soft and taut and she loved the feel of it. Cade stretched out as if giving himself over to her. In fact, he relaxed and closed his eyes.

Maddie was dismayed. "Are going to take a nap?" she asked in an incredulous tone.

Cade's head rose, his eyes cracked open, and one of his dark brows arched.

"Ok," Maddie said. "Good to know."

He closed his eyes again and lay his head down. Maddie ran her hands over him, much the way she did when she was grooming a horse. With her fingertips, she stroked every inch of the man, not being able to get enough of the feel of him. Maddie knew he wasn't sleeping because of the way his nostrils flared and the way he was breathing.

Plus, his cock was jumping around, just begging for attention. Maddie took him in her hands and Cade moaned. There was some pre-cum on the tip of it and Maddie licked the salty-sweet taste from it. Cade sighed and shifted a little on the bed. Maddie flicked her tongue over the head of his cock and Cade moved again.

Smiling, Maddie stroked his shaft up and down, steadily increasing her tempo. The big man's hips rose off the bed and he groaned. Maddie took him deep inside her mouth and sucked as she pulled back and Cade growled. Maddie thought it was one of the sexiest things she'd ever heard.

His cock tasted so good and he was rock-hard. Maddie swirled her tongue around his cock and then took him deep again. She wanted to taste his cum, wanted to give him pleasure the way that he'd given her pleasure. Getting up on her knees, Maddie grasped the base of his cock and moved faster, bobbing her head as she worked him with her mouth.

A fine trembling started in his body and another low moan came from his throat. Cade propped himself up on his elbows and watched her suck him off. Maddie switched to her hand again and looked over to see Cade watching her. He smiled at her, his blue eyes shining and she couldn't help but answer with one of her own.

"You feel so good, Cade. So hard," she told him.

Cade moaned and said, "What you're doing feels incredible."

Maddie smiled. "I want to make you cum. I want to taste it."

"I'll give it to you."

"Good," she said and licked him and sucked him again.

Cade couldn't help but move his lips. His balls tightened up and his loins felt like a fire had been lit inside them. Her touch was driving him crazy, her hot mouth making his desire reach an intense high.

He fisted his hands in the bedsheets and whispered, "Maddie, I'm gonna cum, don't stop whatever you do."

She didn't answer, just kept going. Cade dropped his head back and shuddered as his orgasm ripped through him. Maddie caught every spurt that filled her mouth, loving the taste and kept working him to get every last drop from him. Cade groaned softly and almost pulled the sheet corners off the mattress it was so intense.

Maddie only stopped when she felt Cade begin to relax. He let the sheets go and sighed as his body went limp.

Maddie wiped her mouth and said, "That's one of the best lunches I've had in a while."

It started out as a chuckle and grew, Cade pulling a pillow over his head to muffle his loud laughter. Maddie soon joined him. Cade rolled over and pressed his face harder into the pillow, giving Maddie an unobstructed view of his fine ass. She gave him a playful smack and giggled.

Cade turned back over and grabbed Maddie dragging her down beside him. He was still laughing a little as he kissed her. "Now you're a bad little kitten. I like it. I like you, Maddie."

Maddie rolled her eyes. "Well, obviously."

Cade laughed again. "Obviously."

"I wish I could stay, but someone's going to come looking for me," she said with regret.

"Go on, then. I better get back to work, too, before my boss fires me for screwing on the job," Cade said with an impish smile.

Maddie laughed and scooted off the bed. Cade lay for a moment, watching her get dressed. Then he said, "You better use my comb. Your hair's a little messy."

"Gee, thanks," Maddie said.

"I like it messy, but I don't think you want to leave here looking like you had a sex romp," Cade clarified.

"Right you are," Maddie said and stepped into the miniscule bathroom. She redid her ponytail and straightened up her clothes. "There. How do I look?"

"Delicious," Cade said.

Maddie laughed. "Do I look presentable?"

Cade sat up and said, "Yes, ma'am, boss lady. You look fine. You go ahead and I'll follow shortly. There are some steers that need to be moved to another pasture. That's my plan for this afternoon. That ok?"

"Great," she said as he rose from the bed and came to encircle her waist.

Cade looked down into her brown eyes and then gave her a lingering kiss. "You know, if someone were to leave their door unlocked tonight, there could be some dessert served," he said and arched an eyebrow.

Maddie grinned. "Duly noted," she said. "That door just might be unlocked," she said and stepped out of his embrace.

Cade dressed while she left, smiling to himself as he got ready to go back to work. Maddie's right, he thought, that was one of the best lunches I've had in a long time.

Cade not only got the steers moved, he finished mending the last section of fence that needed fixing and helped shoe two horses. Maddie was impressed with his work ethic and the way his muscles jumped and moved while he was working. He was exceptionally good with the horses and didn't have to talk to them much.

It was as if he had a private language with them. Maddie wondered if that came from his Indian heritage. Either way, she was glad that she'd hired him. It was hard to find good hands, and Maddie hoped Cade would stick around for a while. Briefly she wondered why it was so important for him to have an Internet connection, but then got busy doing all kinds of tasks and forgot about it.

That night, she couldn't sleep for wondering if Cade was going to come to her. She'd left the door open since he'd hinted for her to do so and lay in bed naked, tossing and turning. She finally drifted off at some point and woke to the feel of hands on her body. Maddie smiled and rolled over to see Cade's face illuminated by the light from the full moon pouring in her windows.

He smiled at her and kept running his

hands over her. Then he pulled her against him and kissed her senseless. His hungry mouth and tongue teased and captured hers, drawing moans from Maddie as he sparked a fire deep in her belly. Cade didn't seem to be in any kind of a hurry. He kissed her and stroked her leisurely.

Maddie squirmed against him and returned his fiery kisses. She kneaded the muscles of his back and arms, reveling in the power she felt in them. Maddie ran her fingers through his sleek, black hair. She'd never been one for long hair on guys, but Cade was the exception.

Cade was getting hard. Maddie's touch and sighs drove him crazy and he wanted her badly. He forced himself to go slow, though, wanting to savor their time together. He bit his way down her neck to her breasts and teased her nipples with his tongue, telling her in between bites what he was going to do to her in crude terms.

"I'm gonna fuck that sweet pussy of yours," he told her as he captured a nipple in his mouth and sucked hard.

Maddie moaned and said, "I want you to fuck it. Oh, God, that feels so good," she said. "I never knew until this afternoon that it was possible to have an orgasm just from someone playing with your nipples."

Cade chuckled. "I'm glad you enjoyed it," he said and went back to work on her nipples. He alternated sucking and tweaking with brushing his fingertips against them. Maddie's hands roamed down his stomach until they found his cock. They played with each other, becoming hornier and hornier.

Cade pushed Maddie onto her back and slipped a hand between her legs, stroking her slick cunt. He quickly thrust two fingers into her, sawing in and out in fast, sure motions. Maddie's back arched and she let out a high-pitched moan. Cade moved faster making sure that his palm slapped against her clit.

"Oh, Cade, shit!" Maddie said and spread her legs even further. She thrashed her head from side to side. Her cunt pulsed around Cade's fingers and her swollen clit ached with need. He was forcing her to that point when bliss would sweep through her and she wanted it so badly.

Cade kept up his tempo, all the while whispering to her, telling her how soft and hot and wet she was inside. His words alone excited Maddie and she grew hotter by the second. He started using a trigger motion with his fingers, hitting her G-spot. He massaged the slightly raised patch of skin there and Maddie shot off the mattress, an intense orgasm holding her in its grip.

She cried out, not able to form words as she came. Her pussy juice dampened Cade's hand, and he groaned as the scent of it filled his nostrils. Her scent was intoxicating and he wanted to taste her. Maddie collapsed back onto her pillow, and Cade withdrew his fingers and sucked on them.

Maddie's flavor filled his mouth, making his cock even harder. He fought the temptation to hurry, stamping down on his impulses. He snatched one of the condoms he'd brought with him off the nightstand and rolled it down over his engorged prick.

"On your knees, boss lady," he ordered her.

Maddie smiled and complied. "Yes, sir." She rose up on her knees and spread her legs for him. "Like that?" she said with a shake of her ass.

"Yeah, just like that," Cade concurred. "Brace yourself," he told Maddie and thrust inside her roughly.

"Oh, yeah!" Maddie said. "Damn! That feels so good."

Cade didn't answer. He just kept plunging inside her, rocking to and fro as he filled her cunt over and over. Then he raised one of his legs until he was half-kneeling and rammed into her from another direction, changing the intensity of his strokes.

Maddie could only form an "O" with her mouth as his cock hit a different place inside her. The pleasure was intense already, and then Cade reached one hand around and started playing with one of her nipples, and Maddie screamed as another orgasm shook her to the core.

The sound of her pleasure filled the room, and Cade wanted to hear her cum like that all the time. All of the senses added to his sexual experiences and none more than sound. When Maddie went limp, Cade let her down onto the mattress and had her turn over. He put her legs up over his shoulders and slapped his hard dick against her clit.

It was his intent to excite her again and he did an excellent job. Maddie loved the way his cock made her clit feel when they made contact. Little jolts of electricity shot inside her every time it hit her. Then Cade started stroking crossways with it and that was even more intense. Maddie began needing more, wanting him inside her again.

"Cade, please put that cock inside me and fuck my brains out, will you?" she said with a big smile.

"Yes, ma'am. Anything you want," Cade answered.

He pressed his cock inside her and pumped hard, his ass cheeks clenching and unclenching with each movement. Maddie grabbed his ass and helped drive him harder inside her. They slammed against each other, seeking the ultimate reward, the highest pleasure possible.

They groaned, moaned, and grunted their way to ecstasy, rocketing into a mutual orgasm so explosive that Cade banged Maddie's head on the headboard. She didn't care, didn't even feel it in her state of bliss.

Cade shouted as he filled the condom with his hot cum and thrust inside her a few more times. Maddie had a death grip on Cade's ass as she came and let out a shriek. She quaked against him and her breathing was raspy. They came down from their high in small increments, their hearts beating furiously. Sweat covered their bodies, dripping from them to dampen the sheets.

Gently Cade took Maddie's legs from his shoulders and lay them on the bed. Then he extricated himself from her and fell next to her on the bed. His big chest heaved as his lungs sought oxygen. For long moments, they simply lay there, catching their breath.

Then Cade rolled over to face Maddie, cupping her face and giving her a soft kiss. Maddie kissed him back and looked in his eyes. Somehow she understood that he would be going back to his cabin soon and the reasons why. She appreciated his concern for her reputation. It would go hard for her if she were found sleeping with one of the hands. It would make it seem as though she were playing favorites and complicate her relationship with the other hands.

They lay companionably together, just holding hands for quite a while, and then Cade kissed her and rolled from the bed. His big form blocked out the light from the moon, silhouetting him. Maddie watched him slip on a pair of shorts, all that he'd apparently worn to her house. He came to her side of the bed and kissed her one last time and silently left.

"Wait! I'm stuck!" Cade said.

Maddie said, "It's so big! How'd it even get in there?"

Cade laughed breathlessly. "Just like it always does."

"What do we do with it now?" Maddie asked.

Cade grunted. "It's so slippery, I'm not sure what to do with it."

"We better figure out something quick," Maddie said, growing serious.

Cade grunted and gave a slow pull on the snout of the foal he and Maddie were trying to help into the world. It was breech and they had to get the foal into the correct position to be born. It was not an easy task. It was a good thing that Cade was as strong as he was, Maddie thought as she watched him turn the foal.

She was holding down the head of the mare, talking to the frightened animal who was enduring great pain to bear her young. Maddie looked at the intense expression on Cade's face, admiring his ability to focus on a task so completely. He was as gentle as possible while acting quickly.

Finally, Cade felt the foal slip into place and withdrew his one arm and both hands from the mare's insides. A lot of people would have been disgusted by having their hands in such a place, but Cade just viewed it as a necessity, something that had to be done to save two lives and a boat load of money.

"There. She should be able to finish on her own now," Cade said standing up. He was breathing hard and filthy but had no intention of leaving until he'd seen that the mare had delivered her foal safely.

Maddie let go of the mare's head and joined Cade by the far side of the stall. Ten minutes later, the filly slid effortlessly from her dam onto the straw in the stall. Brown Betty turned immediately to tend to her daughter. When Cade smiled down at Maddie, she was surprised to see tears in his eyes.

"I never tire of seeing a birth," he said, his voice slightly husky.

Maddie's wonder was evident. "Really? I thought most guys were afraid of such stuff."

"I'm not most guys, then. Birth is beautiful no matter what species," Cade answered with a sniff.

Maddie gave him a considering look. "How many species have you seen give birth?"

Cade thought a moment. "Five. Cattle, horses, dogs, cats, and humans."

"Humans? You've seen a human baby being born?" Maddie asked with shock.

"Yeah. I delivered a set of twins once and helped my cousin Trina gave birth to her son," Cade said.

"Wow!" was all that Maddie could say for a few moments. "Your cousin? Really? Wasn't that awkward?"

Cade shrugged. "She didn't have anyone else who would stand by her because she got pregnant really young, so I stepped in. It wasn't fair to punish her for such a thing. The father didn't want anything to do with her or the baby. She needed someone, so I was that someone."

"You're really something, you know that?" Maddie smiled up at him. "And you delivered twins. How'd that happen?"

"It wasn't intentional, of course, but I was actually riding a bus one time on my way to California, and there was a lady who went into labor in the middle of a traffic jam. There weren't any doctors on board and I had delivered other kinds of babies so I figured I was her best shot."

Maddie shook her head as she absorbed what Cade had told her. She knew that Cade was good in an emergency, as evidenced by what had just happened. It would seem that he held up under pressure just about anywhere.

"So you stepped in and saved the day," Maddie said. "That's incredible! So they were all ok?"

Cade nodded. "Twin girls and mother were all doing well when the paramedics arrived." Cade turned his Irish blue eyes on her. "I'm not Superman. I had help. There was an older woman who gave us her scissors and embroidery yarn to cut and tie off the umbilical cords. I also had assistance from a woman who had a lot of children and knew the process very well. So we all helped those babies come into the world. It was a beautiful experience and I'll never forget it. I still keep in touch with them. Her husband was very grateful and we became friends."

"Amazing!" Maddie said as she looked at him with shining, dark eyes.

Cade grew a little bashful. "Thanks!"

They were quiet for a little while as they watched Brown Betty and her filly. The little thing was up on her feet now and trying to nurse. Cade walked over and helped her over to her dam's teats and got her sucking. Brown Betty stood still, content that her foal was feeding.

Cade looked down at himself and cringed. "I'd better go get cleaned up," he said.

"Yeah, me, too," Maddie said. "Meet me in the tack room in an hour. I have something I'd like to discuss with you."

Cade arched an eyebrow. "Oh? Are you going to tell me know what it's about or make me wait?"

"Um, I'm going to make you wait," she said.

"All right. I'll see you in an hour." Cade wanted to kiss her, but there was too big a risk that someone would see, so he just touched her shoulder quickly and left.

Cade panted and groaned as Maddie sucked his cock. He'd cleaned up and met her in the tack room where she'd promptly shut and locked the door. She'd pushed him down in a chain and unzipped his jeans. He'd wiggled out of them, grinning at her daring and aggressiveness.

Maddie smiled back and laughed and then set about giving him a fantastic blowjob. It hadn't taken long to get his dick erect and now Maddie swirled her tongue around the head and took him deep. She sucked and licked and basically drove Cade to the brink, then backed off again.

Maddie was so horny and knew that her panties were soaked. She couldn't take any more. Standing up, Maddie quickly got rid of her jeans and panties. They were as wet as she'd thought. Cade watched hungrily as she straddled his dick and rubbed it on her clit a little.

Maddie moaned and then took him inside, sitting on Cade and taking him all in. They sat like that kissing and touching, until Maddie started to move. Cade growled as Maddie rose and fell, every stroke bringing intense pleasure. Maddie got wild, moving up and down faster, pinching her nipples and riding Cade hard.

Cade loved it, loved the way her pussy stroked him and the way she sounded. Her heart-shaped face was tilted toward the ceiling, mouth open, and her eyes were closed as she enjoyed every sensation. Cade had undone the buttons of her shirt and pulled down her bra. Her full tits bounced as she moved and Cade needed to taste her nipples.

He leaned forward and took one in his mouth, sucking and lapping. Maddie moved even faster, her nails digging into Cade's shoulders. He didn't care; all he cared about was making her cum.

"C'mon, baby. Cum for me," he crooned to Maddie. "I'm gonna give it to you."

Hearing Cade talk that way turned Maddie on even more and she felt the first pulses of her orgasm begin.

"Cade?"

"Yeah?"

"I'm gonna cum. Oh! Shit! I'm cumming, I'm cumming!" she moaned and rocked to and fro with Cade completely inside her. His dick was buried to the hilt. "Cum with me," Maddie said and rocked harder.

Cade grasped her hips and moved with them, pushing his ass off the chair. He felt it build from deep inside. His release was imminent. His balls tightened and then he was cumming, shooting his sperm deep inside Maddie's pussy. Cade muffled his hoarse cry of pleasure in Maddie's breasts and then leaned back, out of breath.

Maddie leaned her forehead on his, smiling

as she caught her own breath.

"Great meeting, Mr. McAllister. Very productive," she joked.

Cade nodded. "Yes. I agree, Ms. Wilson. I do believe we should continue to have these meetings in order to keep abreast of further developments."

"Right. Issues might arise that need attention," Maddie said.

Cade laughed. "Well, you do have great attention to detail."

Maddie laughed, unable to keep up their conversation. She stood up and pulled on her jeans. "Looks like I'm going to have to go shower again," she said. "Not that I mind, believe me."

"Me, neither," Cade said stretching. "Are you open for a visit tonight?"

Maddie smiled and shook her head. "I'm going to a bachelorette party and who knows what time I'll be home. Better make it another night," she said. She would have much rather stayed home to be with Cade, but it was best that she went. Besides, Connie was a great friend and she wouldn't miss the party for anything.

"Need a stripper?" Cade asked, the devil showing in his grin.

Maddie laughed. "You strip?"

"A brief stint. It was pretty fun, actually," Cade told her.

"Is there anything you haven't done?" she asked.

"I've never been married," he said. "There's something I haven't done."

Laughter burst from Maddie. "Good to

know. I gotta go. See you tomorrow."

"See ya," Cade said and pulled his pants up.

Something woke Cade from the sound sleep he'd fallen into after writing until 1 a.m. His book was starting to come along, at least the second draft, and he hadn't wanted to stop. However, he figured that he needed some sleep if he would be worth anything at work, and he wanted to do a good job for Maddie.

He jolted awake and listened. He heard a light knock on his cabin door. He rose and shoved his long legs into a pair of boxer briefs and strode to the door. The moon was high and he could see well through the glass top of the door. It was Maddie and by the looks of it, she wasn't feeling any pain.

When he opened the door, Maddie stumbled in and Cade caught her to keep her from falling. He closed the door and sat her at the kitchen table.

"Hi, handsome," she said. Her voice was slightly raspy as if she'd been shouting a lot and Cade thought that the party must have been a doozy.

He smiled at her disheveled state. Cade never denied anyone the right to have a good time as long as they were responsible about it. "Hi, yourself. Did you drive home?"

Maddie shook her index finger at him. "Oh no. Not me. I would never drink and derv."

Cade understood that "derv" meant "drive."

"Good. That's a relief. Let me make you some coffee," Cade said.

Maddie shook her head. "You shoulda been there tonight. They had a stripper but he wasn't anywhere near as hot as you."

"That's nice," Cade said knowing that his responses weren't going to be given much heed.

"He was skinny and had a big nose," she went on. "Not like you with all your muscles and stuff."

Cade grinned. Maddie was a funny drunk. Better than a nasty one. "Come on, beautiful. Let's get you into bed."

Maddie stood up and swayed on her feet. "That's the best idea I've heard all night."

"C'mon. I'll get you settled." Cade led her to his bed and pushed her down onto it. "Lay down, Maddie."

She did as he told her and then said, "Aren't you lying down with me?"

"Mmm hmm. Scoot over," Cade answered.

He situated himself next to her and Maddie put her head on his shoulder. It wasn't long before she was out, as Cade had known she'd be. She was going to have one hell of a hangover in the morning. He would have to make her some hair of the dog to alleviate her suffering. Cade smiled and kissed Maddie's forehead then dropped into a peaceful slumber.

The next morning, Maddie slowly walked across the driveway to her house. Cade had thoughtfully got her up around 4 a.m. and gave her some hair of the dog and coffee. Her head felt like someone had put it in a nutcracker and was squeezing for all they were worth. He'd also given her some headache pills and she felt a little better.

He'd gotten her out the door by four-thirty so that she would be in her own home before the other hands were up and around. Now as she stood naked in the bathroom, ready to shower, Maddie thought about how sweet Cade had been to her. He was very thoughtful and had anticipated her needs.

Maddie felt a little ashamed that Cade had seen her like that, but it wasn't something she did all the time. Celebrating at the bachelor party had been freeing and refreshing. She hadn't realized how much she'd needed to get out with the girls. Being the boss over a bunch of guys wasn't easy, and with limited female contact, she sometimes lost her femininity. Last night, she'd been able to dress up and be girly.

As she stepped into the shower, Maddie wondered what it would be like to go out with Cade. She envisioned them going to dinner and then dancing at a club. She would love to do that with him, but right now it was impossible. Frowning over that, Maddie knew a moment of frustration because she'd like to date Cade. The next moment, she backpedaled away from that thought since getting emotionally involved with Cade would be a mistake. He'd be moving on after a while, like a lot of the ranch hands did, and falling in love and getting her heart broken would be stupid.

Maddie finished her shower and dressed, getting ready to start her day despite the fact that her head still pounded.

Maddie had unexpected company that night. Her friend Katy from Utah showed up out of the blue. She was passing through on her way to Michigan and couldn't resist stopping to see her good friend. They'd gone to college together and been close ever since.

The bubbly brunette with blue eyes took one look at Cade and the way he and Maddie looked at each other and had known that they were getting it on. Katy always had a good radar for that kind of thing, and it didn't let her down this time. She teased Maddie about it, but promised not to say anything to anyone, including Cade.

"I can see why you're hitting that," Katy said as they worked on demolishing a container of Chunky Monkey ice cream. "He's a hard-bodied dream come true."

Maddie almost blushed. "Yeah, he's pretty awesome."

Katy shook her head. "You are so lucky. I'd give anything for a guy like that and I certainly wouldn't be hiding it. Screw the other hands. There's no evidence that you've played favorites since you guys have been doing it, so what's the big deal?"

Maddie knew that Katy didn't understand ranch society, but her thoughts were aligned with her friend's. She found she didn't want to hide her relationship with Cade any longer.

She thrust her spoon down into her ice cream. "You're right. Why should we have to hide? If they don't like it, they can leave. I want to go out and do things with Cade. Don't get me wrong, the sex is off the charts, but I want to go to a movie or dancing or whatever."

"There you go! That's it!" Katy said, becoming excited. "You keep that attitude even after I'm gone, ok? You gotta enjoy life while you can," she encouraged Maddie.

Maddie nodded. "I will. But for now, let's have a sappy movie marathon," she said. The girls set up to watch movies and got lost in them.

Cade used the evening to work on his book, delving deep into the plot and characters. Maddie kept invading his mind from time to time, and he thought about her lush, lithe body, and the way they moved together. He sat at the table in a pair of shorts, and the more he thought about Maddie, the hornier he got. Finally, he couldn't stand it anymore and decided that a shower was in order.

He stripped and climbed in, the cold spray bouncing off his well-muscled body. Closing his eyes, he imagined the way Maddie's hands felt on his skin, the way her fingers stroked him. He took his dick in his hand and started working it. Cade grew hard as he brought to mind how Maddie's hot pussy tasted and the way it felt when he thrust inside her.

Cade's breathing grew slightly labored as he stroked his cock faster and harder. This wasn't going to be nearly as good as when he was with her, but it would at least let him concentrate on his writing. He remembered the way she looked when she was giving him head in the tack room. Maddie had a very talented mouth, and he could see his cock disappearing into her mouth and feel her tongue licking him.

As he imagined her pussy cumming around his cock, Cade started to cum. His load shot from him in hot spurts, mingling with the water. Cade was quiet as he came because it wasn't nearly as intense as when he was with Maddie. Once he was finished, he showered and then got out and wrapped a towel around himself, prepared to write for as long as he needed.

Katy left the next morning, waving at Cade as she drove by his cabin. He waved back and smiled. The lively Katy was a lot of fun, it seemed. Maddie came walking down from the main house to stand beside him. Cade was on the way to the mare barn to check on Brown Betty and her filly.

"Morning, boss," he said with a smile.

"Morning, sexy," she replied.

Cade grinned. "You're not so bad yourself. I missed you last night."

"Really?" Maddie said as a happy flush stole up her body. "Me, too. Which is why I want to go out tonight. With you."

Cade's expression sobered. "What?"

"I've decided that if anyone has a problem with me dating you, then they can leave. I can always hire more hands. I'm the boss, after all. I want to do more with you than just, well, you know," Maddie said. Her hands had become animated, as she'd become more flustered.

Cade smiled slowly. "You want to date me?

Really?"

Maddie nodded. "That is if you want to–"

Cade grabbed Maddie and kissed her soundly right there, not caring if anyone saw or not. "Tonight. Seven. I know just where to go. I'll pick you up then," Cade said. "Be ready on time. Dress up!"

Maddie watched in stunned silence as Cade took off, whistling as he trotted along to the mare barn. Happiness bubbled up from her throat to emerge as laughter. She turned around and encountered Luke.

Maddie's chin rose and she gave him a level look. "What's the matter? Never see someone make a date before?"

Luke's craggy face softened into a big grin. "'Bout damn time, Maddie. Thought I was gonna have to marry you myself just to save you from becoming a spinster."

"Hey! I'm not old. Besides, I'm not marrying him. Just going on a date," she protested.

"Famous last words, Maddie. Now come with me. I got a bad hoof I need to show you. Called Dr. Ellery already, but I knew you'd want to see it," Luke said and led Maddie away.

When Maddie answered the door that evening, Cade stood staring at the woman before him. Maddie always looked sexy, but the way she looked in the little red number she was wearing made him want to stay home and take it off her.

"You look stunning," he said. He drank her in from head to toe.

Maddie enjoyed his perusal, smiling and teasing him by doing sexy poses.

"Damn, I wish I had a camera," Cade said with a laugh. "You look like you should be on a magazine cover."

"Ah, and so the Irish blarney comes out," Maddie said shaking a finger at him.

Cade shook his head. "No, I mean it. Are you ready?"

Maddie grabbed her clutch. "Yes. Where are you taking me?"

"You'll see," Cade said with an enigmatic smile.

Cade took Maddie to Q's Place, an upscale establishment that featured fine dining and dancing. They ate succulent fillet mignon and drank a fine cabernet. Maddie had been worried that they wouldn't have anything to talk about, but her fears were groundless.

Both of them shared stories of their childhood: she of what it was like growing up on a ranch and then taking over the reins and he told her about growing up part-time on an Indian reservation. His father was Irish Catholic and his mother Indian. So Cade had grown up with one foot in both worlds, and Maddie could see that he'd taken somewhat more after his mother's side.

Maddie had learned responsibility at an early age. Her father had begun grooming her at the age of fifteen to take over later on. They had been so close, especially after her mother had died.

Cade and Maddie danced, moving together naturally, as if they had been created for one another. As their bodies swayed together, brushing against each other, both of them grew aroused. The look in Cade's vibrant blue eyes told Maddie how much he wanted her. After a few more dances, they left by silent mutual consent.

They started kissing almost as soon as they were out of Cade's truck, hands urgently roaming over each other. They kissed all the way onto Maddie's porch and through her front door. Clothes started coming off until they were naked by the time they hit the upstairs hall.

Maddie broke away from Cade and ran down the hall to her bedroom and into her bathroom. Several years ago she'd had a whirlpool installed to help ease sore muscles after a long day of hard labor. She turned on the faucet to fill it up just as Cade caught her around the waist and hauled her back against him.

"Oh, my, Mr. McAllister. It feels as though you have something pointed at me. Are you trying to hold me up?" she teased.

Cade bit her earlobe, making her shiver. "Yes. I have something that will hold you up and something sharp to poke you with, too."

"You say the nicest things," Maddie told him as she tested the water. The whirlpool was ready. "C'mon, I want to soap you up," she said.

Cade went willingly, the idea of her hands all over his soap-slick body highly appealing. They sank down in the water, getting wet. Then Maddie chose a soap that was a neutral scent so that Cade didn't smell like a woman. Cade relaxed back in the tub as Maddie began washing him. She didn't miss an inch of his skin. Once she had washed him, she just ran her hands over him, loving the feel of his hard muscles under her hands.

Cade's dick was throbbing now and Maddie stroked him and played with Cade's balls. It felt so different wet and she was incredibly turned on. She felt in the mood to try something new. She put his dick between her full tits and pushed them together around it.

She smiled up at Cade who was grinning down at her. He began moving his hips while she kept her breasts pressed around his cock. It felt so good to Cade, so slippery and tight, and he would have been happy to cream her tits, but he wanted her satisfied as well. Still, he was enjoying the experience and groaned as the sensitive head slid between her tits.

For Maddie, it looked so erotic when his cock emerged from the valley between them, almost touching her chin. After a few moments, she released him and sidled up to Cade, tracing his mouth with her tongue and slipped it inside his mouth, capturing his in a languorous kiss.

Cade brushed his fingers across Maddie's nipples, eliciting a gasp from her as she kissed him. He pinched them and caressed her breasts, loving the feel of them in his hands. He wanted to be inside of her intensely. Cade grasped Maddie by the waist and turned the both of them around until her back was pressed up against the wall.

Maddie spread her legs, ready for what he was going to do. She wanted it, craved it. She wanted to feel that big, hard dick of his thrust deep inside her cunt and knew that Cade would deliver. Cade found her entrance and pressed inside her pussy, the water lubricating the process. She was tight and hot and Cade began thrusting right away because he was so excited.

Their foreplay during dancing had aroused both of them to a fever pitch and they didn't need a lot of lead up to the main event at this point. Cade humped her like a dog humping a bitch in heat. Maddie held on to Cade's shoulders for the ride, gasping and whimpering in bliss with every plunge he made.

"Fuck me, Cade, fuck me hard!" Maddie yelled.

"Oh, yeah, baby. I'm gonna screw that twat of yours good," Cade said and pounded into her.

Maddie came then, her nails scoring Cade's shoulders as it ripped through her. Cade didn't stop his assault. He was intent on giving her another orgasm and drove on with his rock-hard dick. Maddie felt her body begin the ascent to ecstasy again and wanted to cum again. She was so horny.

Cade shifted the angle of his thrust slightly, and Maddie moaned loudly as his dick started hitting her G-spot.

"Oh, shit! Cade! Oh, I'm cumming!" Maddie yelled as her cunt clenched around his cock in pulses of pleasure.

Cade felt his own climax beginning and his moans joined hers as his intense release roared down on him. His hot cum shot deep inside her and Maddie relished the sensation. They shuddered against each other as they came, whispering hot words of passion to one another.

It seemed to them that the ecstasy went on for a long time before it began to fade, leaving them both weak and shaken. Carefully, Cade extricated himself from Maddie and set her on her feet. The water was turning cold so they rinsed off and got out. They dried each other off and then fell into Maddie's bed. Wrapped in each other's arms, they drifted off, dreaming of a future together under the Montana skies.

9 ELECTRIC BLUE

"Listen, Jason," Blue said in a patient southern accent. "I'm a P.I., not a bodyguard." He leaned back in his desk chair and propped his feet up on it. His scuffed boots reflected a man who was on the move a lot and did hard work.

Jason Deavers smiled at his cousin. "Yeah, but you need the money. You might as well admit it, and this woman can pay really well. You could name your price, really," he said. His brown eyes shone with good nature.

Blue blew out a sigh and folded his hands across his ripped stomach. His plain black T-shirt showed off his well-muscled arms. Faded jeans completed his relaxed look. The fact was that he needed the money, but was he desperate enough to take a bodyguard position?

"Look, Blue, you've done this sort of work before. What's the big deal?" Jason asked.

"I know, but I got out of that line of work because I was tired of getting shot at," Blue responded.

"She's really pretty, too," Jason coaxed. He knew how much of a sucker Blue was for a good-looking woman.

Blue cocked his head at Jason. "How pretty?"

"Model pretty."

"Hmmm. Let me think about it, ok?" Blue replied.

Jason stood up. "Ok, but don't take too long. She's shopping around and wants to hire someone quickly. Here's her number."

Blue took the piece of paper that Jason handed him and looked at the name. Cassie Riggs. Nice name, he thought. "All right. I'll keep that in mind."

"Good. See ya."

"See y'all," Blue said as his cousin walked out the door.

Blue sat staring at the paper for a few minutes trying to make up his mind what to do. Finally, he decided to call the woman and get her story. He'd make up his mind after having some more information about the situation.

He picked up his phone and dialed the number.

She picked up on the third ring. "Hello?"

Blue liked her voice immediately. It was low and husky for a woman. Very sexy.

"Hello. Is this Cassie Riggs?" he asked.

"Yes. Who is this?" Cassie asked suspiciously. With everything that was going on in her life, she was wary of strangers.

"My name is Blue Spalding, and I'm a private investigator. Jason Deavers gave me your name and number and said you were in need of some protective services," he said putting on his most professional voice. He wanted her to know that he was legit and that she could trust him.

Cassie felt relieved when she heard Blue's reason for calling. Jason was a good friend and had promised that he could help her. He'd told her about Blue and said that he would have Blue contact her.

"Oh, yes. Jason said that you'd be calling."

Blue frowned. Jason always did know how to con him into doing what he wanted. "Yeah. He's my cousin, actually. So why don't you tell me what's going on?"

Cassie told him how she was going to be testifying against her former employer because she'd discovered that he was laundering money and had mob ties. As a result, she was being targeted by some of Gino Cimerelli's men to change her mind and forget about testifying.

She wasn't backing down, however, and had decided that protection was in order. The police could only do so much, so she thought that a private firm was the way to go. Jason had assured her that Blue was the best and would be able to keep her safe.

"So what do you think?" Cassie asked when she was finished with her tale. "Do you want the job?"

"What does it pay?" Blue wanted to know.

"Three hundred a day, plus expenses. I'm willing to pay for good services," Cassie informed him.

Blue thought that her pay rate was very generous. He could really use that money. Business had been a little slow and the last client he'd had had welched on his bill and skipped town. "How far away is the trial?"

"A week."

Seven days at three hundred came to twenty-one hundred dollars. A nice chunk of change. He could get caught up on some bills and have money besides.

"All right," he said. "I'm yours until the trial."

Cassie's relief came over the line. "Oh, thank you. I can't tell you what a relief this is."

"You're welcome. Now here's the deal. I need you to pack enough stuff for a week. You're going to come stay at my place," Blue said.

Cassie jerked a little as she sat at her kitchen table. "I'm staying at your place? Why?" She didn't want to stay with a total stranger. She'd thought that he would stay at her house.

"Because they don't know me, and they won't know where you are. Plus, my place is alarmed to the hilt and it's my home turf. I'll know if something is wrong or out of place. Your house is unfamiliar territory, and I wouldn't know if there was anything amiss," Blue explained.

Cassie thought about that for a moment and decided that what he was saying made sense. "All right. I'll pack some things."

"Great. I'll pick you up around six-thirty

this evening. I want to do it after dark. We'll leave out your back, too. I want to get away without anyone seeing us," Blue told her.

"I understand. I'll be ready."

"See ya then," Blue said and hung up.

Blue pulled up in the back of Cassie's house in a slightly beat up, nondescript, dark blue Buick sedan. It would blend in with other cars. He didn't want to stand out to anyone. The house was a real beauty. White with green shutters, a sunroom in the back and a pool off to one side; it was a house he envied.

He was afraid that Cassie would be disappointed in his small lived-in house. It was a fixer-upper, and there were a lot of things that needed fixing. His state-of-the-art alarm system wasn't one of them. He had surveillance cameras hidden outside, too. She would be very safe there.

Blue parked and cut the engine. He scanned the street for anyone suspicious but found everything in order. He got out and closed the door quietly. He hated it when people slammed car doors. It was one of his pet peeves.

He loped up the steps that led to the sunroom and rang the doorbell. A woman came through a doorway into the sunroom to the door. She opened the door and smiled at him, and Blue was instantly lost in her green eyes. Jason hadn't been kidding when he said that Cassie was very pretty. In fact, Jason's description didn't do the woman justice.

"Hi. You must be Blue," she said and held out her hand.

Blue took it and noted that her handshake was firm. He felt some kind of current flow between them. Cassie seemed to notice it, too. "That's right, ma'am," he said. "It's nice to meet you, Ms. Riggs."

"And you as well. Come on in," she said and led him through the sunroom into a large kitchen. Stainless steel appliances and white cabinets dominated the room. An island stove and workspace completed the room.

As he followed her further into the house, Blue looked at all of the art on the walls of the tastefully decorated dining room and finally the living room. Fine luggage stood in the center of the room, two suitcases and two overnight bags.

Blue looked at her with a slightly crooked smile. "Are you gonna take the kitchen sink, too?" he teased.

Cassie looked in Blue's eyes and was mesmerized. In the lamplight, she got a good look at the color of them. They were the most startling blue she'd ever seen. They reminded her of the neon signs in bars. They were so vivid, and Cassie felt like they were penetrating to her very soul.

She smiled back and shrugged. "What can I say? I'm a girl."

Blue grew serious. "Well, make sure you have everything because we won't be coming back."

Cassie didn't answer right away because she was thinking about everything she had packed and making sure there wasn't anything she was missing. She was also checking out Blue. He was one nice piece of eye candy with those bedroom eyes, sandy blonde hair and long, lean body. She had a sudden urge to pull up his shirt so she could see his chest.

"I have everything," she said finally.

Blue had pretended to look around the room while Cassie was thinking, but he'd been looking her over. Her black hair was long and luxurious. He judged her to be about five-foot-five. She was voluptuous and curvy. She had a killer rack, and he bet that her legs were sinfully sexy beneath her expensive looking pants.

She turned around and bent to get her purse, and Blue admired her shapely ass. As she straightened, Blue shifted his gaze to a picture on the wall.

"All ready then?" he asked.

"Yes. Ready," she said, suddenly nervous. Cassie was apprehensive about staying with a strange, single man. "You do have a guest room, right?"

Blue gave her a wolfish grin. "Afraid I'm going to try to hop in bed with you?"

Cassie blushed.

Blue took pity on her. "There's a guest room, ma'am. No worries."

Cassie smiled at him. "I'm sorry. It's just that this is all so unsettling."

"I understand," Blue said. "But you're in good hands with me. Don't worry about a thing."

"All right," Cassie said.

"Let's get a move on so we can get you settled," Blue said and grabbed the two larger suitcases. He was a very strong guy, but he felt the weight of them and wondered what the hell she had in them.

He trudged out to his car and hefted them into the trunk. Cassie came out of the door with the two smaller bags and Blue took them from her. They locked up and Blue held the passenger side door for her.

Cassie looked around at the interior of Blue's car. Blue caught her at it and grinned. "Probably not what you're used to, but it runs. Plus, it blends in. For a job like this, I make sure not to stand out. We don't want to draw attention to ourselves," he explained.

"Makes sense. You really do know what you're doing," she complimented him. "That makes me feel better."

Blue looked over at her as he turned the ignition switch and the dashboard lights came on. The light and shadows emphasized his chiseled features, and Cassie wondered how the man wasn't married with those kinds of looks.

"Thanks. I have a lot of training. I was in the army, and I also was a cop for a while," he told her and backed out of the driveway.

"A cop, huh? What happened there?" she asked as they turned the corner and Blue sped up.

"Didn't care for all the rules and sucky pay. I wanted to do my own thing, make my own rules," he said.

Cassie was amused. "I can see that about you. You strike me as the kind of guy who marches to the beat of his own drum."

"You got it," he agreed. "Now, I gotta warn you about my house. I'm fixing it up, so it's not nearly as nice as yours. Your room is nice, though, and the bathroom is right across the hall from it. All the plumbing works, so that's a plus."

"All right. I'll deal with it. I'm sure it's not as bad as you think it is. Besides, roughing it a little is worth it if I get to stay alive," Cassie responded.

Blue gave her a sharp look. "You really are afraid, aren't you? It's really that bad?"

A frowned marred her beautiful face and Blue regretted his question.

Cassie nodded. "I'm afraid so, Mr. Spalding."

"Please call me Blue. Mr. Spalding is my dad," he quipped.

"Blue it is then. You have to call me Cassie," she said.

"Done," Blue agreed as he turned another corner. He looked in the rearview mirror making sure they weren't being tailed.

They drove the rest of the way in silence. Presently, they pulled into a long driveway and parked in front of a modest, two-story house. The porch sagged slightly and a shutter hung haphazardly outside one of the front windows. Cassie thought the house was gray but couldn't be sure in the dark.

"Home sweet home," Blue said as he got out. He came around and opened her door for her.

"My, you are a gentleman. That's rare these days," Cassie commented with a smile.

"My daddy drummed manners into us. It's second nature to me now," Blue said with a shrug. "C'mon. I'll show you the place."

Cassie followed him onto the porch and unlocked the regular doorknob lock and a deadbolt. He turned to her before opening the door.

"Rebel likes company, but he can be a little intimidating at first. He's a pit bull, but I assure you he's totally safe... to his friends," Blue said.

Cassie backed up slightly. "You didn't tell me you had a dog, much less a pit bull. Aren't they dangerous?"

Blue frowned. He hated that pits got such a bad rap. "No more dangerous than any other dog that's trained to fight. Poodles can be trained to be nasty, just like any dog. He's not going to hurt you, I promise you. You gotta trust me Cassie, or else, this is never going to work."

Cassie swallowed, took a deep breath, and squared her shoulders. "All right. I'm putting my life in your hands. I'll trust you."

"Good," Blue said and grinned. "Besides, I don't get paid if you're dead."

Cassie opened her mouth to make a retort when Blue opened the door and a huge dog bounded towards them. Blue held his hand up to the dog like a traffic cop stopping traffic and the big mutt slid to a stop on the hallway floor. It was comical to see the eighty-plus pound dog ungracefully obeying the command.

Cassie smiled in spite of her fear. Blue entered the house and turned on a light. An alarm panel blinked on the wall and Blue quickly entered the code, silencing it. He pointed to the floor and Rebel lay down. His whiplike tail was going a mile a minute, though, and his hind end squirmed as he held his happiness in check.

He kept looking at Cassie and switching his ears back and forth and sniffing the air getting her scent. Cassie wasn't certain that he wasn't sizing her up to see if she would make a good meal.

Blue turned towards Cassie and held out his hand. "Shake my hand. That's how he knows you're my friend," he said.

Cassie took Blue's strong hand and shook it for the second time that night. The difference was that Blue didn't release it right away. Instead, he seemed to be studying it.

Blue was indeed studying her hand. It was pretty, with nicely shaped nails. It was strong and feminine at the same time. After a few moments, Blue let her go and turned towards Rebel. Cassie could see that he was an attractive brindle and white dog.

"Sniff," Blue commanded. "Gentle."

The big dog rose and walked slowly to Cassie.

"Hold out your hand and let him get your scent good," Blue instructed her.

"All right." Cassie did as he told her. Her hand shook a little.

Rebel's cold nose went all over her hand and finally licked it in approval.

"Tell him to shake. That's another sign that you're a friend," Blue told her.

Cassie put her hand out again and said,

"Shake, Rebel."

Rebel complied immediately, putting his huge white paw in Cassie's palm. She closed her hand over it and gave it a ginger shake before letting it go.

"Good," Blue said. "See? Now you're friends."

Cassie was still unsure.

"Guard," Blue told Rebel and then went back out the front door to retrieve the suitcases.

Instantly, Rebel's attitude changed and his ears pricked up. Cassie moved to follow Blue, but the big dog blocked her path and nuzzled her hand. Cassie tried to move around him, but Rebel gently grabbed her wrist and held her in place. She understood then that she was supposed to stay in the house.

She backed up and Rebel let her go. Cassie decided to look around a little bit. Off to the right was a doorway that led to a kitchen. It needed to be painted, but all of the appliances looked to be in working order. She flipped a switch she found on the wall and recessed lighting came on underneath the cabinets. They were brand new, and she thought they were walnut.

The floor has an ugly brown and white design, and Cassie surmised it must be one of the things that Blue was working on fixing. A scarred wooden table and chairs sat off to the left.

Cassie backed out of the room and collided with Blue who had just come back into the front hall.

"Oh, I'm sorry!" she said after registering

the contact with his hard body.

Blue laughed. "That's ok. No worries." He jerked his chin towards the kitchen. "Isn't that the most shitty-assed floor you've ever seen?"

Cassie laughed at his turn of phrase. "'Shitty-assed?'" she said. "If that means ugly then yes, it is."

"Yeah, it's ugly all right," Blue said. "Ok, follow me. I'll show you your room."

He took off up the stairs at a fast clip even with two big suitcases in each hand. Cassie followed him, but couldn't quite keep up. Rebel padded up the stairs behind her. Blue waited for her in the upstairs hallway outside a doorway.

"Here y'all are," he said and entered the room.

Cassie noted that there were two windows that faced west and would catch the morning light. A large four-poster bed held court in the center of the room. Nautical pictures added a whimsical touch and color to the cream-colored walls. A large bureau took up the most of one wall. Blue opened a door and showed her a good-sized closet, in which hangers hung.

"I think you'll be comfortable here. It's not the Ritz, but it'll do temporarily," he said with a smile.

Cassie nodded. "It's very charming, Blue. Um, where is your room? In case I need you in an emergency that is," she clarified quickly. Oh shit! What is it about this man that makes me as tongue tied as a schoolgirl? It isn't like I haven't been around sexy guys before. My husband was quite nice to look at and good in bed. So what makes this guy so different?

Dimples appeared in Blue's cheeks as he smiled. "My room is off the kitchen. It's closer to any point of entry so that I can guard you better. They'll have to get through me and Rebel here to get to you. So that's where my room is if you need me... only in an emergency, of course."

That wolfish grin of his did something to Cassie, and she could feel the pulse at the base of her neck throb a little harder.

"O-ok. Good to know," she said in a businesslike voice.

Blue laughed softly and said, "I'll be back with your other bags. Rebel, come."

Once he'd left, Cassie distracted herself from her attraction to him by hanging her blouses and pants in the closet and putting her other things in the bureau drawers. Rebel came bounding back up the stairs and jumped on her bed. He snatched a pair of her underwear right out of her suitcase and took off with them.

"Hey!" she shouted. "Come back here!"

Cassie chased him out into the hallway, almost knocking over Blue, who was bringing up her other bags down to her room.

"What happened?" he asked and put the bags down.

"Your dog stole my underwear, that's what!" she called back over her shoulder as she chased Rebel down the stairs.

Blue laughed and followed them down. All he needed to do was command Rebel to stop and drop, but he wasn't going to tell Cassie that. This was going to be too much fun, he decided.

Rebel led Cassie on a merry chase around the house, jumping just out of reach. He growled and showed his teeth to her, but she understood that he was only playing. Rebel would bow down, shake the underwear in challenge, and then take off running again when she advanced toward him.

She shouted and laughed and became breathless as she chased him. Finally, Blue decided that she'd had enough and whistled for Rebel. Ever obedient, the dog came to his master and sat down. Blue took the underwear from Rebel and held them up. They were black silk thongs, and Blue could easily see Cassie in them.

Cassie stared at Blue in disbelief and anger. "You could have done that the whole time? He'd have stopped for you, wouldn't he?"

Blue nodded, a huge smile on his handsome face. "Yep. I have to confess. I could have stopped him long ago, but there's a couple of reasons that I didn't—no, make that three reasons," he said.

Cassie crossed her arms over her chest and glared at Blue. "What would those reasons be?"

"First off, you needed to get used to Rebel, and there's no better way to do that than to play with a dog. Second, he got used to you, too. Third, I wouldn't have had the fun of watching you chase him all over the place. Oh, and four? I may not have had the chance to see your undies. Very nice, by the way," Blue said.

Cassie's face was red as she yanked her

panties from Blue's hand. "I'll thank you to not worry about my underwear, Mr. Spalding. Good night," she said and stomped up the stairs to her room. Her bedroom door slammed.

Rebel looked at Blue as if to say, "Uh oh. You did it now."

"Shut up," he said to the dog. He did a perimeter check and then watched some TV as he nursed a beer. Around 11:30 p.m., he put Rebel on guard in his bed in the front hallway and went to bed himself.

In the morning, Cassie was awakened by the smell of coffee and bacon. Her stomach rumbled as she got up. She'd forgotten where she was for a moment and then remembered. She also remembered the romp with Rebel and her embarrassment over Blue's perusal of her thong.

She laughed to herself, able to see the humor in the morning light. Cassie pulled her journal out of her purse and wrote about it briefly then gathered her things to shower. Half an hour later, she joined Blue downstairs.

The sight of him standing shirtless at the stove stopped Cassie in her tracks. His body was a study in lean muscle. A smattering of dark hair graced his broad chest. The muscles and sinews in his forearms rippled as he flipped an omelet in a frying pan and tended bacon in another.

Cassie's mouth watered more from watching such a delicious man than the great-looking food he was cooking. Blue looked up and smiled at her.

"Sleep ok?" he asked.

She'd forgotten how vivid his eyes were and was struck anew by their intensity. Sitting at the kitchen table she said, "Yes. Thank you."

Blue nodded. "I hope you're hungry."

"Starving, actually. That romp with Rebel gave me quite an appetite," she said with a smile.

"Yeah, playing with him will do that," Blue said and laughed. "I'm sorry about that. I should've stopped him, but it was so damn funny, I just couldn't."

Cassie laughed with him. "I know. I got up laughing this morning thinking about it. It was funny. You're forgiven. So where is the thief this morning?"

Blue chin-nodded towards the kitchen door that led to the back yard. "Outside chasing a squirrel or something." Blue loaded an omelet and some bacon onto a plate and set it in front of Cassie. Then he poured her a cup of coffee. "Cream? Sugar?"

"Just cream, thanks," she said.

Blue turned to the fridge and opened it. He bent over to get the cream and Cassie couldn't help but look at his tight ass. She bowed her head and paid attention to her breakfast to keep from gawking at him. She didn't want him to see her staring at him.

Blue smiled inside as he turned from the fridge and saw Cassie's head suddenly duck and her eyes quickly shift to her plate. She was checking me out, he surmised.

"Here you go." He sat the cream down in front of her. "So where is your husband?"

His abrupt question startled Cassie. "Well, he passed away about a year ago," she told Blue.

He said, "I'm really sorry. I didn't know. I was just wondering where he was in all of this." Blue went back to the stove to see to his own breakfast.

"It's ok. Really. You couldn't have known. I'm doing ok with it. I've worked through a lot of stuff and I'm fine," Cassie told him.

Blue just nodded and filled another plate. He turned the stove burners off and brought his breakfast to the table. Rebel chose right then to scratch at the door to come in.

Blue let the pit bull in and the mutt greeted Cassie with much tail wagging and sniffing. Cassie pet him, no longer afraid. He was actually a beautiful animal, Cassie thought. His slightly slanted eyes were looking hopefully at her bacon.

"Rebel. Corner," Blue said.

Rebel reluctantly went and lay down on a carpet in one of the corners. He still watched them intently just in case they sent something his way.

"I don't feed him a lot of table scraps. Pits are prone to digestive issues and a lot of people foods don't agree with them," Blue explained.

Cassie nodded. "I see. So they're a little high maintenance then?"

"Somewhat. Not too bad. It's like any animal. They need certain things to survive and be healthy. Just like people," Blue said.

"I understand. This is delicious. You're a good cook," Cassie said.

Blue smiled at the compliment. "Thank you, ma'am."

Cassie thought his drawl was very out of place in Philadelphia. "So where are you from because your accent gives you away."

"I'm originally from South Carolina. I moved here about six months ago because my cousin Jason lives here and said that I'd be able to build up a good P.I. business here. At first, I had more work than I could handle, but after about three months, it started dwindling off," Blue said.

"That's a shame. I hope it picks up for you," Cassie said.

Blue smiled. "Yeah. Me, too. Since business is slow, I was available to help you out."

"That's good for me," Cassie said. "I'm grateful to you."

Blue said, "You're welcome."

"So what's on your agenda today?" Cassie asked.

"Guarding you," Blue replied.

Cassie laughed. "Besides that, do you have any other cases to work on?"

"Well, I'm not letting you out of my sight, so I'm just gonna work from home. I have some skip-tracing to do, but I can do that on the computer and phone," he informed Cassie.

"Do you have Wi-Fi?"

Blue nodded. "Yep. I'll put you on the network. It's all kinds of secure so don't worry about that."

"Great! I have some business to do myself,

so that will be great," Cassie said.

The other thing I plan to do is get you into bed, Blue thought. Cassie was one hell of a desirable woman with her black hair, gray eyes, and killer body. Blue felt a quickening in his loins just thinking about that body naked.

"When we're finished here, I'll get your laptop set up for you," he told her and worked on eating his food.

Cassie hadn't missed the desire in his eyes and found that her body responded to it. Her nipples tightened a little, and there was a slight flutter in her lower abdomen. She lowered her eyes to her plate wondering if she was ready for that kind of relationship again. It had been a long time since she'd been with a man.

Once their food was eaten and the kitchen cleaned up, Blue led Cassie upstairs.

"I'll need to take your laptop into my office to get it hooked up to the network," he told her.

"Ok. I'll get it," Cassie said, suddenly nervous around him. There was something in the air between them and it made her feel unsettled.

She retrieved the computer and found Blue in one of the other rooms in the upstairs. His computer, printer, and other electronic equipment were scattered around the room on various pieces of furniture. Files and papers of all kinds covered many surfaces.

"Sorry for the mess," Blue said following her gaze. "I just never seem to have time to get organized."

"It's ok. I like it," she said.

He took the computer from her. Their hands brushed each other and Cassie felt like a spark had been set off. Blue obviously felt it, too, because his eyes locked on hers and then lowered to look at her mouth. He wanted to kiss her in the worst way. Her full, pink mouth begged to be kissed.

Blue sat the computer aside and closed the short distance between them.

"Cassie, you are a beautiful woman. I can tell that you're as attracted to me as I am to you. I want to kiss you. Right now," he said.

Cassie couldn't look away from those electric blue eyes. She was lost in them and wanted him to kiss her. A powerful yearning rose in her chest and she nodded her permission.

Slowly, ever so slowly, Blue slid his hand under her dark hair and cupped the back of her head. His touch set off goose bumps along Cassie's neck, and she shivered a little. Blue's eyes never left hers as his thumb rubbed her neck. Then he buried his fingers in her satiny hair and pulled her towards him.

He lowered his head and brushed his lips across hers, barely touching her, and Cassie's eyes fluttered shut as a sense of weakness settled in her legs. Blue put his other arm around her waist and slowly drew her against his hard body. She was soft and womanly and Blue wanted her intensely. He took her mouth in a bold kiss, tasting her sweet lips and nibbling at them.

With a moan and a probing of his tongue, he urged Cassie to open her mouth. Cassie was happy to oblige. Their mouths fused together and Cassie encircled his neck with her arms and slid her fingers up into his wavy, blonde hair. Her breasts flattened against his chest, and Blue had trouble thinking of anything but the way she felt against him.

He brought both hands down to her ass, cupped her cheeks and pressed her harder against him so she could feel his hardening dick. Cassie moaned and moved her hips against him. It had been so long since she'd felt a penis, and she was suddenly voraciously hungry for this ultra-sexy man.

Blue let her ass go and ran his hands up under her button-down blouse and found her breasts. He covered the bra-encased orbs with his hands and squeezed them. They more than filled his palms and felt so good that he groaned.

"Shit, Darlin', you feel so good," he whispered in her ear.

Cassie made a little noise in her throat. "So do you." She laid her head on his chest. "Blue?"

"Yeah?"

"I have a confession to make," she said.

Blue said, "All right. I'm listening."

"I haven't been with anyone since my husband died. I'm kind of nervous," Cassie told him in a soft voice.

"That's ok, honey. Don't worry; we'll take this nice and slow," he said. Blue tipped her chin up so she had to look at him. "It's going to be all right," he promised.

Cassie nodded and then sighed as his mouth claimed hers again. He began to move them out the door and into the hallway. He pinned her up against the wall at one point, his hands roaming over her, touching her breasts, delving between her legs and kissing her neck and mouth. Cassie could feel her panties getting damp and marveled at how much she ached for him.

They reached her room, and they sat down on her bed, kissing the whole time. "You're so beautiful, Cassie. I want you so much," Blue told her and sucked on her earlobe.

"Oh, Blue, I want you, too," Cassie responded.

Growing suddenly bold, she began running her hands over his bare chest. The hair on his chest felt good against her palms. She played with his nipples and smiled when he growled his pleasure. Then her hands strayed to his jeans. She wanted him naked and Blue was happy to comply. He stood up and stripped quickly, his proud cock jutting out from his body.

Cassie stood as well and undid the buttons of her blouse and parted it when they were all freed. She slid the shirt off revealing a sexy white bra.

"Allow me," Blue said and came to encircle her waist and undo the clasp in the back with deft fingers.

He drew the bra straps down over her arms and let the garment fall to the floor. Cassie's nipples contracted in the cooler air and Blue watched in fascination as the dusky pink peaks hardened. He palmed them and toyed with them a little but didn't pinch them or squeeze them. At this point, he just wanted to tantalize her.

Blue then unsnapped her pants and unzipped them. They fell from her and Cassie stepped out of them. Her panties soon followed, and they were completely naked together. Blue thought she was the most beautiful thing he'd ever seen. She had such womanly curves, shapely legs and full breasts. He was a breast man and her large tits turned him on immeasurably.

Blue backed her up to the bed and urged her to get on it. They lay down together, and Blue ran his hands over every inch of her, taking his time to tickle behind her knees and the backs of her thighs. His dick was getting harder by the second as he touched and teased her.

Her hips moved up, and she moaned as he stroked her body. Cassie felt like a liquid fire was spreading through her limbs and settling in her pussy. When Blue finally touched her most secret place, she was so slick that he had no trouble sliding two fingers inside her cunt.

Cassie rose up and urged him inside farther. Blue complied and slid his fingers in all the way.

"Oh, God, Blue," she said. She wanted to come so bad, needed it, but Blue was intent on drawing things out.

He didn't want to rush her since this was the first time she'd been with anyone in a year. Blue felt that it should be special and didn't want her to feel rushed.

He withdrew his fingers and sucked them. "Damn, baby, you taste good," he said as she watched him.

Cassie thought that was incredibly erotic. "I'm glad you think so. Nobody's ever done that with me before."

"That's a shame. You have a delicious pussy," he told her honestly.

Blue had her spread her legs and positioned himself between them. He rubbed the inside of her thighs and tickled them with his fingertips. She quivered and moaned. He laid his hands on either side of her sex and rubbed her pussy lips.

"Oh, God, Blue. I'm so horny," she said. "It's been so long since I've felt this way."

"Don't worry. I'm gonna take care of that for you," he promised as he laid his throbbing cock against her clit and began making little thrusts with his hips. Her clit was swollen and pink and felt so good against the head of his penis every time he hit it.

Little flames of pleasure sparked inside her pussy with each thrust of Blue's hips, and it was driving Cassie wild. She moved her hips, urging Blue faster as her need increased. Blue wasn't interested in going fast and didn't speed up his rhythm. He took ahold of his cock and began moving it back and forth over her clit. Now, he moved faster and Cassie's movements became frantic as she sought her release.

"Yeah, baby, that's right," Blue crooned to her in that sexy southern drawl. "I'm gonna make you cum now," he said and moved even faster.

He was true to his word and Cassie felt it building. Oh how she needed it, wanted it. Her orgasm crashed over her in heavy waves, and she cried out sharply and arched her back as she came hard. Blue didn't even give her time to come down from her climax before he moved inside her, burying his cock deep while the pleasure was still fresh for her.

"Yes, Blue, please fuck me. Oh God that felt so good. Fuck me now, please," she pleaded with him.

"Oh yeah, I'm gonna fuck you, Darlin'. Don't worry about that. I'm gonna make you cum and cum," Blue promised.

Cassie was so hot and wet inside. Blue glided in and out in practiced strokes meant to elicit the most pleasure possible, and Cassie thought she was going to cum every time he moved. Blue slowed the rhythm and then took one of Cassie's and legs and flipped her over on her side. He was experienced at this and never slipped out of her pussy.

He lay on his side behind her and raised her leg into the air, holding it up with his powerful arm. Cassie had wondered what he was doing, but just went with it. She'd never been in this position, and she was curious and sensed that she was going to enjoy it. She wasn't wrong. Blue began stroking her from the back, and the sensation was different.

Blue penetrated her at an angle where his cock kept hitting her G-spot.

"Now, when I tell you, I want you to stroke your clit, understand?" he murmured in her ear.

"I can't. I've hardly ever done that," she confessed.

That shocked Blue. A lot of women he knew

masturbated. "Really? Not even by yourself?"

Cassie shook her head as pleasure snaked along her body from his cock filling her repeatedly. "I'm a little sexually repressed," she said.

Blue chuckled and the sound made Cassie even hornier. "We're gonna change that, baby. By the time this week is up, you'll be well versed in a lot of the ways a man and a woman can pleasure each other. Sound good to you?" he asked with a hard thrust.

"Oh yes!" Cassie called out as her pussy tightened around his dick.

"Stroke it now, baby, fast," Blue ordered as he moved faster.

Cassie was a little apprehensive about touching herself but did as he said. When she touched her clit, a hot spear of pleasure shot through her pussy, surprising her.

Blue felt her jerk. "See? Feels fucking good don't it?"

"Uh huh," she said and did it again. It felt so incredible that she was soon doing it faster and faster without even thinking about it. She was rapidly approaching climax.

"You gonna cum for me, you sexy bitch?" Blue said with a laugh to let her know that he was just playing.

"Oh yeah. I'm gonna cum. I'm your sexy bitch and I'm gonna cum if you keep fucking me!"

Blue laughed and said, "Damn, girl, I like it when you talk dirty. Do you like my cock thrusting inside of you?" he asked.

"Yes! Harder!" she ordered. She was becoming wild with desire and didn't care what she said anymore.

Blue pumped harder and faster, and Cassie abruptly rocketed into a shattering climax.

"Oh! Oh! Blue! Blue!" was all she could manage to get out as she came harder than she ever remembered cumming.

Blue held her while she shimmied against him and her pussy juice covered his cock. He growled and told her to hold on tight. Blue rocked them and plunged into her tight cunt. His orgasm was long, hard, and hot, burning through him slowly at first and then swiftly moving him along over the peak. He was suspended there for long moments and he had no idea of his surroundings.

He bit the back of Cassie's neck in a primal signal of the male animal dominating the female in a mating ritual as old as time. Cassie shivered as his teeth lightly scored her, and she felt proud that she could make a man feel like that. Blue's climax began to ebb and he started relaxing as the tension left his long body.

Cassie relaxed along with him. They slumped onto the bed together, their breathing harsh in their chests. For several minutes, neither of them spoke as they caught their breath.

Then Blue tightened his arms around Cassie and asked, "How you doing, Darlin'?"

Cassie laughed. "I'm doing amazing. How could I not be after that?"

"Just checking," Blue teased. "I know what you mean. That was hot. I'm honored to be the first guy after your husband." He frowned. "I'm not sure how that sounds, but I think you get my drift."

"Yeah, I do," Cassie said with a smile and kissed his forearm. "I have to tell you, though, not even Shane made me feel like that."

"That's a shame. Men and women should always pleasure their mates," Blue said matter-of-factly.

"Mates? Sounds like animals," Cassie said.

Blue nodded against her inky hair. "We are animals. Wouldn't you say that what happened was animalistic?"

"Well, yeah, but…"

"And after a bit we weren't thinking, just feeling? That's what happens with animals. All they know is what they want, and it has to do with the pleasure center of their brains. We're not much different. It's just that we attach emotions to the physical act of mating and we're much more imaginative about it. Much more creative."

Cassie turned in his arms so she could see his face. "You sound like a professor," she said.

Blue grinned. "My father is a biology and anthropology professor, so a lot of that has rubbed off on me."

"So you don't believe in love? Just physical lust?" she asked.

Blue frowned. "I didn't say that at all."

Cassie grinned at his defensive tone. "No but you didn't say that you do believe in it either."

Blue cleared his throat as he thought about his answer. "My father may be a man of science, but he has been in love with my mother for forty years and vice versa. I've watched them over the years and have wanted the same kind of relationship that they've had. I just haven't found the right one yet," he said by way of an answer.

Cassie shifted. "Yes, it's hard to find love sometimes," she agreed. "It took me a long time and then he died."

Blue hated the shadow that fell over her face as the memory of sadness came to her.

"I'm sorry you had to go through that. You must have loved him very much," Blue said in a comforting tone.

"Me, too. But I can't dwell in the past. He wouldn't want me to do that." Cassie kissed him softly and then sat up. "Well, I've worked up a sweat and need another shower."

The sight of her naked, curvy body made Blue want to start all over again, but he sensed that she wasn't in the right frame of mind. He'd get her there again, though. He smiled up at her. "Ok. I'm just gonna lay here a moment longer and then do that myself."

"Ok," she said with a little smile.

Cassie walked down the hall to the bathroom, not caring that she was naked. She relished the slight soreness in leg muscles that she had used in a while. All through her shower, she wondered what the rest of the week would be like.

"Gotcha, fucker!" Blue shouted. He sat behind his piled-down desk, working on some skip tracing. After his sexual interlude with

Cassie, he had been energized. That's what sex did for him; it gave him energy. Most men were tired after sex, but not Blue.

He hit the print button and hummed to himself while the paper printed that contained one of his suspect's address and phone number. Blue loved it when he found one of his bail-jumpers. The hunt excited him. He was a southern boy, brought up on hunting and fishing and that hadn't changed since moving to the city. It was only the type of prey that had changed.

He hit a speed dial number on his phone. "Streeter, get your ass over to my place. I got a client I'm guarding here, but I need to go after a perp. I need you to babysit her for me." Blue listened for a moment, laughed and hung up.

He walked swiftly down the hall to Cassie's room. The memory of their lovemaking from that morning hit him as if he'd walked into a brick wall. She was sitting on the bed, working. Rebel lay beside her and started wagging his tail furiously when Blue walked in the room.

Cassie looked up and said, "Hi. Is everything all right? I heard you swearing in there."

Blue laughed. "Yeah, it's fine. In fact it's great. I have to go out, but a good friend of mine is coming over to stay with you. You'll like Streeter. He'll keep you safe, I can guarantee you that. We work together sometimes. He'll be here in about ten minutes," he told Cassie.

"Oh, ok. If you say he's good then I'll take your word for it," she answered.

"Good. I'll bring us back some dinner once I drop this guy I'm after off at the police station," Blue said.

"You're a bounty hunter, too?" Cassie asked. "Isn't that dangerous?"

"No more dangerous than playing bodyguard, Darlin'. Besides, it pays big bucks sometimes. This guy is worth a cool grand."

A loud, knock that had a rhythm to it sounded downstairs on the front door. Rebel shot off the bed and flew down the stairs, barking and growling like he was going to tear someone limb from limb.

"Good boy, Rebel. That's right, do your job, old boy." Blue followed him down, made sure it was Streeter on the other side of the door and then called Rebel off.

Cassie had come downstairs, too and now stood in the front hall. She curious about what her next guard was like. Streeter was like no one Cassie had ever met in person before. He looked to be about six-six and was broad with it. He sported a black Mohawk, nose, lip, and eyebrow piercings and lots of tattoos.

Cassie backed up a little and looked at Blue as if to say, "This is the guy you're leaving me with?"

Streeter caught her look and laughed in a low throaty tone that reminded Cassie of a motorcycle. "It's ok, sweet cheeks. I'm not gonna eat you up or anything. I'm at your service," he said in a London accent that surprised Cassie. "I'm Lionel Streeter, love."

His friendly grin made Cassie feel a little better as she looked into his dark eyes. "I'm

Cassie Riggs," she said.

"Well, Ms. Riggs, it's a pleasure to meet you," Streeter said.

"All right," Blue said. "Now that we've had our introductions, I gotta get going before someone else nabs this guy. Be back soon," he said and took off out the back door.

Streeter smiled at Cassie and said, "How about a spot of tea and a game of chess? Do you play?"

"Yes, I do, actually," she answered and smiled. This man was full of surprises. Looking at him, she would have never guessed that beneath his frightening exterior beat the heart of an intellectual and a gentleman.

"Splendid. I'll get the tea going and you can set up," he said, handing her a chess set, which she hadn't noticed before.

"All right. You're on," she said.

Streeter had turned out to be both excellent company and an excellent protector. He was adept at handling Rebel as Blue was and it was obvious that the dog loved him. As it became dark, Streeter began drawing blinds and only turning on what lights they absolutely needed. Rebel was on the prowl, pacing around the downstairs. Several times, Streeter had put the dog out so he could patrol the yards. The dog hadn't given any alarm and all was quiet when Blue returned.

He'd called Streeter from outside so that Streeter could turn the alarm off for a few minutes while he came in. The smell of Chinese hit Cassie's nostrils and her stomach rumbled. She hadn't realized how hungry she was.

Blue set the food on the kitchen table, slapped Streeter on the back and told him that he wasn't company and to get plates out. Streeter smacked Blue upside the head but got the plates. Cassie laughed at their roughhousing.

Rebel wanted in on the action and jumped up on both men, barking and whining. Finally, Streeter gave the dog what he wanted and had a good romp with him, which set the dog off on a running fit.

Cassie didn't have much experience with animals, and she was scared by Rebel's antics at first. He raced out into the hall into the living room then back to the kitchen where he slid on the floor and snapped at Blue or Streeter who just laughed and watched the dog do it all over again.

Once Rebel had had enough, he flopped down on his rug in the corner and the three of them settled down to eat. The two men told Cassie how they'd met as bouncers working at a nightclub and had become friends almost immediately.

Once the meal was over, Streeter took off, promising Cassie he'd be back for a chess rematch. Blue reset the alarm once Streeter had left and turned back to Cassie.

"He's a character, huh?" he said fondly.

Cassie smiled. "Yes, he is. He's such a nice guy. And a great chess player," she said.

"Yeah," Blue said stretching.

Cassie watched Blue's red Phillies T-shirt rid up revealing his six-pack abs. Her hands itched to touch him.

"I'm glad you got your man," she quipped.

Blue hadn't missed the way she was watching him. His own awareness of her grew as he watched her tongue wet her bottom lip. It was such a small thing but so erotic, too.

"Yeah, I got him," he said lowering his arms. "But I'd rather get my woman."

Cassie was unprepared for Blue's sudden assault, but welcomed it. She'd been too shy to initiate it on her own. He cupped her face, kissing her deeply, his tongue plundering her mouth, tasting the Chinese and beer on her and thinking it delicious. His obvious desire for her unleashed Cassie's for him, and she shoved her hands up under his T-shirt, letting her fingers explore the muscled contours of his back.

"Damn, Cassie, you're like a drug," Blue said when he dragged his mouth from hers. "I've been thinking about this all day, wanting you like crazy."

"Me, too," Cassie said as she brought her hands around to play with Blue's nipples.

He gasped and then groaned as he took her mouth again. They stood in the kitchen necking for several minutes until neither of them could stand any more.

"My room, now," Blue commanded.

Cassie went through the doorway Blue indicated. He flipped a wall switch and soft light filled the room. It was a beautiful room, Cassie saw. It was large with three windows and its own bathroom. The light green and white trim was calming, and the slightly darker green drapes were the perfect accent to the room.

Blue's king-sized bed occupied one wall.

Two nightstands flanked the bed. The floor was a beautiful hardwood. An old Persian rug covered the center of the floor.

Cassie barely had time to register these details when Blue embraced her from behind, cupping her breasts in his hands.

"Do you know how beautiful you are? How sexy? God, these drive me crazy," Blue rasped in her ear.

Cassie shook her head. "I've never thought about myself that way. I've always been a little too..." she couldn't finish the statement.

"Too what? Shaped the way a woman should be? Curves and toned muscles instead of all sharp edges and bones?" Blue turned her around and made her look at him. "Don't you ever think about yourself like that again. You are so fucking hot, it's not even funny."

Cassie laughed and ducked her head a little. "Ok, if you say so."

A hot light flared in Blue's eyes as he brought Cassie's gaze to meet his again. "I say so. Don't ever doubt how beautiful you are," he said and brought her hand to his crotch.

Even through his jeans, Cassie could tell that Blue was hardening. She unfastened them and tugged down on them. Blue laughed and just let her do it.

"That's right, girl. You take what you want," he encouraged her.

Cassie pulled them all the way off him and then pushed up his shirt. "Off," she commanded.

"Yes, ma'am." Blue removed it and tossed it aside. "What now?"

Cassie looked at Blue standing there in

nothing but his underwear. "Take them off. I want to see all of you."

Again, Blue did as he was told and stood proudly before Cassie. She drank in the sight of his male beauty. The fact that he was already at half-mast told Cassie how much he desired her. She came forward to fondle him and so thoroughly enjoyed touching him that she forgot that she wasn't naked yet.

Blue reminded her of that fact by reaching behind her to pull up her T-shirt. Cassie helped him pull it off and then unlatched her bra. Blue bent and took a nipple in his mouth and sucked hard. Cassie pressed his face harder against her tit, loving the electric sensations coursing through her body straight to her pussy.

He released her and then practically tore at her jeans to get them off. Between the two of them, they succeeded in removing the garments, and then Cassie pushed Blue onto the bed, still in an aggressive mood.

"Oooh, kitty's got claws," Blue remarked with a big grin. "I love it. Do your worst, baby."

Cassie smiled at him and crawled between his legs. Kneeling, she took him in her mouth, flicking her tongue over the head of his big cock and dipping into the tiny divot in its tip. Blue groaned and smiled at her. Cassie kept going, circling the head faster and faster. She was so glad to feel him growing rock hard in her hands and mouth.

She grasped his dick at the base and worked up and down his stiff shaft. He tasted musky and salty, and then she noticed that there was some pre-cum liquid seeping out of his cock and she licked up.

"Mmmm," she murmured. "You taste so good."

Blue smiled. "I'm glad you think so. Damn, baby, you give good head."

Cassie colored at his compliment. "I'm not that experienced at doing it."

"Couldn't tell it by me," Blue said.

Cassie ran her tongue up and down him and then went back to work on sucking him. Her pace picked up and Blue sucked in a breath as his loins quickened. He let her go on for several minutes loving each pleasurable sensation she brought him.

"Shit, you do that so well," he told her. "I wanna do that to you, too, baby. Swing your ass around her so I can lick your cunt."

Cassie did as he told her and Blue had his face filled with her wet pussy. He loved it. He made his tongue stiff and thrust it inside her cunt, loving the taste of her. Cassie gasped and jerked a bit as the first sensation hit her. Blue kept tongue fucking her, wanting to taste her pussy juice when she came.

He replaced his tongue with two fingers and then began licking her clit. Cassie moaned and stopped what she was doing for a few moments. Blue grinned when he understood that it was hard for her to concentrate. He had the same problem when she started sucking and licking his cock again.

Cassie couldn't stop moving her hips as Blue kept licking. He was making her so horny and making her pussy feels so good. She knew she was going to cum soon and didn't think it was fair, so she increased her pace and suction.

Blue thrust upwards as Cassie performed her act of seduction and groaned against her pussy. He was trying to decide if he was going to let his orgasm happen this way or stop and switch to something else. His control was shattered when Cassie took him deep, squeezed the base of his dick and then came back sucking hard and kept repeating the motions.

"Oh, shit, Cassie, I'm gonna cum," he said against her pussy and then kept licking.

"Mmm hmm," Cassie murmured, not stopping what she was doing.

She began quivering against Blue, her moans becoming high pitched and urgent. Blue felt his orgasm rip through his body at the same time that Cassie's overtook her. Both of them cried out either around or against the other's genitals as they came together.

Cassie surprised herself by swallowing Blue's cum, having only done it once in the past. She found that she actually enjoyed it and wondered why. Blue lapped up the warm liquid that dripped from Cassie's hot pussy and then licked her cunt, wanting every drop of the sweet juice.

Cassie sank down onto Blue's big body, sated for the moment. Blue laid his head back on the bed and rubbed Cassie's back and ass cheeks. He loved the feel of her and slapped her ass.

Cassie squealed in surprise and then laughed. Blue did it again and Cassie laughed even more. Then Blue started tickling and a tickle fight ensued at the end of which both of them were out of breath. Laying down on the bed together, they kissed and talked, telling each other more about their lives.

Suddenly, Blue sat up. "I am fucking starved. How about you?"

Cassie's stomach growled at the mention of food and she laughed. "What's that tell you?"

"Great. I'll make us some club sandwiches. You like Swiss cheese?" Blue asked.

"Yeah, I do," she slid off the bed with Blue and pulled on her T-shirt and undies.

Blue put his underwear back on, and they walked back out to the kitchen. Several things happened at once: Rebel growled and let out a vicious bark, a window shattered in the living room, and the alarm system started screaming.

Blue leaped in Cassie's direction and dragged her down to the floor with him. He curled his body around hers, covering her. Rebel was barking his head off, the alarm kept screaming and more windows were shot out.

Finally, the shooting stopped and Rebel began to calm down. Blue disentangled himself from Cassie and sat up. She went to sit up, but Blue pushed her down and motioned for her to stay. Rebel came into the kitchen, and Blue made several hand signals to the dog. Rebel came and lay down on Cassie and Blue got up.

He went into his bedroom, yanked on his jeans and stuffed his feet into a pair of sneakers. Opening his closet door, Blue chose a long-range rifle with a night vision scope and stomped back through the kitchen.

Cassie saw the lethal weapon and shrank back a little.

Blue barely even looked at her, but gave her a little wink as he did. That wink assured her that Blue knew what he was doing and that she would be safe. Blue silenced the alarm and then went into the living room making sure to stay well back from the window. Glass crackled as he walked. Ducking down low, Blue placed the barrel of his gun in a lower corner of the blown out window and took a look through his scope.

He scanned the street but saw no one. There were no cars, either. Blue knew they were gone. This was merely another message for Cassie. Blue knew he was going to have to take desperate measures now.

Flashing lights announced the arrival of the cops. Blue mainly dealt with them, preferring not to upset Cassie more than was necessary. She was scared and nervous and kept pacing in Blue's room. The cops finished gathering their ballistics and made them promise to come to the station right away to give a statement.

Blue waited until they left and then had Cassie pack her bags. He threw some stuff in a duffel bag for himself and Rebel and then called Streeter. It wasn't long before the huge man showed up in a big SUV and picked them up.

"Where are we going?" Cassie asked.

Blue sat in the back seat with her and made sure there was no tail on them. "Somewhere safe that these assholes won't be able to find us," he told her.

Cassie saw the dangerous light in Blue's eyes and wondered just what kind of man he really was for a moment. Should she trust him and this man in the front seat to take care of her? Were they trustworthy? She'd slept with Blue. Twice. Well, kind of one and a half, she guessed. She pushed those thoughts away. She shouldn't be thinking about that right now.

Then common sense kicked in and she realized that Jason wouldn't have entrusted her to just anyone. He would have made sure that Blue was a professional of the highest standing. Plus, Blue was Jason's cousin. Jason knew Blue extremely well. She was just seeing a different side of Blue right now: his professional, no-nonsense side. After thinking about it for a moment, Cassie felt reassured that Blue was acting this way. It meant that he was taking things seriously.

"How'd they know where she was?" Streeter asked Blue.

"I don't know. I've only used burner phones to talk about her with Jason. Shit, she ain't been with me two days and they found her. These guys are serious."

"Right," Streeter agreed. "We need to find the common denominator, mate."

Blue shifted in the seat so he was facing forward again. "Yeah, like what? You think Jason's line was bugged? No, he's only used burner phones, too."

"Where did he ask you to take the job?" Streeter asked.

"Fuck! My office phone! I called Cassie from my office phone!" Blue hit the back of the passenger seat hard enough to make it buck. "I'm so fucking stupid!"

"No, mate. You just didn't think they'd get a lock on it right then. Hindsight, remember?" Streeter said in an effort to comfort Blue. He knew it was useless but he felt he had to try.

"They were able to trace me through her phone line. They had to have it tapped. Her house might be bugged, too." Blue hit the seat again, his rage needing some form of release. "Nothing I can do about that now except to correct the mistake and use the backup plan," Blue said.

One of the most important lessons in life his father had ever taught him was that focusing on mistakes was useless. You had to move forward and correct the situation and learn from the mistake. Blue put this lesson into practice right then. He worked through the problem, running through every contingency until he had a concrete plan.

During this time, Cassie kept silent, just watching the look of concentration on Blue's face. He kept looking behind them and in front of them, making sure no suspicious cars approached them.

Blue shifted yet again and he caught Cassie looking at him. He locked onto her eyes. He didn't wink, didn't smile, he just reached out to hold her hand in a gesture of comfort. They held hands the whole rest of the way to their destination.

Cassie stared in wonder at the large cabin in the woods. It was beautiful and brought to mind the frontier houses. The cabin was made all natural wood and stained with a clear stain to preserve it. A deck ran around three sides of the cabin.

The inside was as impressive at the exterior, and Cassie was delighted with the huge beams and fine furnishings.

"It's gorgeous," she told Blue.

Blue smiled down at her and said, "Yeah. This is my Uncle Fred's cabin. He's my mother's brother. We always used to come here as kids. He gave me a key years ago and told me that I was always welcomed to use it. I come for a vacation every year."

"I can understand why you'd come here. It's very homey and relaxing," Cassie commented.

Streeter came in with Cassie's other two bags. "There you are, love," he said. His smile was warm and reassuring.

Blue turned to his best friend and said, "Thanks, Streeter. For everything."

"No worries," Streeter returned with a clap on Blue's back. "I'll be back in the morning. Make sure all the cameras and alarms are on."

Blue rolled his eyes. "Yeah, like I don't know to do that."

Streeter laughed. "All right, then. See you in the morning," he said to them both and left.

Blue smiled and shook his head. "That man is a piece of work."

"He's a good guy," Cassie said.

"The best," Blue concurred.

He grabbed her bags and took them to the master bedroom then returned. He went into the large great room and touched a knot in the wood on one of the walls. A panel slid open revealing a row of TV screens. Cassie stepped up to them, fascination settled on her beautiful features.

"Is this a surveillance system?" she asked.

"Bingo," Blue said. "The road here is monitored in several places, and there are sensors in the road that let you know if someone has driven over them. There are cameras equipped with night vision in several places around the house. I also installed several motion detectors around the perimeter of the clearing where the cabins sit that will tell us if someone tries to get here on foot."

"It's like a fortress," Cassie said with wonder.

Blue nodded. "We should be safe here. I don't think they're going to be able to find it. There are several ways in and out of here. Streeter won't come the same way twice, and he's able to spot a tail a mile away, so I know he won't let anyone follow him here."

"Good to know," Cassie said and then yawned.

Blue caressed her cheek. "You must be exhausted. Why don't you go get some sleep? I'll join you in a little while."

Cassie gave him a haughty look. "So you're just assuming that we're sharing the same room? Rather presumptuous of you, Mr. Spalding."

Blue gave her that sexy smile of his. "So Ms. Riggs, you're telling me that you don't want my company?"

Cassie grinned. "I didn't say that. I just said

you were presumptuous."

Blue embraced her and gave her a light kiss. "Yeah, but that's part of my charm. I see something I want and I go after it."

Cassie's body reacted to the contact with his. "And you want me?"

"Yeah, I want you."

"I see. Well, I'll go to bed and maybe when you join me, you can show me how much you want me," she said and stepped out of his arms. She gave him a come-hither look and then entered the bedroom leaving Blue to stare after her.

He'd never had such a strong reaction to a woman before. Cassie was quickly becoming addicted to Blue, and he was filled with wonder over it. He did want her, very badly. Thinking about them naked together got him excited, but he went through setting all of the alarms and surveillance equipment properly. He wasn't going to have anything happen because he wasn't thorough enough.

After turning off the lights in the great room and the kitchen area, Blue took a pair of night vision binoculars and did a perimeter check. He let Rebel, who had been doing his own surveillance outside, in for the night. Rebel hadn't indicated that anything was amiss, so Blue felt reasonably sure that everything was all right.

When he entered the master bedroom, Cassie lay under the sheet, and it looked to Blue as if she were naked. She smiled at him and crooked her finger at him.

Blue shed his clothes in record time and jumped in the bed making Cassie laugh loudly. She ran her hands up his chest and raised her face for a kiss. Blue obliged very willingly, taking charge quickly. His tongue delved into her mouth, her sweet taste intoxicating. He wanted more, wanted everything all at once and had to remind himself to slow down a little. The woman made him so horny that his brain got fogged from desire.

Cassie didn't seem to mind that Blue was wild that night. She went along with him, twining her tongue with his and caressing him everywhere she could touch. Blue whipped the sheet back so he could see her sexy body. He played with her nipples, squeezing them and brushing his fingers over them in turn.

Cassie's pussy was throbbing and she knew she was wet. She moaned into Blue's mouth as he played with her tits. He broke the kiss and playfully pushed her down on the bed. Cassie liked the roughhousing and pushed him back. Blue laughed in surprise and then pushed her again. She caught a pillow and whacked him in the face.

That brought on a full-scale naked pillow fight that ended with Cassie pinned beneath Blue on her stomach.

"Now what, Cass?" Blue asked. "Now I got you."

Cassie wiggled around trying to get free. She laughed as she felt Blue's hard dick against her ass. "You don't have me yet, but I hope you do soon."

"Ah, there's the kitty in you coming out again," Blue remarked with a laugh. "So just what do you want me to do here?"

"I want you to fuck me. Do it now. Ride me hard," Cassie said not believing the things that were coming out of her mouth. She'd never had the guts to say stuff like that before, but Blue gave her that confidence.

Blue didn't answer, just hauled her up onto her knees and slid his fingers up and down her pussy slit to make sure she was wet enough and then positioned his dick at her opening.

"You ready, Darlin'?" he asked. "Cause it's gonna be a bumpy ride."

Cassie wanted him so badly and said, "Hell, yeah. Go for it."

Blue penetrated her quickly, drawing a moan from her that indicated how good it felt. Cassie relished the way his cock filled her and moved back to meet him. She wanted it to be wild and rough. Blue grasped her shoulders and began plunging forward over and over. With every stroke, Cassie whimpered or mewled her pleasure. Her cunt was slick, hot, and tight, and Blue had no trouble gliding in and out. The rhythm he created was fast and hard and suited Cassie just fine.

Blue groaned as Cassie pulse around him. He squeezed her tits and played with her nipples, exciting her even more. Fuck, but he loved her tits.

"Oh, shit, Blue!" Cassie growled. "I'm gonna cum, baby."

"I want you to cum. I want you to cum all over my dick. You hear?" Blue said as he drove even harder into her.

"Oh! Yeah! Don't stop! Blue!" Her words dissolved into loud moans and shouts of sheer bliss as her orgasm spread through her body at a shattering intensity.

Blue gritted his teeth and kept going. He wanted another climax for her. Cassie's cunt was even slicker after cumming, and he was able to increase his speed again, his hips smacking against her ass. He slapped her ass, grabbed it and squeezed it.

Cassie whimpered and dropped her head. "Oh God, Blue. Yeah, fuck me again."

"Yeah? You want it?" Blue snagged her hair with a hand and pulled her head back.

Cassie had never had rough sex before and was so turned on by what Blue was doing. She loved the pleasure-pain he was creating and didn't want it to stop.

"Yeah, I want it. You gonna give it to me?"

Blue chuckled. "I'm gonna give it to you all right. I'm gonna fuck you 'til you cry uncle, 'til your pussy can't take any more, you got it?"

"Mmm hmm. Blue, it feels so good, so, so erotic!" Cassie moaned as she came again and screamed at the sensation that was almost too much to handle.

Her body convulsed and shook with her release and still Blue pounded on. She didn't know if she could handle another orgasm, but she was going to try. Cassie was surprised when her body responded, the tension building once again within her.

"Oh, baby! Fuck it, fuck it, fuck it!" she shouted.

Blue was sweating by this time but kept going. "Don't worry, Darlin'. I told you I'm not done yet." He grabbed her around the waist and pumped like a dog humping a bitch.

The change in angle made Cassie gasp and moan as the intensity grew. Then she felt Blue's hand slide down her abdomen and his fingers stroke her clit. She jerked as new sensations ran through her body like jolts of electricity, exciting every nerve, every synapse in her brain coming alive.

Blue moved his hand faster and was rewarded by her pussy clenching around his cock, almost milking it.

"Is it good, baby?" he crooned to her.

"So good, so good. Cum, baby," she urged him. "Cum inside my cunt. I want to feel you cum deep inside of me!"

"No problem, Darlin'."

Blue stopped holding back. He pumped and stroked and growled as his own orgasm neared.

"C'mon, you fucking stud. Do it for me!" Cassie cried out.

Her dirty talk excited Blue beyond belief, and he shot over the edge into an orgasm so intense that all he could do was hump her and groan loudly. Cassie loved the fact that she made him feel so good. His movements slowed and then stopped altogether. Slowly, Cassie slid down onto the bed, Blue still on top of her.

They lay that way for several moments, basking in the wonder of what they'd just shared. It had been untamed and fierce, fiery and raw, but underneath that, there was a deeper connection. They'd both felt it.

Blue rolled off of Cassie, afraid she wouldn't be able to breathe with his full weight resting on her. She shifted so she could face him, a big smile on her face, and Blue thought she was the most beautiful woman alive.

"Oh, Blue. That was amazing. I've never experienced anything like that before," she said as she stroked her face.

Blue took her hand and kissed it. "I know what you mean. I didn't even know my own name for a minute there."

Cassie laughed. "Me, neither." She snuggled up close to him, completely sated and getting sleepy already.

Blue smiled when her eyes drooped and her breathing slowed. She had a soft little snore and he found it adorable. He drew the covers up over them and let himself drift off as well.

The rest of the week passed without incident, much to Blue's relief. Streeter came often to check in and relieve Blue if he needed to go somewhere. He never returned to his office. He figured he wouldn't do that until after the trial was over. This way, there would be no chance that anything could be overheard on a bug.

Blue hadn't even told Jason where he was taking Cassie. In fact, he hadn't told Jason anything that had happened or that he was going anywhere: the less people who knew, the better. Right now, it was only the three of them and that suited Blue just fine.

When Monday came, Blue found Cassie already awake at 5 a.m., sipping coffee in the great room. She was nervous as hell and Blue couldn't blame her. He was nervous on her behalf. He comforted her as best he could and promised to protect her throughout the trial.

Cassie was somewhat reassured and could

only hope for the best. Her resolve hadn't been shaken, and they left in good time to get to the courthouse. Blue drove directly to the police station where he informed them of what was going on, and they had a police escort to the courthouse.

The trial was mercifully only about a week long. During that time, Blue and Cassie stayed in a different hotel each night. Blue used an alias and always paid with cash. Once Cassie's testimony was given, under very stressful conditions, she was free to go, but Blue wouldn't stop protecting her and stayed at her place. By this time, Blue knew that his heart belonged to her and that he'd do anything for her. Cassie felt the same way about Blue, but neither of them was ready to voice their feelings.

When the guilty verdict came, Cassie sat and cried in relief with Blue holding her. The nightmare was over, and she could resume her normal life. Blue knew it was time to say something and knew that this was what they'd both been waiting for.

He'd had repairs made to his house and all of the alarms upgraded even though he vowed that he was done with bodyguard work for good. He decked the newly remodeled kitchen out with romantic candlelight and other touches and made a filet mignon dinner for the two of them.

Cassie thought they were going out for dinner when she showed up. She was so impressed that Blue was so romantic and thoughtful that she almost cried. They enjoyed a fantastic dinner, after which, Blue took her hand and led her upstairs to her old room.

Cassie was confused and a little apprehensive, but Blue's easy smile reassured her.

"This is where it all began with you and me," he said. "I wasn't planning on you coming into my life, but I can't tell you how happy I am that you did. You know, when Jason first told me about the job, I didn't want it, but I think it was meant to be."

Cassie smiled at him. "You do, huh?"

Blue nodded. "Yeah. I fell head over heels for you, Cass, and I love you so much. I can't really tell you how much. I want to be with you and only you."

Blue's words were honest and direct and Cassie could tell that he meant them. "I love you, too, Blue. I really didn't think I'd find love after my husband died, and then I meet you and I'm proven wrong. I don't know how I could be happier."

Blue swept her up, fancy dress, heels and all, and deposited her softly on the bed. He proceeded to take off her shoes and put them on the floor. His electric blue eyes watched her as he gave her his devil's grin and said, "Oh, I have some ideas about that. Let me show you."

10 PASSION RAIN

Rob O'Conner eyed the darkening sky with a sense of foreboding. It wasn't looking good. His four big bay horses were acting nervous, which was another indication that the coming storm was going to be a nasty one.

It had been a long time since this part of the state had seen rain and Rob was afraid that if there was a big downpour the road would become a quagmire. The coach would get stuck.

As that last thought went through his mind, lightening streaked down from the roiling gray clouds. The flash startled the horses and the following roll of thunder didn't help. He talked to his horses, calling them each by name. Rob could tell that they were listening by the way their ears flicked back and forth. They settled down and kept on going.

Raindrops started peppering him and the horses and the wind kicked up. Rob could smell the rain on the wind along with a faint tinge of ozone from the lightening. The clouds seemed to get closer to the horizon and the skies lit up again.

One of the horses snorted and tossed its head. Rob had a lot of experience with these kinds of storms and knew that they needed to find shelter quickly. Rob thought about the raven-haired beauty who rode in the coach. He was to deliver her to Austin by tomorrow evening but it looked like they were going to be delayed. Her safety was more important than taking chances to be on time. He started scouting around for somewhere to hole up.

Meanwhile, inside the coach, Jenna Boyd was glued to the window next to her. She loved storms and loved that they were outside while one was brewing. Suddenly the storm broke and the lightning strikes came in a rapid sequence.

Jenna heard the driver yell to the horses as the carriage lurched. The horses must be spooked, Jenna thought with concern. Then the coach swayed as they made a left hand turn onto another road. Having gone over the route with her father, Jenna knew that this was a deviation from that path.

As they traveled along the new road, a large farmhouse came into view and Jenna understood that the driver meant for them to take shelter there. The horses whinnied at the next flash of lightning and she heard Rob's voice again. There was another lurch as he urged the team faster.

They reached the farmhouse a few minutes later and came to an abrupt halt that made the coach springs squeak. Rob secured the reins and jumped down. He opened the coach door, rain dripping from his hat.

"Miss Boyd, we're going to have to stay here for the night. It's too dangerous to keep going in this storm," he told her.

Jenna nodded her understanding. "All right," she said and moved to the door of the carriage. She gathered her skirts and then Rob helped her down.

The hard rain began to pummel her and her shoes squelched in the water. She gave a gasp of surprise when Rob picked her up and trotted to the porch. He sat her down lightly on the wooden surface.

Jenna had the chance to get a good look at Rob. His eyes were a rich hazel and he had dark hair under his hat. It brushed his shoulders and rain dripped from it onto his coat.

"There you are, Miss Boyd. I doubt anyone lives here. Go on in and see if there's anything to start a fire with," he said. "We need to get dry and warm."

Jenna nodded as a resounding clap of thunder rolled. When Rob bounded back down the stairs to the coach, Jenna turned to the front door. She rapped on it twice but there was no response. Feeling vaguely guilty, she turned the knob of the faded green door and opened it. She walked into a large foyer. There was a large room on either side of it. Catching sight of a large fireplace in the one on the left, Jenna headed to it.

There were no logs in the hearth, but the fireplace was still intact. Knowing that most farmhouses had a room off the kitchen where wood was stored, Jenna made her way down a long hall to the kitchen. It was a large, airy room. An old scarred table stood in the middle of the floor. A huge black stove took up a corner.

They were in luck. The mudroom held enough wood to get them through the night, Jenna surmised. When she picked some up, she noticed that it was good and dry; it would light easily.

She carried a good armload back to the living room and arranged some in the grate. After carrying a second armload to the fireplace, Jenna started rummaging around in the kitchen for some matches. Finding none in the drawers there, she returned to what she assumed was the living room to wait for Rob.

A half hour later, Rob returned to the house. He'd put the horses in the barn and given them a good rub down. After gathering up one of Jenna's smaller cases, his own pack, and a food sack, he ran hard to the house. He wasn't worried about himself getting wet, but rather he was concerned with Jenna's things getting ruined by the rain.

He took off his hat and coat and hung them on a peg by the front door to dry. Rob saw that Jenna had done the same thing with her wrap.

"What a hell of a storm," he said as he sat their luggage down. "I hope you don't mind the language, Miss Boyd."

Jenna smiled and her beauty mesmerized

Rob. "Not at all. I have three brothers and was quite the tomboy," she informed him.

Rob nodded. "I wasn't sure which suitcase to bring, so I hope there are some things in here that you can use."

Jenna knew what the case contained and was glad that Rob had chosen it.

"There are. You chose well. Thank you, Mr. O'Conner."

Rob jerked his chin towards the fireplace. "I see you found some wood."

"Yes, and it's very dry. It will burn well. There's more in the mudroom off the kitchen," she said.

"You should have left it for me to carry," Rob said with a frown. He was the one providing service, not Jenna. Plus, he didn't want her to get hurt.

Jenna's expression turned haughty. "I'll have you know that I have a strong back and two good arms. I'm not some coddled girl who can't do anything for herself," she said.

Rob grinned at her cheeky response. He liked a woman with spirit. "I stand corrected. Forgive me?"

After regarding him thoughtfully for a moment, Jenna said, "Very well. I hope you have matches. I searched but I didn't find any."

"Sure do. I have to camp out a lot so I always keep plenty on hand. Let's get that fire going," Rob said, producing a box of matches from his pack.

Jenna couldn't help but notice the way his wet, white shirt clung to his back as he bent over to light the fire. Soon a blaze burned in the hearth, its heat spreading into the room.

"I'll be right back," Rob said and went back out to the front porch. He returned a moment later with two lanterns. Jenna watched in silence as Rob lit them.

"There," he said, sitting one on the floor. It created more brightness in the darkening room. "We need to get out of these wet clothes. I'm going to go change in the kitchen and you can change in here. Just give a holler when you're finished and the coast is clear."

"All right," Jenna said. She was relieved to see that he was a gentleman.

Rob hefted his pack, picked up the other lantern and left the room. Twenty minutes later, Jenna called to him that she was finished dressing.

"I'm sorry for the delay," she said, "but it was difficult to get everything off since it was soaked so badly."

The image of Jenna stripping down layer by layer stopped Rob at the doorway. He could just imagine the lushness of her body under her dress and petticoats. As it was, she looked beautiful in a simple blue calico day dress. He smiled when he saw that she wore no shoes, just stockings. Her feet were small and nicely shaped.

Jenna saw his smile and frowned a little. "What's wrong?" she asked. She looked down at herself and smoothed her dress. "Don't I look all right?"

Rob laughed and shook his head. Leave it to a woman to be worried about her appearance even during a raging storm.

"You look very pretty, Miss Boyd. I was

simply amused by your bare feet. They're very pretty, too, if you don't mind me saying so."

Rob crossed to the fire and knelt down to stoke it some more. Jenna caught herself admiring the way his trousers pulled tight across his backside. She turned away quickly. A betrothed woman shouldn't be looking at other men that way.

"No, no. I don't mind at all. I don't think anyone has ever complimented my feet before," she said with a laugh.

"Well, I tend to notice things. Even the small things," he quipped.

Jenna laughed as she caught his joke. "You're teasing me, Mr. O'Conner," she said.

He stood and turned to her and Jenna was struck by his handsomeness. His wet hair looked black and brushed his shoulders. The white shirt he wore accented his powerful chest and arms. His waist was trim and his hips lean. The man had long legs, too.

Despite not being married, Jenna was not unacquainted with the male body. She and her fiancé, Gregory, had succumbed to their passion a couple of times once they'd become engaged. Gregory was tall and slim, very elegant. With his blond hair and blue eyes, he cut a very dapper figure.

He'd been very gentle with her both times and she had enjoyed it. Their lovemaking had been pleasant but Jenna had felt that something was missing. However, she had no idea what it was.

Rob was a different kind of man: muscular, rugged and quietly confident. She hadn't missed the male appreciation in his eyes as he'd looked at her. It gave her a little thrill to think about it. Then she felt guilty and she blushed.

Rob was smiling at her. "I hope you don't mind a little ribbing," he said.

"Three brothers, remember?" she replied.

"That's right. Are you hungry?"

"Famished," Jenna admitted.

Rob crossed in front of her to get to his pack and Jenna caught a whiff of his scent. He smelled of soap, horses, and hay. It was a pleasant combination.

"It's not fancy, but I have some bacon and beans," Rob said as he unpacked the food and cooking supplies.

"Anything is fine," Jenna assured him.

"Good. Now, Miss Boyd, if you'd be so kind as to open these cans, I'll get the bacon ready."

"Please, call me Jenna. It's much simpler," she said.

"Ok. Call me Rob," he replied.

Then they set about fixing their dinner. They worked well together and it wasn't long until they were sitting down to eat.

Their conversation was pleasant and they enjoyed each other's company.

"How did you come to drive a stage coach?" Jenna wanted to know.

"It's our family business," he said. "We own the stage coach company. My father doesn't drive much anymore. He handles the business end of things."

"Really? That's very interesting," Jenna said honestly.

"I like it. I get to see a lot of the country and

meet a lot of different people."

Jenna's blue eyes grew wide. "It must be so exciting traveling to places you've never been or going back to the ones that you really enjoyed." Her active imagination took over. "Have you ever been attacked by Indians? Or robbed? Or escaped from desperados?"

Rob burst out laughing. He couldn't help it. She was so excited, so adorable, and her questions so outrageous, that he was helpless against the laughter.

"Don't laugh!" she said with a giggle of her own. "Well, have you?"

"Well," Rob said as he tried to sober a little. "Let's see. If Indians had ever attacked me, like as not, I wouldn't be sitting here. I've never seen a desperado, but I have been robbed."

Jenna's excited, sharp intake of breath made Rob laugh again.

"Don't look so happy about it," he chided her.

Jenna placed a hand on his forearm. "Tell me about it and don't leave out a single detail!"

Her touch sent a small sizzle of awareness up Rob's arm, but he didn't move it. "Oh, so you don't want the shortened version then?" he teased.

Her dinner forgotten, Jenna scooted around the table to sit at his side and face him. "No! Everything. I want to hear it all," she insisted. Her father had always read her stories of adventure and intrigue and Jenna loved a good story, especially one that was true.

Rob gave her a sly glance. "People get paid

to tell stories sometimes," he said.

"I'll pay you whatever you want," Jenna said immediately.

"Not sure you'll like my terms," Rob said.

Forgetting propriety, Jenna grabbed his arm with both hands and shook him a little. "Rob! What are your terms?"

"Are you sure?"

Her female sound of frustration bounced off the walls of the empty room and Rob laughed again.

"Ok. I want a kiss," he said. His keen eyes watched her face closely.

Jenna's eyes blinked a few times. "A kiss?"

"Mmmhmm. And I mean a real kiss, not a peck on the cheek. Just one," he said.

Jenna couldn't deny she was attracted to the man, but she was a little unsure about submitting to such a request. Then she thought about the pros and cons of such an arrangement. Not only would she get to hear an exciting story, but also she would have the further excitement of kissing a handsome stranger. No one ever had to know, she reasoned.

"Deal!" she asserted. "But only one."

Rob was stunned. He hadn't expected her to agree to such a thing. He'd only been kidding her, but she was willing to do it. God help him, he wasn't about to turn her down, either.

"Right. Only one," he agreed.

"Yes. Now, on with the story," she urged.

Rob cleared his throat and told her how he'd been traveling along the route to Galveston, which was a very desolate stretch of road, when a group of three bandits showed up out of nowhere. Their ambush was sudden and brutal. They'd thrown Rob from the coach, raided it and took off. As they rode away, Rob had managed to shoot one of them. Fortunately, he had already dropped off his passenger, so there was only his safety to consider.

Jenna's face registered her shock and wonder. "Were you badly injured?"

Rob shrugged. "A few broken ribs and bumps and bruises. It made me feel good that I at least got one of them. The thing was, they didn't realize that there was a hidden compartment in the coach where I kept the money. The locked cash box was just for show. So they didn't get any money for their troubles and one of their men lost his life for nothing."

"That is so exciting! You tell the story very well, too," Jenna said with a dazzling smile.

"Thanks," Rob said. His gaze zeroed in on her full mouth. "Now about that payment..."

Jenna was suddenly nervous. "Yes. I never welch on a deal."

"Don't be scared. It's just a kiss," Rob teased.

"I have kissed a man before, you know. I know what it's like," Jenna informed him in a cool tone.

Rob smiled. "Good. I won't have to break you in then."

"No," Jenna said looking steadily into his hazel eyes.

Rob slid a hand around the nape of Jenna's neck underneath her still-damp hair. Slowly he brought his mouth to hers. He brushed his lips across hers, testing her. When her eyes closed, Rob kissed her more firmly, pressing his lips against her soft mouth. His arms wrapped around her waist and he pulled her closer so he could angle his mouth over hers.

With the tip of his tongue, Rob teased her lips, asking for entry. She yielded to him, parting her lips and placing her hands on his shoulders. Mercilessly Rob plundered the sweet recess of her mouth, twining his tongue with hers, running his tongue along her bottom lip.

Jenna had never been kissed like this. Rob was setting her on fire with unfamiliar feelings. His kiss was alternately wild and gentle and went on forever. Jenna didn't want it to stop. She moaned and gripped his shoulders harder.

Rob deepened the kiss even further and felt his loins constrict as her breasts came in contact with his chest. Without realizing that he was doing it, Rob brought a hand around and cupped her left breast. It was full and firm. His thumb toyed with her nipple and Jenna arched into his hand.

Jenna sighed when Rob's mouth left hers to trail kisses along her jawline and leave bites down her neck. When his tongue licked her collarbone, Jenna mewled and pressed a hand over the one with which he was squeezing her breast.

Rob raised his head and looked into her passion-filled eyes.

"Jenna," he whispered. "Should I stop? Tell me now or else," he said.

She shook her head. "No. Don't stop. Please."

Rob gave her a sexy smile and stood up. "Stay right there," he instructed her.

He went to his pack and withdrew two blankets which he placed one on top of the other near the fire. Then he came back to her and drew her up on her feet. Rob gathered her soft hair and draped it over her shoulder so it hung down over her chest. He turned her around and began undoing the buttons of her dress. He gently scored the back of her neck with his teeth, making Jenna shiver.

She'd never had anyone bite her like that and loved the way it made her feel. Every time Rob's fingertips grazed the skin of her back, a frisson of desire snaked through her veins. His clever fingers soon had the buttons undone and he slid the dress down over her shoulders revealing her chemise. Jenna tugged the arms the rest of the way down her arms until they were free.

Rob brought both his hands around to cup her breasts and played with Jenna's nipples through the thin cotton material. Jenna thought she was going to collapse as intense heat sprung between her legs. Holding her firmly against him, Rob's hands never stopped as he kissed her shoulders. He was growing hard and understood Jenna's excitement.

His hands traveled down her torso and pushed her dress completely off her. Her petticoats followed quickly, leaving her calves bare. The air felt delicious to Jenna.

"Turn around, Darlin'," Rob drawled.

Jenna did so, her eyes locking on his. They

had turned a deep, bottle green in the firelight and Jenna was transfixed by the hot desire she saw in them. Gregory had never looked at her like that.

"Take my shirt off," Rob said.

Jenna's fingers trembled a little as she worked the buttons on the shirt, but then she parted it and sucked in her breath as she saw the powerfully muscled chest beneath it. Rob took her hands and placed them flat against his chest and Jenna was amazed that his skin was so hot. She ran her fingers down his rippling muscles, fascinated with how they looked and felt.

She wanted to see more of him and pushed the shirt from his shoulders. Thick ropes of muscle moved under his skin as Rob shrugged out of the shirt and tossed it to the floor. Jenna's mouth made an "O" of admiration. Rob brought her hands to his belt.

"Go ahead. It's all right," he said softly.

His reassurance worked and Jenna deftly released the buckle and unzipped his trousers. She looked questioningly up at Rob who smiled broadly at her and nodded. Her cheeks turned crimson but she pressed on, pulling the pants down over his lean hips and letting them fall to the floor. Rob neatly sidestepped them, then grabbed Jenna around the waist playfully, making her squeal in surprise.

Jenna laughed then and Rob loved the sound.

"Think that's funny, huh?" he said through his own laughter.

"Yes! You scared me!" she said. "Shame on

you."

Rob hauled her against him and Jenna immediately felt his cock press against her stomach. She remembered Gregory's member doing the same type of thing, but his hadn't felt as firm as Rob's. His reaction made her bold.

She reached between them and rubbed him through his underpants. Rob's eyes widened in shock. He hadn't expected her to do that.

Jenna gave Rob saucy smile and said, "I'm not a virgin, Rob. I've not been with a man many times, but I know some things," she said.

Rob arched an eyebrow at her. "Really? Well, that changes things a bit then," he told her.

It meant that he wasn't going to have to be quite as gentle with her. Not that he was going to hurt her, by any means, but he didn't need to go incredibly slow.

"How?" Jenna asked.

Rob answered by covering her mouth with his and setting her on fire again with a searing kiss. The whole time they kissed, their hands roamed over each other with increasing speed. When Rob broke the kiss, both of them were breathing rapidly. He grasped the bottom of her chemise and pulled it over her head. She, in turn, ran her hands under his underpants and slid them off him.

Then they stood back and admired each other. Rob didn't think he'd ever seen a more beautiful woman. High full breasts with dusky nipples, lovely shoulders, a waist that dipped in then flared out into curving hips and melted into shapely thighs and calves.

Jenna couldn't help but stare. Everything about Rob was powerful and chiseled. His chest and abdomen looked like they'd been cut from some kind of rock and some of the pieces of art she'd seen in galleries depicting the male form came to her mind. His hips were perfectly formed and his legs strong and slightly hairy.

Rob took Jenna's hand and led her to the blankets, pulling her down with him. He stretched out beside her and stroked his hand over her breasts, playing with her nipples. He kissed her lazily, teasing her tongue with his. Then he ran his tongue down her neck to the nipple closest to him. Jenna arched her back when his hot mouth closed around her hard peak and sucked. The fingers of his other hand pinched and rolled her other nipple and Jenna was drawn down into a world of bliss and wanting.

Rob let go of her one breast but kept sucking the other one. His fingers skimmed down her stomach, playing with her navel before delving into the soft, dark curls between her legs. Jenna gasped and spread her thighs for him, wanting whatever he would do to her.

Finding Jenna wet, Rob growled as he slipped a finger inside her and stroked the slick, satiny flesh there.

"Oh!" Jenna said.

Rob smiled against her breast then resumed his sucking. Jenna felt like a jolt of lightning was running between her breast and pussy. Her fingers curled into the blankets as an urgent need rose inside her. She'd felt something like it with Gregory, but nothing as intense as this. She moaned and tossed her head to the side.

Stroking faster, Rob reveled in how good she felt to his touch. She was hot and wet and he could tell that she was tight. When Jenna's hips began to move, Rob placed his thumb on her clit and stroked it, too. Jenna cried out and moved faster.

Jenna thought she was going to burn up over what he was doing to her. She needed that unknown something. Suddenly she felt on the brink of it and started panting and uttering high-pitched moans. Then she shot over the edge and a pleasure unlike anything she'd ever known flowed over her.

Jenna wasn't able to move or utter a sound at first, so powerful was her orgasm. Then she was practically screaming with the erotic sensations Rob was creating in her. Rob growled as she constricted around his finger. His cock throbbed with need. Damn, she makes me so horny, he thought.

The tide within Jenna ebbed and she relaxed. Her heavy breathing filled the room.

"I've never felt anything like that," she told Rob. "What do you call it?"

"It's called coming. An orgasm," he informed her.

"Coming," she said experimentally. "I like the sound of that." She smiled at him and Rob grinned back.

"There's a lot more where that came from," Rob said.

Jenna's eyes widened. "More? We can do

that again?"

"Hell, yeah! Come on. Up on your knees," Rob instructed.

"On my knees?"

Rob laughed. "Yeah. You ever see horses or dogs mate?"

Jenna nodded. "I was sometimes around when my father was having one of his horses bred. It's quite the process."

"Well, that's just the way I want you," he said.

"All right." Jenna was a little tentative about what Rob wanted her to do, but figured that he wouldn't hurt her or anything. So she rolled over and got up on all fours. "Like this?"

The sight of her pretty pink pussy illuminated by the fire did something fantastic to Rob. "Oh yeah. Just like that."

His cock was so hard and so ready, but he knew he had to keep control of himself if he wanted things to last. Rob knelt down behind Jenna and pressed kisses to her pussy. He got a taste of her when he licked his lips and it was amazing.

"Your pussy tastes so good, Darlin'," he told her and licked her clit, flicking his tongue back and forth over it.

"Oh, Rob! That feels so good. That's new, too. I'm finding that there's much about lovemaking that I don't know," Jenna commented after gasping. "So my, er, private is called a pussy?"

Rob stopped as he laughed. "Yeah, that's just one name for it."

"There are more?" Jenna asked. "Tell me," she said.

"Cunt, snatch, beaver, snapper, twat," Rob rattle the names off quickly.

"Beaver?" Jenna giggled. "Why that name?"

"Because of the hair. Kinda like fur, you see?" Rob grinned. Explaining this stuff to her was so fun because she was so curious and willing to learn.

The connection clicked in her mind. "Oh yes. I understand now."

"Good. Now, back to what we were doing," Rob said and began licking in earnest.

Jenna's back arched as that delicious heat spread through her again. She liked having her pussy-that's how she thought of it now-exposed to the air. It felt... naughty and decadent, she decided. She made a disapproving whimper when Rob stopped again.

"Don't worry, Darlin'. I got something here that I know you'll like," he told her.

Rob moved up close behind her and ran his cock up her wet slit, hitting her clit repeatedly. "You feel that?"

"Uh huh. Yes. I like it."

"This little spot right here is called your clit."

Jenna smiled. "I think I like my clit."

"I like it, too," Rob agreed.

Then he positioned the head of his cock at her entrance and slid inside slowly. Jenna's eyes became big as he filled her. Rob groaned in pleasure. She was as tight as he'd thought she'd be and it felt incredible. He withdrew and stroked in again, faster this time. Jenna moaned and moved back to meet him.

Rob took it from her motion that she'd be

all right with really getting down to it.

"I'm gonna fuck you, sweetheart. I'm gonna fuck you good," Rob said through clenched teeth.

"Is that what we're doing? Fucking?" Jenna said in a husky voice.

"Yeah."

Grasping her hips, Rob drove inside her over and over, increasing his tempo and thrusting harder. He smacked her ass a couple of times, which made her giggle and him laugh. Lord, she was a lusty one despite being green. Jenna was nearing an orgasm and wanted it desperately.

"More. Harder. Something," she pleaded.

Rob gave her more and gave it harder. His body slapped against her ass and his fingers dug into her flesh. Jenna was loving every second and then she shot over the precipice and her orgasm was fast upon her. She almost screamed as she came and she could feel how wet she'd become. It dripped from her onto the blanket and she marveled at it.

Rob barely held back his own orgasm. Slowly, he withdrew, his breathing ragged.

Jenna felt like a rag doll. She lowered herself to the blanket and sprawled out. Her legs were delightfully weak. She shrieked when Rob unexpectedly flipped her over on her back. She returned Rob's devilish grin and then looked down at his cock. It was bigger than Gregory's - not that she'd seen it very long.

"I want to touch you," she said.

"Go right ahead, sweetheart," Rob replied.

Jenna sat up then and ran her fingers

lightly along his shaft. It was still damp from her pussy and the skin was very soft. Instinct took over and Jenna closed her hand around Rob's cock, fascinated by the feel of it in her hand. Slowly she began stroking up and down. Rob's groan of pleasure made Jenna smile.

"Do you like that? Am I doing it right?" she wanted to know.

"Oh yeah. Shit, Darlin', that feels so fucking good. If you do it faster, I'm going to come. Do you want to watch me come?" he asked in a tight voice.

"Yes. Yes," Jenna said as she moved so she was on her knees. "I want to watch your cock come, Rob. Please?"

"I will, baby, I will," he promised her.

Jenna worked his cock harder, more sure of herself with every moan of pleasure Rob released. Rob felt the blissful pressure build in his loins as Jenna continued to stroke him. She was a fantastic student, he briefly thought. Then it was his turn to shout as a mighty orgasm rocked him. His cum shot forth, hitting Jenna's chin and neck.

"Oh, Rob! Yes, come, honey!" she crooned as she watched the hot liquid spurt from his cock. It was warm on her skin and had a pleasant, musky scent. She kept stroking Rob until his hips stopped thrusting and then released him.

"Oh, my Lord, Jenna," he said looking down at her with his hazel eyes. "That was amazing."

Jenna nodded with a big smile on her beautiful face. "Yes, it was."

Rob stepped to his pack and drew out a couple of his handkerchiefs. Tenderly, he cleaned her up. He would teach her about blowjobs before they left here. He figured they might not be able to leave until the day after tomorrow because the road was probably impassable near the riverbed several miles down the road.

"I think I saw a pump out back. I'll get us some water, Darlin," he said. He bent down and kissed Jenna and wished he could start all over again. Soon, he thought.

Jenna lost herself in his kiss, wanting him to kiss her always. Rob ended the kiss and dressed quickly. Without Rob there, she was cold. Jenna put on her chemise and warmed herself by the fire. Rob soon returned with a bucket of water and a big pot.

"Where did you find that?" she asked.

"In the barn," he said. "I went to check on the horses and saw the bucket. The pump is near the barn. Plus, there was all this stuff stored out there from the house. Furniture and the like." He planted a kiss on her pretty nose. "Speaking of which, I'll be right back."

He ran from the room before Jenna could speak, leaving her to wonder what he was up to. Jenna yanked her dress over her head and took the bucket of water and the pot to the kitchen. She checked the cook stove to see if it was in working order. She didn't have much experience with them, but it looked safe.

She got some wood from the mudroom and put it in the stove, then went back for Rob's matches. By the time Rob returned, Jenna had a nice fire going in the stove and the water she'd poured into the pot was just beginning to heat.

Rob eyed the stove and the pot and then looked at Jenna with a surprised expression on his face.

She cocked an eyebrow at him. "I do know how a household is run, you know. Just because I don't normally cook doesn't mean that I don't know how to work a stove."

Rob smiled. "I apologize for my previous misconceptions," he said. "Seems like we're gonna be comfortable here for a couple of days."

Jenna straightened. "What? A couple of days?" That meant she was going to be getting to Galveston very late. "Why? And what is that that you're carrying?" she asked indicating what looked like a bunch of bed sheets hanging over his shoulder.

A wicked grin lit his face and Jenna's heart did a little lurch as desire sprung within her again.

"Help me carry it to the living room and I'll show you," Rob instructed.

Jenna grabbed hold of the thing and they got it to the living room fairly intact. She'd noticed that pieces of straw had dropped from it along the way. Rob worked for a few minutes and Jenna was pleasantly surprised when a makeshift bed began to take shape. She pitched in and soon they had a nice straw-tick bed set up.

She smiled up at Rob. "This is rather fun, don't you think?"

"Oh yeah."

Rob tipped her face up and planted a soft

kiss on her mouth and Jenna could feel herself melt as he deepened the kiss and his arms encircled her waist. She opened her mouth and ran her tongue along Rob's bottom lip. He groaned and opened to her request and their tongues danced and teased each other.

Reluctantly, Rob pulled back. Jenna could see her desire mirrored in his eyes.

"We better check that water on the stove. Sorry we don't have any soap, but at least we can freshen up," he said.

Jenna shrugged. "It's better than nothing. I have an old chemise that I can rip up for cloths. That way we can wash up better," Jenna told Rob.

He frowned down at her. He didn't like the idea of her having to destroy a piece of her clothing. "I'd rather go back out to the barn and see what I can find. I don't want you to have to ruin your clothing."

Jenna smiled at him. "All right, but if you can't find something, we can use my chemise."

"Ok. I'll be back shortly," Rob said as they walked to the kitchen.

He returned in fifteen minutes with some towels and washcloths.

"Here we go," he said handing her some. "Glad I went back out there."

"Me, too. I can't believe all of this stuff is out there. Why didn't they just leave it in here?" Jenna said. It was very curious to hear why someone would move all of their valuable possessions to the barn.

"I don't know, but I'm glad it's here," Rob said as he started stripping down.

Jenna watched his nimble fingers undo the

buttons of his shirt. His bare upper half looked good enough to eat. Then he took off his boots and pants and Jenna's heart thumped in her chest as she took in those lean hips and his cock.

Without thinking about it, Jenna wet one of the cloths with the warm water and started washing Rob. He smiled and closed his eyes. She slowly ran the cloth over his arms and back, not forgetting his ass. She came around to his front, refreshed the cloth and washed his broad chest. Rob's nipples hardened as the cool air hit his chest.

Jenna wondered if men liked their nipples sucked like women did. She decided to find out. She leaned forward and flicked a tongue over one of Rob's nipples. His sharp intake of breath told her that he did indeed like it. Next she bit is slightly and Rob shifted his feet a little.

Then she placed her mouth over the nipple and sucked. Rob gasped and his hands came up to cup her head. Her mouth and tongue worked his nipple and Rob felt his cock start to harden. Lord, what she did to him.

Jenna repeated the procedure with his other nipple. By the time she was done, Rob was breathing a little faster. Jenna dipped her cloth in the water again and began washing Rob's privates and thighs. He groaned and shifted restlessly again.

Jenna saw that he was growing hard and took him in her hand. She was surprised when Rob's hand closed around her wrist.

"Huh uh. Not yet, Darlin'," he drawled in his sexy voice. "It's your turn," he said.

Jenna gave him a saucy smile. "All right."

Rob picked up a cloth and soaked it. He washed Jenna from head to toe, skimming over all of her private places, not missing an inch of smooth skin. He treated her breasts to the same treatment that she'd given his and it was Jenna's turn to squirm.

No sooner was Rob done than Jenna was on him, kissing him and running her hands over his body. Kissing and caressing they made their way down the hall. Rob was so horny that he couldn't wait and stopped. He pressed Jenna up against a wall and ran his hands over her. Then he grasped her ass and said, "Wrap your legs around me when I lift you up."

Jenna did as he instructed when his powerful arms hauled her off the floor. As she settled down on his hips, she felt his cock fill her pussy and moaned loudly.

"Oh God, Rob, that feels so good."

Rob practically slammed her against the wall and thrust upwards, burying himself deep inside her pussy.

"Yes! Yes! I want to come, Rob. Make me come!" Jenna pleaded.

"Don't worry, I will," Rob grunted as he set up a fast rhythm. She was so wet and had such a tight pussy. It was incredible the way her pussy gripped his cock.

Jenna grasped Rob's shoulders and held on as he drove them down the fiery road to completion. Rob ground against Jenna in earnest and she plunged over the edge into a tremendous orgasm. She screamed her joy and tightened her legs around Rob, preventing him from pulling out when his climax began. His hot cum shot forth inside her and Jenna loved the sensation.

Spent, Rob leaned against Jenna for a few moments to catch his breath. Jenna held him close and kissed his neck. She ran her hands through his long hair and over the smooth skin of his strong shoulders.

Rob lifted his head. No one had ever made him feel like this and he was hit by a sharp stab of jealousy at the thought of her fiancé ever possessing her. He wanted her for his own. He knew it was unreasonable and impossible, but it was like that old saying: the heart wants what the heart wants.

He gazed into her soft blue eyes and saw that she felt the same. Rob knew better than to get ahead of himself, though. Great sex didn't equal love. It was easy to get caught up in passion but hard to get out of the trouble it could cause.

Slowly, he let Jenna slide down and he set her on her feet. She leaned against him until her slightly wobbly legs were a little more stable.

"That was unbelievable," she said nuzzling his chest. She planted kisses there, loving the taste of his skin on her lips.

"Mmmhmm," Rob agreed. "Come on, let's clean up again and get something to eat. I don't know about you, but I've worked up a hell of an appetite."

Jenna agreed and they made their way to the kitchen.

Two days later, the rain had finally stopped and Rob knew the road would be passable.

Rob had decided that they would be able to start out the next morning. This fact filled Jenna with both relief and sadness. She'd enjoyed their romantic interlude and found that she would be perfectly content to stay there with Rob.

Jenna realized that that could never happen. She was engaged to another man, but surprisingly felt no guilt in what had happened with Rob. They had agreed that neither of them would ever speak of their time together.

That night after supper, Rob and Jenna lay down on their straw bed and held each other. Neither one of them talked about how they were feeling, but they knew what the other felt. Without a word, Rob turned Jenna's face to his and kissed her long and tenderly.

Their lips sealed together and their tongues twined and tasted. Rob rolled Jenna over on her back and trailed little bites down her neck. Jenna shivered and rubbed his shoulders, loving the muscle play under his smooth skin. Rob licked his way down her chest. He began toying with her breasts, teasing the areas around her nipples but not touching them.

Jenna felt a slow fire spreading along her limbs. She wanted him to suck on her nipples and knew that he was prolonging the sweet torture to excite her. With his fingers, Rob circled her areolas, watching in fascination as her nipples contracted into tight buds. Finally he skimmed his fingers over her nipple and Jenna's back arched. She buried her fingers in his hair and urged him toward her nipple.

Rob smiled at her eagerness and gave in. He took a hard peak in his mouth and sucked and licked and bit gently. Jenna moved her hips as the fire inside her roared into an inferno.

"Oh, Rob! It's so... incredible," she said in a husky voice.

"I know," Rob agreed as he switched to her other breast.

It was true. The passion between them was unlike anything Rob had ever felt before. He'd been with his share of women, but none of them had ever made him as hard as Jenna did and so fast. With her he found that he had to double his control so that things weren't always over so quickly.

For Jenna, the couple of times she'd been with Gregory couldn't compare by far to what she and Rob shared. Any other man would never match the intense pleasure he gave her, she knew.

Rob rose up and continued sucking on her nipple. He settled himself between her thighs and Jenna rose her hips, wanting him to enter her. Rob had other ideas. He ran his tongue down over her ribcage and flat stomach. When he kissed her down-covered pussy, Jenna moaned and moved restlessly.

Gently, Rob spread open her lips and looked at the beautiful pink center that was revealed. He could see that she was wet and relished the fact that he excited her. He dipped his tongue into her sweet well and found her clit. Jenna gasped and thrust her hips upward.

Rob flicked his tongue over her sensitive

nub, going back and forth and up and down. He circled her clit and felt it swell. It felt so good against his tongue and she tasted salty-sweet. He pressed a little harder with his tongue and Jenna fisted her hands on the sheet that covered the straw bed.

As he continued his ministrations, Jenna began to tremble against his mouth. He sensed that she was close to coming and moved his tongue faster and harder against her clit. Jenna began to mewl and make high-pitched moans. She couldn't hold still. She needed to come and was almost there. She wanted to feel that soaring ecstasy and knew that Rob would deliver it.

Just when she thought she couldn't stand it anymore, Jenna broke through and roared into a shattering orgasm. Rob tasted her cum and licked faster. Jenna writhed and cried out loudly as she came. She came so hard that she was breathless and her muscles were fantastically tense. As she reached the peak of her climax, she screamed with pleasure and bucked under Rob.

He held her down and continued his tongue movements, drawing out her pleasure. As her orgasm started to slowly subside, Jenna began to relax. Rob raised his head and smiled at the sated sleepy look on Jenna's beautiful face. She was incredibly beautiful with her deep blue eyes, full mouth, and well-formed cheekbones. Her chin was pretty and her jawline created a slightly heart-shaped form to her face.

Rob lay down next to her, his cock throbbing with his own need. "Stroke me," he said when she'd caught her breath.

Jenna smiled and took him in her hand. She loved how hard he was, loved touching him this way. Her deft fingers explored his shaft and gently touched the head of his dick. She enjoyed feeling the different textures of the various parts of his cock. She noticed that there was a little liquid seeping out of the tip of his cock and she wanted to taste it. She'd never done that yet and had a sudden hunger to do so.

Rob read her face and saw how her eyes were trained on his cock.

"Go ahead," he told her.

Jenna looked into Rob's eyes. "I've never done that before."

Rob rubbed her shoulder in an encouraging manner. "I'll teach you. It's all right."

"What do I do?"

"Just start by licking and then we'll get to the rest," Rob said.

Jenna got up on her knees and bent over his penis. She flicked her tongue over the tip of his cock tasting the liquid. It was rather salty and she liked it. She licked around the head of it and then getting braver when Rob made noises of pleasure, she ran her tongue down the length of him to his ball sac.

She cupped it and felt its weight in her hand. His skin was so soft there. Then she licked her way back up him and circled the head with her tongue.

"Take me in your mouth and lick around my head," Rob instructed her. "Think of it like an ice cream cone."

Jenna smiled as that image came into her

head. "What flavor are you?" she asked playfully.

Rob laughed. "Me. The flavor is all me."

"Mmmm," Jenna said as she licked him and then closed her mouth over him. He tasted so good and the way he filled her mouth was exciting. She felt her pussy reacting to the sensation of him in her mouth. Instinctively, Jenna took him deeper and then sucked on his cock a little.

Rob couldn't hold still. Her mouth was so hot and she seemed to be getting the idea. He felt his cock swell even more. "Suck harder, honey. It's ok."

Jenna did as he said and put more suction into her motions.

"Yeah, that's it. Now take it back in and then suck as you pull it back out again. Do it a little faster."

Jenna was incredibly horny again. Doing this for him was erotic and she was enjoying it immensely. She began working him faster and sucking harder. Rob couldn't help but thrust his hips as she drove him crazy with desire.

"Oh, shit, honey, that's so good. So good."

Rob's encouragement gave Jenna the confidence to be bold and she played with his balls with one hand while her other hand held his cock steady. She felt his balls tighten and then Rob grabbed her hair and pulled slightly.

"Whoa, Darling. Gotta stop or it's gonna be over and I have something else I wanna do with you," Rob said.

Jenna released him and smiled up at him. "I'm glad that I make you feel good."

Rob gave a short laugh. "Good ain't the

word. Fantastic is more like it."

"Good."

"Now I want you to come up here and sit on me."

Jenna's brows puckered with confusion. "You want me on top?"

"Yeah. It'll be all right. You'll see. Come on," Rob urged her. "Pretend I'm a wild stallion and you're gonna tame me."

Jenna giggled at that. "That sounds fun."

"It is, trust me," Rob told her.

"All right," Jenna said and put a leg over Rob's stomach. She squealed when Rob just lifted her up and settled her over his hips.

"Now lift up a little."

Jenna's hips rose and Rob positioned his cock at the entrance of Jenna's cunt.

"Ok, now sit back down."

She did and was amazed at the different sensation as he filled her from this position. Slowly she took him in completely.

Rob gritted his teeth and told her to stay still for a minute. He was close to coming and didn't want that to happen yet. Once his control was in place again, he began moving his hips upwards and told her to press down when he thrust upwards.

Jenna soon caught on to the rhythm and Rob thought that was one of the things he loved about Jenna the most: her willingness to learn and the way she caught on so fast. Rob grasped Jenna's hips and really began hitting her hard.

"I'm gonna pound that pussy," he told her.

Jenna moaned. "Yes, please. Pound it!"

She gave as good as she got and they

slapped their bodies together, riding the tide of passion and pleasure as they sought the ultimate reward. Rob began playing with her nipples and Jenna felt the jolts of pleasure travel to her cunt and moved even faster.

"Yes, Rob, oh God! I'm going to come!" Jenna announced.

"Yeah, do it, Darlin'. Come for me," Rob growled as he looked into her eyes. "Keep looking at me. I wanna watch you come," he said.

Jenna held his gaze as her release swept through her and even as she cried his name and shuddered on top of him, she looked deep into his beautiful hazel eyes. At that moment she knew that she loved this man who was indeed all man. She jerked as the spasms of her orgasm rocked her.

Rob kept moving his hips. "I'm gonna come, Jenna. I'm gonna come for you."

"Yes! I want you to come. I want to feel you come inside of me," Jenna said still feeling the effects of her climax.

Rob thrust inside her over and over and he felt the intense pressure build. It was a sweet torment as she took him in again and again. Then he knew he was going to come and worked his hips faster. As he did he felt Jenna clench around him in another orgasm and he was lost. His hot seed filled her pussy and his cock throbbed with pleasure.

His strong hands gripped her thighs as he held her still while his climax shook him. He called out her name and growled as he came. Finally their mutual release ebbed and Jenna collapsed on top of Rob. Their labored breathing filled the room as they rested together.

Rob rubbed Jenna's sexy back and then hugged her to him.

"Oh, Darlin', what you do to me. No one has ever made me feel like this," he murmured to her.

Jenna raised her head so she could look into his eyes. "I feel the same way. Rob, I love you. I do. It's not just the... lovemaking. I love the man you are. I don't want to go to Galveston. I don't love Gregory. I won't marry a man I don't love. I thought I loved him, but that was before I met you," Jenna said, pouring her heart out to Rob.

He was stunned. He hadn't expected this. How did he feel about her? Rob's heart swelled and he suddenly knew that he loved this woman who'd come into his life so unexpectedly.

"Jenna, sweet Jenna, I love you, too. Don't ask me how it happened, but it did. These past couple days have been the best days of my life. I don't want you to marry him, either. I want you to come to Houston with me. That's where I live."

Rob gently rolled her over and then propped himself up on his elbow.

"I know that you're not supposed to do this in bed, but since nothing else about how we've gotten involved has been unusual, why not this? Jenna, will you marry me? I want to be your husband and I would be so proud to have you as my wife."

He waited nervously for her answer.

Jenna's eyes filled with tears and her throat

grew tight. She couldn't get the words out at first but pushed through. "Yes. I'll marry you. I would love to be your wife. I love you so much. I can't imagine being without you now."

Rob whooped and swept her up against him, kissing her fiercely and leaving Jenna breathless. Rob grew serious then. He took her engagement ring off, setting it aside on the floor.

"I don't want you wearing that anymore," Rob told her.

"I don't want to wear it anymore. I don't belong to him. I belong to you," she said. She gazed into his eyes and smoothed back his slightly sweaty hair from his brow. "I'm yours."

"We'll leave in the morning for Galveston and you can end things with Gregory," Rob said.

Jenna nodded. "Yes. I owe him that much and I want to give back his ring."

They made their plans for going to Houston after that and throughout the night they gave themselves to each other again and again, sealing their union and their future together.

AUTHOR'S NOTE

Readers: I want to expand a few of the stories to see where the characters can be explored further. If there are any of the stories that you would like to read more about again, I'd love to hear from you!

Visit my blog at www.faederose.com

Join my newsletter for free exclusive previews
www.faederose.com/in

Follow me on Twitter at
www.twitter.com/faederose

Like my page on Facebook at
www.facebook.com/faederose

Discover my books at major ebook retailers everywhere.